I've travelled the world twice over,
Met the famous: saints and sinners,
Poets and artists, kings and queens,
Old stars and hopeful beginners,
I've been where no-one's been before,
Learned secrets from writers and cooks
All with one library ticket
To the wonderful world of books.

© Janice James.

The wisdom of the ages
Is there for you and me,
The wisdom of the ages,
In your local library.

There's large print books
And talking books,
For those who cannot see,
The wisdom of the ages,
It's fantastic, and it's free.

Written by Sam Wood, aged 92

THE DROWNING MARK

The corpse of a Chinese man drifts with the incoming tide till it scrapes against the newly moored boat. On board are Dr Alexandra Kennedy, with her lover Mike Harley, an ex-London copper. Their gruesome discovery initiates a full-scale police investigation — but their own continuing curiosity stirs up hostility and resentment among the inhabitants of the remote village of Lexton on the Suffolk coast. As Alex is increasingly confronted with inexplicable and frightening occurrences, she realises that in this isolated village there hides an evil intelligence which is terrifyingly dangerous.

ALAN SCHOLEFIELD

THE DROWNING MARK

Complete and Unabridged

ULVERSCROFT
Leicester

First published in Great Britain in 1997 by
Macmillan Publishers Limited
London

First Large Print Edition
published 1998
by arrangement with
Macmillan Publishers Limited
London

British Library CIP Data

Scholefield, Alan
    The drowning mark.—Large print ed.—
Ulverscroft large print series: mystery
    1. East Anglia (England)—Fiction
    2. Detective and mystery stories
    3. Large type books
    I. Title
    823 [F]

ISBN 0–7089–3885–X

Published by
F. A. Thorpe (Publishing) Ltd.
Anstey, Leicestershire
Set by Words & Graphics Ltd.
Anstey, Leicestershire
Printed and bound in Great Britain by
T. J. International Ltd., Padstow, Cornwall

This book is printed on acid-free paper

For Peter Lavery

He hath no drowning mark upon
    him;
his complexion is perfect gallows.

The Tempest

1

A GOLDEN morning and the North Sea is at its most benevolent. Along the beaches there is a susurration of light surf on shingle and the smell of seaweed. The sun is rising in Holland and casting long shadows along the English coast, especially here at Lexton in Suffolk, with its cliffs and its river and its reedy creeks.

On the long beach below the crumbling cliffs there are half a dozen rod fishermen after dabs and codling.

This is a lost and lonely place where few people live and there are few roads to get here. It is a mysterious place of ruined abbeys, of sea marsh, of bird sanctuaries, and scrubby pine forests. It lies at the end of huge flat plains and the land is slowly being devoured by a hungry sea. It is a place where bitter winds come racing off the North Sea and great waves batter the headlands. A few hundred yards out to sea is

1

an almost permanent fog bank. Often it moves onto the land and enshrouds the little town, then it withdraws again to cover the area where the old town of Lexton stood before it slid under the waves and drowned.

But this is a golden September day, the last of summer, and nothing, you would think, could harm it. Except, that is, for the body. The body is still out of sight in the fog bank. It is floating gently along on the current and will, in its own good time, reach the shore.

If a person drowns the lungs fill with water and the body sinks. If a person dies from other causes, the lungs retain air and together with the air in the stomach and the oxygen trapped in the muscles the body is kept partially afloat. This body is also wearing a life jacket. It floats on its stomach and sometimes on its back. Waves turn it over. At one point, when it was on its back, a cormorant picked out its eyes. The eye sockets are left with small trailing fibres and these have attracted both fish and sea lice. The fish, tiny little things, have pulled at the fibres and eaten them, the lice have entered the eye sockets and are making their way into the tissues of the face.

The body floats with the current. This particular current is called the Haringstroom and it sweeps towards the Suffolk shore at three knots. It starts far out in the North Sea near Flushing in Holland, swings down towards Ostend in Belgium and then turns west and sets out for England like an aquatic thoroughfare.

In the centuries before boats had engines to drive them against the wind, it was this current which helped many travellers to reach the coast of England.

And now it is bringing along the body, and carrying it over a very strange place. Below it in the depths, covered by mud and seaweed and limpet-encrusted wrecks, lies the old town of Lexton, and the body is passing over the remains of what was once the cornmarket.

It has come a long way, and considering its movement is unassisted by anything other than the Haringstroom it has done pretty well.

What is bothering it now is its clothes.

3

They have become saturated with water and are weighing it down.

It has also lost some of the oxygen in its muscles. So it has sunk a little and floats just below the surface.

While it has been on the surface birds have attacked not only its eyes but its face, so there are breaks in the skin. Under the clothing, which is badly torn, there are other breaks, and some of them are large and deep and have not been caused by birds.

In this semi-immersed condition the body is not visible to the rod fishermen on the beach. Fishermen on the boats might have seen it had they been coming or going. But the boats are snugly tied up with not a noise or a movement between them on this summer Sunday morning.

So the body drifts slowly and unobserved into the mouth of Lexton River just as though it is coming home, but that isn't so at all.

* * *

Mike was watching her. Alexandra wasn't sure how long his eyes had been open

4

but they were staring at her in that concentrated way he had. There was no half awake look about Mike. He was either asleep or suddenly, bang!, awake, and she wondered if this had anything to do with his former work.

"Hi," he said.

"Hi, yourself. I won't ask if you've slept well. You were out like a light."

"What's the time?"

"Just past seven and I've been awake for hours. Minutes anyway and I want my coffee."

"You should have made some."

"Didn't want to wake you. I'll make it now."

She went to the galley. It was, like the rest of the boat, in serious need of tender loving care.

"There's only instant," she said.

"I only drink instant."

"Well, I don't."

"Élitist."

She lit the gas and waited for the kettle to boil. In front of her was a porthole and from it she could see in the distance the outline of Lexton Church, a great flint structure that was more

5

cathedral than church and had been nicknamed the Church of the Meres because it was surrounded by marshland and small creeks. To one side of it she could see Lexton River with the fishing boats tied up. Closer at hand above the tops of the reeds which almost touched the boat, the land rose to form the cliffs that ran along the beach. On the nearest spur was the mansion, Lexton House, which dominated the town. It was a large three-storey house which dated, in part, from the fourteenth century, and in other parts from the seventeenth and nineteenth. Some walls were of flint and stone mixed, some of brick. It had two Dutch gables, and unlike a modern house, it was built with its back to the sea and the main rooms faced the marshes.

People used the word 'town', she thought, when describing Lexton, but in fact it wasn't much more than half a town. The other half, the bigger half, was below the waves.

The scenes she looked at now she knew of old, for it had been in her Aunt Hannah's house, less than twenty miles away in Southwold, that she had grown from a teenager into maturity, and they had sometimes come here for picnics on the beach. Lexton was old and it was beautiful but its main attraction for her was that it was unspoilt.

She glanced through at Mike. He was doing his exercises, bringing his legs slowly up off the big brass bedstead, bending the knees, straightening the legs, bending the knees, straightening the legs. She could hear the inhalation of breath each time and wondered whether it came from effort or pain. A bit of both, probably.

How different he looked now from those early days. A different person completely.

She had first seen him in London, but that had been at night under sodium lights with guns going off and blood on the road. Then he had looked like any other man with dark hair and dark eyes who was above middle height and dressed in jeans and a bomber jacket. Later, in the physiotherapy pool at Effingham, where she had helped . . . no, not helped, he'd never stand for a word like that . . . where she had . . . assisted . . . him to use his legs . . . she had seen his body for the first time. White. Dead white because it was the middle of winter, but trim and flat-bellied.

The revelation of his physical potential had come later on. She had already registered the power of his personality and his obsessive determination to get well again but in the sea he had taught himself to swim like a fish and even to body surf. It was as though he was showing her: Hey! Look what I can do.

She wished, though, that he had decided to go in for something safer than diving on old cities and old wrecks and trying to find the pot of gold. But what was safe for an ex-Scotland Yard detective who couldn't walk properly?

She had tried to explain this to Hannah and at the same time to explain it to herself. "He's got to be his own man," she had said. "Can't you see that?"

Hannah had said, "But isn't it going to be terribly expensive, I mean for the boat and everything, and then what's he likely to find?"

Alex said, "It's not the finding, it's

the doing that's the important thing. I'm surprised that someone like you should have to be told that."

Hannah had looked at her over her cigarette and flicked back her short grey hair. "No one said psychiatrists were perfect."

She herself had asked Mike why he wanted to buy a boat and he had thrown the question back at her. "Why the hell not? It's only money."

Now she realized he had right on his side. This is what interested him and she thanked God he did have an interest. There had been times when she had despaired of him ever being interested in anything again.

But even at his lowest ebb he was still, she thought, the man you wanted to be sitting next to on an aircraft when the captain said they had just developed engine trouble and were coming down in the sea. With Mike in the neighbouring seat she would have felt just that little bit less terrified. If she had been sitting next to her ex-husband, Freddy, and the same set of circumstances arose, she would have had to look after *him*. The point about Mike was that he didn't complain. He had once actually bent the old phrase into 'never apologize, never complain'. And he didn't as a rule do much apologizing either, so he was at least being true to his own philosophy even if it did make things difficult from time to time.

She put three sugars into his mug. She used none and it made her feel slightly queasy to think of the sweetness.

The stateroom, as he sometimes grandly called his cabin, was part of what had once been the fish room. Fish *hold* she had called it and he had corrected her. "You're very nautical now," she had said. "Do I give you a cap and blazer?"

"You wanting to dress up your bit of rough?"

Sometimes there was an edge to his remarks that stopped her from saying anything further.

The daylight strengthened. There was a slight breeze which she could hear in the reeds. And she could hear the cries of the gulls and smell the heavy sea smell in the humid air. For a second it took her back to her childhood in Cape

Town where the same smell often lay over the suburbs. Then, she remembered, her parents had called it ozone. Now, for her, that represented not a lovely sea smell, but pollution and people coming to her with asthma.

Well, she didn't have to worry about asthmatic patients, not today and not for a month. Part of that month would be spent here on the boat and another part at Southwold with Hannah, near enough for Mike to visit her or she to visit him, but based with Hannah so she did not feel neglected. How lovely for everyone that I'm spreading my favours like this, she thought, with self-mockery.

She said to Mike, "I'm going to have a swim in the creek. Have you swum here?"

He shook his head. "I have off the beach. The water's quite warm."

"What are we going to do today? And don't say paint the boat."

She looked around the cabin. Instead of bunks it had an enormous brass bedstead, built-in cupboards and a desk with a swivel seat. Very nice. But the metal bulkheads were covered in rust and livid scratches. They would have to rub these down and paint them. That was only part of the work they would have to do. Mike had decided to pay just so much for the boat and he and the yard had come to an agreement: they would do the structural alterations and make it seaworthy, he would do the finishing off. That meant not only painting the bulkheads and hull but rubbing down the woodwork in the wheelhouse and varnishing it and replacing cracked and discoloured glass and all sorts of things which needed the willing hands of a female London doctor who had come down on holiday.

"What do you want to do?" Mike asked.

"It's the first day of my holiday so I don't want to do much. I want to lie in the sun and — "

"Not supposed to lie in the sun. You should know that."

"A little bit of what you fancy is what they taught us at medical school."

"A little bit of what I fancy?"

"I was hoping we'd get round to that."

"Take your nightdress off."

"Let's finish our coffee."

"Take it off."

She took it off. The sun coming in from the porthole lit the faint downy hairs on her breasts. He touched her on the shoulder letting his hand drop down to her breast then leaned forward and kissed it. She stroked his shoulder. His skin was smooth and elastic, quite unlike Freddy's, which had been rough.

At that moment there was a slight scraping noise on the side of the boat.

"Did you hear that?" She picked up the nightdress ready to cover herself.

"Probably Dommie."

"Who's Dommie?"

"From the big house on the cliff. He's been paying me visits."

"Why didn't you say so?" She leaned over and closed the curtains on the porthole.

The scraping came again. Mike pulled on a pair of jeans and made for the companionway. He paused at the bottom as though steeling himself, and then began to climb. His legs were always worse in the mornings and she put this down to stiffness.

"There's no one," he called.

She followed him onto the deck. The sun was up and warmed her through the nightdress. They were almost completely engulfed by tall reeds.

"Let's go down," he said. "We've got unfinished business."

Just then the scraping came again, followed by a slight bump. She bent over the rail and looked directly into a face just below the surface of the water. It had no eyes and parts of the lips had vanished making the teeth seem huge.

"Oh, God! Mike! There's something here!"

He came to her. "Jesus!"

The body slowly moved in the current, the metal buckle of its belt scraping along the steel hull. Mike grabbed a boat-hook and twisted it into the body's shirt holding it where it was. Then he got onto the creek bank and waded into the water. He took the body by its shoulders and began to work it to a little beach about forty feet away.

All this was watched by a figure hidden in the tall reeds. He stood, craning to see, parting the reeds ahead of him

14

with a knobbly stick. He saw the body being pulled to the little beach. He saw the woman, whom he had seen arriving the previous night, come out onto the bank and watch. He saw the sun shining through her nightdress. He saw her breasts and her pubic hair. Then he turned and ran through the reeds on paths only he knew. He crossed little streams and ran alongside the larger ones. He came to a path, then a road, then a gate, then a drive, then a house. He ran into the house and shouted, "Grannie! Grannie! There's a funny man!"

He went to the big windows of the drawing room. Below was the creek where the new boat, the one he had been watching, was moored.

But his grandmother didn't come and he ran into the kitchen. "Grannie!" he shouted. "A funny man has come from the sea."

Ellen Blackhurst was having her breakfast. She was sitting in the huge old kitchen eating her toast and reading *The Times.*

"What man, Dommie?"

"A man!" Dommie stamped his foot.

15

"A man from the sea. He's lying on the little beach."

Something inside her seemed to shrivel. "Where? Show me?"

She followed him into the drawing room and looked down at the beds of reeds that spread out from the Lexton River into the marshy ground of the small delta.

"Give me the glasses."

Dommie handed her the binoculars.

As she raised them to her eyes a chill went through her body. She focused on the boat. She saw the man and the woman. She saw the body lying face up on the little shingly beach. This is where it had happened the last time. This is how it had happened. Was it all happening again?

"What are you going to do?" Dommie was looking up at her with intense interest on his strange un-English face.

"I don't know, darling."

Absently she patted him on the head, her fingers touching the taut hairless skin. Dommie was thirty-five years old and going bald.

2

ALEX rose from the shingly beach where she had been examining the body and said, "There was never any chance he was alive. He's been dead for more than a day. I'm not sure how long, we'd need a pathologist for that."

"We'll have to tell the local bobbies," Mike said.

"I'm going to get some clothes on."

"He's not a pretty sight, is he? How old do you think he is?"

"Late thirties possibly."

"Christ, those teeth!"

She clambered up into the boat and Mike was left with the body. It wasn't much of a body; a small man dressed in what had once been a dark suit, blue shirt open at the neck. Here too the birds had been active and there were cuts and holes near the windpipe. It was the face that held his attention. It was badly cut up but there was no

17

doubt the man was Chinese or Japanese. For a moment his mind was jerked back to a film called *Breakfast at Tiffany's* in which Mickey Rooney had taken the part of a Japanese gentleman and had worn a set of outlandish teeth which had pushed his upper jaw and lip forward. This man looked a little like that except that these were his own teeth and he no longer had an upper lip.

There were other things Mike saw as he carefully studied what the sea had brought in. The clothing was torn and there were serious cuts in the torso. He assumed that at some time the body must have been washed against limpets or mussels on a reef.

A voice said, "Having trouble?"

Mike looked up and saw a big man watching him. He was in his late sixties or early seventies, wearing a pair of old khaki trousers and a short-sleeved shirt. Under the shirt was a big chest and powerful shoulders. The face was square, the grey hair still thick and tousled.

"He's dead," Mike said. "He was in the creek. I've only just got him out. Poor sod."

18

"My name's Maitland," the man said. "Bill Maitland. I live across the river. What can I do to help?"

"I've got to let the local police know and — "

Alex came down the companionway. She was wearing jeans, a yellow sweatshirt and boat shoes. Mike said, "This is Dr Kennedy. She's examined him. Says he's been dead for days. I'll phone the police." He went back on board and left Alex with the big man.

"We heard him scraping along the boat," she said as though she owed him an explanation.

"I was taking my morning walk," Maitland said, as though he owed one too. "I've seen your boat, of course. Everyone has. It's been quite a talking point. We don't usually have a boat moored in here."

"They wouldn't let Mike moor her in the river. I'm not sure why, but they wouldn't."

"Yes . . . well . . . "

They stood in embarrassed silence on either side of the dead body, neither quite knowing what to say next.

19

Mike saved the moment. He came down the companionway without his usual care and Alex remembered his fall down the stairs of her London flat. "I got through to the police," he said. "One of them is on his way. Is it likely to take long?"

"Nothing takes too long in Lexton. We're not very big and Philip — "

"Philip?"

"Philip Somers, the local police sergeant. He's just across the river too. We all are. There's only the big house on this side."

Although it was still short of eight o'clock in the morning it didn't take long for people to start arriving and soon there was a small crowd trampling down the reeds near the little beach. Alex watched Mike. She could see him becoming more and more irritated.

"Bloody gawpers," he said and fetched a sheet from the boat with which he covered the body.

Alex and Bill Maitland were standing together at the bottom of the gangplank. Alex said, "I don't suppose you can blame them."

The crowd grew. A couple of small boats arrived. The policeman Somers arrived and Mike went to talk to him. Alex and Maitland stayed where they were.

"Not a lot happens here," Maitland said, "but when it does it's . . . " She waited for him to finish but he stopped and she saw that his face had become grimmer.

A man in the small crowd called out, "Who found him, Philip?"

The policeman stopped writing, and said, "This gentleman here, Chris." He indicated Mike. "He found him."

Alex saw a glance go between Mike and the man in the crowd. He was another big man, a little older than Mike, but swarthy, with a black ponytail. It was as though they recognized each other and the glance was hostile.

"Excuse me," the police sergeant said to Alex, "you the doctor who examined him?"

"Yes."

"Could I have your name and details, please?"

She obliged and was just finishing

21

when there was the deep thrum of a powerful engine and a motor cruiser nosed slowly into the creek.

"There's Frank Spender," Maitland said. "Morning, Frank."

The engine note died and the boat drifted closer. The man on board threw a rope and someone tied the cruiser to a small tree.

Spender raised a hand in greeting. "Morning, Bill. Morning, Philip. What have we got here?"

Somers pulled back the sheet and let him see. The crowd craned forward. Somers dropped the sheet.

"Who found him?"

It was the same question that had just been asked but this time it held weight, which the first one hadn't.

"I did," Mike said. "Who are you?" Alex had heard that tone before. It was the tone of the Scotland Yard man who wasn't about to be placed in any position he didn't want to be placed in.

"My name's Spender. Frank Spender." He put out his hand. Mike waited a fraction of a second then took it. "I saw you come in a couple of days ago."

He nodded at the boat. "Welcome to Lexton."

It was said with a pleasant warmth.

Somers said, "He's been examined by a doctor, Frank. She's here."

Alex found herself shaking hands with a man who was much older than she but who still had a magnetism she recognized. His face was sunburnt and lined, his hair was grey, and his eyes matched the expensive denim shirt he was wearing. There was a tensile strength about him.

"What was the verdict, Doctor?"

"He's been dead a couple of days."

She spoke without thinking. A few seconds later she thought how odd it was that she was answering the questions of someone who had no official position yet who was asking them and expecting answers in the presence of a policeman who had.

Spender looked across at Somers and said, "What are you going to do, Phil?"

"Let them know at headquarters and phone for an ambulance."

"Right. You want me to take the body across."

"I'd be grateful, Frank."

Spender turned to Mike. "That all right with you?"

It was said with courtesy and Mike shrugged slightly. "Sure. If it's all right with the sergeant."

"Right, then," Spender said. "Bill, if you and Philip . . . " His voice trailed off and Alex caught him looking across at the crowd. On the edge of it stood an elderly woman with a strange-looking man at her side.

Spender broke off from the little group round the body and went to her. They moved off a short way in the reeds and talked for a few minutes. During that time the woman looked several times at the body and so did the man next to her, whose arm she was holding. Alex noticed he was carrying a heavy black stick and once he pointed it at the body and said something. Spender listened and answered then went on talking to the woman. The man broke away from her grip and came down to the water's edge. He pointed the stick at the body and said, "He's come from the sea."

Somers nodded. "That's right, Dommie. From the sea."

"I saw him. I saw him come from the sea. I ran and told Grannie."

"That's a good boy, Dommie."

"Yes, a good boy. Take it off." He poked at the sheet with his stick.

One of the women in the crowd put her arm round him and said, "You don't want to look at dead bodies, Dommie."

"Take it off!"

Bill Maitland stood between Dommie and the body. "Look what I've got, Dommie." He held up his two hands made into fists, then put them behind his back.

Dommie's face lit up. "It's my turn!"

"Yes, it's your turn."

"Three."

Alex saw two fingers emerge from one hand and one from the other then Bill held them in front of him.

"I win!" Dommie said. "Grannie!" He turned back to the woman who was talking to Spender. "I won, Grannie."

Mike and Maitland and Somers lifted the body and put it on the cruiser.

Somers said to Mike, "I'll need a proper statement from you."

"I'm not going anywhere."

The policeman's head came up sharply. "You can't stay here, you know."

"Why not?"

"It's private."

"That's what they said about the river." Mike lowered his voice. "Everything around here can't be private."

"Well, this creek is. It's owned by Mrs Blackhurst."

"Where do I see her?"

Somers pointed to the big house on the cliff. "Up there, but I can tell you it won't be any use."

He moved off and so did the crowd and soon Mike and Alex and Bill Maitland were the only ones left except for a few young people who were on the small beach looking at the marks in the sand made by the body's feet.

Spender came back as the woman he'd been talking to turned away. "Want a lift, Bill?" he said.

"You'll need some help at the jetty. I'll come with you." He turned to Alex. "Would you and Mr . . . "

"Harley. Mike Harley."

"Would you and Mr Harley have a sherry with me this evening? My cottage

26

is over on the other side of the river. Below the church. Flint and thatch."

Alex paused. She didn't like answering for Mike, who was now checking the moorings of his own boat. Maitland mistook her silence and said hastily, "If you're not doing anything else."

"Thank you. It's kind of you."

"About six."

She watched the cruiser turn slowly in the narrow creek and make off to the wider river, a strangely modern bier carrier.

★ ★ ★

"Eat your fruit, Dommie," Ellen Blackhurst said.

"Don't like fruit."

"Yes you do, and it's good for you."

"Don't want to."

"Oh, all right. Just the banana, then."

"Can I see in the dark?"

"That's carrots."

They were in the big kitchen.

"What are you going to do today?" she asked.

"Going fishing."

"That's good."

She started to clear the table and stack the dishes in the sink. "But not down by the creek."

"Not down by the creek. The beach."

Dommie went out and fetched a sea pole made from the branch of a tree on which a long piece of nylon had been tied. He also collected the rest of his fishing gear. He loved doing this, it had a formula. There was his coat, which he fetched from the downstairs cloakroom, and his green beanie hat which he pulled down to just above his eyes. Then there was his bottle of water and his packet of biscuits to be put in the fishing bag that he slung over his shoulder. If one of these things was not available, if for example he had mislaid his water bottle, he would become angry until Ellen had found it. So she kept a couple of spare bottles just in case. Today everything was in order and soon he had all his gear.

She said, "Don't stay out too long. I know it's warm now but when the sun goes it may be cold."

He went out by the conservatory door.

Ellen followed and watched him go along the path and down the cliffside. He walked with such confidence yet other people avoided that part of the house and grounds. And it wasn't surprising. The 'conservatory' was just a twisted framework now. The glass had come crashing down the last time the house had moved and it had all been picked up and taken away. The tiled floor had cracked and there were cracks in the path to the cliff edge. When she had first married John Blackhurst and come to live here the conservatory had been intact and so had the path. Now it resembled a roller coaster.

She went down it to the top of the cliff and looked over. These were not the granite buttresses she knew from western coasts; these were a mixture of soil and sand and peat and sea grass; soft, crumbling cliffs. Dommie was halfway down the zigzag cliff path. He stopped and waved and she waved back. This was also traditional when he was going fishing.

'Going fishing' was his phrase. He had picked it up from the real fishermen on the beach and it had given him something to do, for which she was grateful. Most of the rod fishermen knew him and would keep an eye on him.

It had started years before. Dommie had gone down to talk to the men, then he had wanted to hold their rods and that had been a problem. So one of them had cut the branch and made him a simple rod and after that it had been much easier. Dommie would cast his line into the water and would sit on the beach with the other fishermen. Naturally he never caught anything for the line only went in a few yards but if their bags were decent they would give him a flatfish or a small cod and Dommie would take it home to his grandmother and she would cook it for him. It would be a big day for them both.

She watched him now. He looked so normal as he reached the beach and went to talk to one of the fishermen. Anyone else viewing him from where she stood would never give him a second thought. Her mind went back to what she had seen earlier that day. Thank God Frank had been there. He'd understood and that had made a difference.

She turned back to the house. This, the east side, was whitened and scoured by the freezing winter winds. There were cracks in the walls from the subsidence. There was the scar of the conservatory. Well, there was nothing to be done. And that was that.

She heard a knocking coming from the other side of the house and walked through the conservatory into the main passage. She opened the door. A man on the drive was turning as though about to leave.

"I'm sorry, I didn't hear you," she said.

"My name's Mike Harley, can I see you for a minute?"

"You're from the boat, aren't you?"

"I was the one who found him."

"What's happened?"

"They got an ambulance and he was taken to Bury St Edmunds. They'll do a post-mortem there."

"Why? Oh yes, of course, they have to, don't they."

"To find out how he died."

"He drowned, didn't he?"

"It's only formal."

"Come in."

She took him to the drawing room and from the windows he could see his boat tucked up in the reeds. Beyond it was the river. Some of the fishing boats were putting out to sea.

"It's about my boat," he said.

She had not asked him to sit down and she stood near the door as though waiting to let him out again. She was a woman of medium height, thin and with her grey hair caught in a bun. She had clear eyes and strong bones and he thought she must have been good-looking when she was young. She was dressed in faded cords and a man's shirt and had scuffed walking shoes on her feet.

"I've come to ask your permission to moor my boat in the creek," he said. "I didn't know it was yours or I would have come up sooner."

She opened her mouth but he said, "I wanted to get a berth in the river but there were none. At least that's what they told me."

"I'm sorry, but I never allow anyone to moor in the creek. If I let you leave your boat there, dozens of holidaymakers would come along and soon the marsh would be full of boats."

"I'm not a holidaymaker. I've come to live in Lexton. I'd pay you, of course."

She hesitated. "I'm afraid — "

"Look, I've got to stay while the police in Bury find out what's happened. There's no other place for me to tie up."

"How long is it likely to take, this investigation?"

"A few days. A week."

She was silent for a moment and then said, "How much would you pay?"

"Whatever's the going rate."

"I've never charged anyone so I don't know myself, but I'll find out. And only for a few days."

"That'll give me time to find somewhere else."

He walked to the door. "It must have been a shock," she said.

"Not nice at breakfast time."

He looked down on the marsh once again. This time a man was standing

33

near his boat looking at it. He was a big man with dark hair but that was all Mike could see without binoculars. Then the man turned into the reeds and vanished.

★ ★ ★

Alex was cooking prawns in butter when he got back to the boat. She said, "Isn't it incredible, here we are at the seaside and I had to buy these in a shop. Not a piece of fresh fish anywhere."

"It's Sunday."

"Even so."

"Did you see someone standing by the little beach looking at the boat?"

"When?"

"Twenty minutes ago."

She shook her head. "People will be coming down to look at the place he was brought from the water. It always happens. How did you get on?"

He shrugged. "She's letting us stay here for the time being. I offered her rent and she seemed interested. I think she could do with the money."

Alex looked up towards the house.

"But she must be very well off, it's huge."

"And it's got huge cracks in it and huge holes in the carpets. It looks as though nobody loves it. My God, if it was mine I'd have it looking good."

3

"I KNOW I had a bottle . . . good sherry too."

Bill Maitland began another search of his desk, or what Alex thought might be a desk if the papers and books on it were ever cleared and she could see it.

Maitland, whose grey hair was brushed and who looked slightly less rough than he had that morning, had changed into a cream fisherman's smock over chino trousers. He said, "Why do you think people like me are always asking folk in to take sherry? No one seems to drink it any more, but it's a kind of tradition. I think it's what vicars are supposed to do. Vicars and university dons. At least they did in my time."

"You're not a don, are you?" Alex asked.

"No, no."

He went on searching. They were in his cottage between Lexton Church and the river. It was a beautiful thatched cottage

36

with a garden completely overgrown by rambler roses and grass. The three of them, Alex, Mike, and Bill, were in his large front room, which overlooked the garden and was the most untidy room Alex had ever seen. It was encased in overflowing bookshelves from floor to ceiling and there were more books on the floor, on chairs and tables and on the window seats and the window sills. She had never seen so many books in one room.

"You're not a vicar?" Mike said.

"Ex-vicar. Do vicars ever become ex? Retired, then. Look, I'm sorry I can't find this damned sherry. I'll go to the pub and get something. You make yourselves comfortable." He cleared a couple of chairs and stood for a moment holding a pile of books, stared at the full bookshelves and finally put the pile on the floor. "I'll find a place for them later."

"We'll walk with you," Alex said.

They went up the road to the Lexton Arms. It was an old pub with several small interconnecting rooms. The wood was dark, almost black, and there was little light.

"Doesn't look as though anyone's touched this for a hundred years," Mike said.

"I wouldn't be surprised," Maitland said. "What I want to know is do we want sherry? What about you, Doctor? What do you prescribe for six o'clock on a late summer's day?"

"For myself, I prescribe white wine, but my patient Michael Harley usually likes beer when he can get it."

"Splendid. That's what I like too." He turned to the barman. "Let's have a bottle of dry white wine and a jug of Old Snorter and I'll bring the jug back later."

As he said it Alex looked past him into one of the rooms and saw the man called Chris. This was the third time she had seen him that day. The first had been when the body was found, the second when Mike had been up at the big house. The fact that she had denied seeing him standing there on the creek bank looking at the boat had seemed a good idea at the time. But was she being too sensitive? She didn't know. She equally didn't know how Mike would react to him. Mike, she had to keep reminding herself, wasn't like Freddy, her ex-husband. Freddy would have gone to great lengths to avoid trouble. She wasn't sure Mike, with his background, would. Chris was playing dominoes with another man. He looked up and caught her eye. She moved ahead of Mike, blocking his view, and they picked up the liquor and walked the hundred yards back to the cottage.

The early evening light was soft and the air silky. "Let's sit out in the garden," Bill said. They found a broken table and a few rickety chairs and sat overlooking the river. The boats were tied up and the fishing huts locked.

"I keep on thinking how sad it was you should have found him on a day like this," Maitland said. "Bloody sad for the poor chap, too. What do you think happened?"

Mike said, "I suppose he fell overboard, but there hasn't been much of a sea."

"Or slipped and fell," Alex said.

"Or was pushed," Mike said.

"God preserve us!" Bill said.

Alex said, "Could be a suicide."

Mike said, "What we're forgetting is he was wearing a life jacket. Anyway, it's too nice an evening for this sort of talk."

"Sorry," Bill said, "that was my fault. I brought it up."

Mike pointed to the fishing boats. "They don't seem to do very much, do they?"

"The fishing's been terrible these last few years. God knows how they keep going."

Mike said, "I've been up to see Mrs Blackhurst. I can stay in the creek for a few days or at least until the police don't want to interview me any longer."

Maitland took a gulp of Old Snorter and licked his lips. "What did she actually say to you?"

"That she couldn't let me have a mooring there because others would come along too and soon the creeks would be stuffed with boats."

"That's not very likely. According to my research the creek has never been used for permanent moorings."

Alex watched Mike. He was shifting his legs every now and then but his eyes were full of interest. "What research?" he said.

"On the history of this part of the coast. It's been a hobby of mine for years. This was my first parish after the war."

"You're writing a book?" Alex said.

Maitland smiled. "That's what I tell myself. It's one of those projects that has grown and grown. I started off doing a little mild research about the church — it's the only survivor, once there were a couple of dozen — and that led me on to the whole story of the town itself and what happened to it. And the treasure and — "

"What treasure?" Mike said.

"Oh, most of these places have some story of treasure. There's been so much erosion here over the centuries that Lexton isn't the only town under the waves. There are half a dozen drowned villages. And there's Dunwich, of course, another medieval town. It was even bigger than Lexton, with its own shipbuilding industry. But nothing could save it."

"What about the treasure?" Mike persisted.

"There's certainly something about that word that sparks people's interest. There's supposed to be a hoard of silver and gold plate buried here. Or that's what the stories say. I've been looking for it for more than forty years and never found a thing."

"Whose treasure was it?" Alex said.

"The Templars were said to have brought it. There was a preceptory here. But that's under the water too. It's a well-known story and occasionally it draws people here. A man called Howarth came to look for it a year or so ago. Came in his own boat with a lot of high-tech equipment but he drowned himself in a storm." He looked at Mike. "Is that why you've come?"

"It's the first I've heard of any treasure. No, I wanted to start what they call diving safaris out in Africa. I want to take divers out to the drowned city. There's also a wreck out there and — "

"The *Friesland*. But she didn't have anything special in her holds."

"No, but she only went down a few years ago and she'd be interesting. I wanted to have a double attraction."

"The water's pretty murky."

"Not all the time. In Africa I dived and worked on a wreck in cloudy water

42

but we were able to see with lights."

Maitland nodded. "But isn't this a bad time of year to start? Autumn's around the corner."

"I'll get a working knowledge of the area during the winter and be ready to start in spring."

"I wish you luck. People have dived on the old town before, of course, and brought up stonework from one of the old priories. I must say I envy you. I wish I had a boat."

"Where would you moor it?" Mike said, his voice acid.

"I'd probably get a mooring in the river."

"I couldn't."

"That's not surprising. I come from here, you see, and the fishermen know they won't have any competition."

"They won't have any from me either."

"They don't know that. It's the English village attitude exaggerated somewhat. You see, this is a lonely coast. The village, that's all we are really, has gone in on itself. People come here and talk about it being unspoilt and it is unspoilt but that's only because visitors have not been welcomed. Howarth found it a problem too. He had to find a berth at Hallows up the coast — "

"But that's nearly twelve miles away."

"I know. And that's what did him in. He was going back to it in a storm when he sank. If he'd had a mooring here he would have been all right."

Alex noticed the tightening of his mouth and said, hurriedly, "Almost no one knows much about Lexton. Mike told me a bit, but he tells it as though he's giving evidence in court. I like the detail." Mike's habit of giving only the bare facts of any subject had irritated her at first but then she had grown used to the idea that that was how Mike was: a man whose first option given most situations was one of . . . not quite secrecy, but certainly he did not reveal information about himself to strangers.

She watched now as Maitland's face adjusted to the fact that someone else was interested in the subject he loved most in the world.

"Yes," he said, "people don't know a lot about Lexton. I'm not saying a great deal hasn't been written about it, because it has, but a lot of it has been technical. You know the kind of thing: how many buildings in Bird Street and how many in Sheep Lane? And what they were made of. And how big they were. And when they collapsed. All jolly interesting to someone like me but not to most people. The romance is lacking."

"You said there had been Templars and treasure," Alex said, "surely those are romantic enough for most people?"

He waved a hand the size of a knuckle of ham and said, "The whole place is romantic. It started, we think, as a Roman coastal station. The roads that lead away to Bury St Edmunds are straight as rulers. That's typical of the times. It had become one of the biggest trading ports in Britain by the fourteenth century. At one time it was a Royal Demesne and . . . Hang on, I'll find it . . . " He went to his desk and picked up a piece of paper with handwriting on it. "Here it is. I copied it out only yesterday. It's by the chronicler William of Newbury and he calls Lexton, 'A town of good note abounding with much riches and sundry kinds of merchandise.'" He went to the window and said, "Look over there to the Blackhurst house."

Alex and Mike looked over the river and the creek where Mike's boat was tied and the marshes that surrounded it. The house perched on the edge of the cliff and looked stark and lonely against the evening sky.

Maitland said, "You've got to imagine that the cliffs went out from there into the sea for perhaps three-quarters of a mile or more and that the area on the cliffs was covered in buildings. That was the medieval town. And the whole place has gone. This area, the area of the church where we live, barely existed at that time. It was just farmland and scrub."

"You can hardly imagine a whole town going down," Alex said.

"It didn't go down all at once, did it?" Mike said.

"Not at all. But the Domesday Book records that by at least the time of the Norman Conquest several pieces of land had been washed away."

"Storms?" Alex said.

"And the movement of sand spits.

Lexton was a great port but just out to sea are a number of big sand spits, and storms moved them so that on several occasions they blocked the river mouth, i.e., blocked the port. The river's much smaller now than in those days. The burghers cut new channels and after the third or fourth reshaping of the port the sea began to cut into the cliffs. Ironic, really. If boats couldn't get into the river the town would die, so they cut channels which changed the tides and caused the cliffs to erode and the town to die anyway. I suppose you could say it was fated."

"How long did it last?" Alex said.

Mike cut in. "Seventeen hundred and something, wasn't it?"

Maitland was not to be rushed. "By the end of the fifteenth century most of it had already been swept away. The leper hospital was gone, so was the Temple, so was All Saints Church and most of Hen Street and Middlegate and the Grey Friars monastery. By that time Lexton was losing a church to the sea every ten years."

"I'd have got out," Alex said.

"People did. But some stayed on. You can see the same thing today. On the Yorkshire coast and the Isle of Wight buildings are being washed away every year. People stay in their houses as long as they can."

"Is that what's happening to the Blackhurst house?" Mike said. "I was up there this morning and I could see cracks and dust."

"We've all spoken to Ellen. The police have been on to her and the coastguard and the local council. Everyone you can think of, but she won't leave. Like many of the inhabitants of the old town."

"I thought they began to demolish it," Mike said.

"They did, but later. In 1688 the market place went down the hill and into the sea and I think that was a seminal moment. I mean, it was just a matter of time, and they knew it. The Maison Dieu hospital went next, then the town hall and people started demolishing buildings and built rubble barriers, in other words sea walls to try and keep the waves out. But it was no use. In November 1750 a massive storm brought away great pieces of cliff together with portions of the town including the cemeteries of St John and St Mark. There's a contemporary account of bones from coffins being mixed up with drowned bodies on the beach after the storm was over. Not a very nice ending, was it?"

★ ★ ★

"What did you catch, Dommie?" Frank Spender said.

"Lots and lots. Fifty. A hundred."

"That's good."

Ellen Blackhurst, Frank Spender, and Dommie were in the drawing room of Lexton house. The sun had gone and below them was the shadowy area of the marshes and the creek. Frank's big Bentley stood outside the windows blocking part of the view. Once there had been a proper parking area where cars could not be seen from the windows, but now it was buckled and full of gaping cracks as though there had been an earthquake and Frank no longer parked on that side of the house.

"I'll show you." Dommie went to the kitchen.

"Is he all right?" Frank said.

"Same as usual. He's been out most of the day. One of the fishermen on the beach gave him an eel."

"Does he like eels?"

"Dommie eats anything."

He came back into the room and held out the eel. "That's what I caught."

"I bet that took some landing," Frank said.

"Feeeeeeeeiiiiii," Dommie said, making the sound of a screaming reel.

"I thought so."

"Put it back in the fridge, darling, you can have it for breakfast. And then you'd better look at your stamp books. I left some stamps from yesterday's post."

They watched him go and Ellen said, "He loves his stamp albums. He keeps them well, too."

There was a pause and then Frank said, "I told you this morning I'd be up to give you whatever news there was."

She nodded. "It's been like living in the past."

"I know. For me too."

They were of an age. Ellen had changed out of her day clothes into a dark frock with a high neckline that set off her grey hair, and Frank was in a white polo neck and black corduroys. His hair was shaped over his ears as though he had just come from a hairdresser.

"Mind if I smoke?" He held up a small cigar.

"Have I ever?" It was when she said words like 'ever' that her county accent was at its most noticeable. By contrast Spender's had an East Anglian twang.

He smiled. "People change." He lit the cigar and then said, "They took him to Bury. They'll do a post-mortem, of course, and there'll have to be a coroner's hearing. But that'll be the end of it. Formalities, that's all."

"But who was he, Frank? And why did he come in here like that?"

"Who he was may remain a mystery. He's Chinese or Japanese, that's for certain, but how he got here . . . well, he might have fallen overboard from a passing vessel. Could be a crew member or a passenger. It's the most likely explanation. Fell and drowned and was picked up by the Herringstream and brought into the river on the tide."

Ellen said, "It gave me a terrible fright."

"It must've."

"The other one was on a day like this too."

"Was it? I'd forgotten."

"Oh, yes, end of summer."

"It was a long time ago and nothing to do with today at all. It's just coincidence. There have been other drownings. There was that man Howarth when his boat sank and we've had the odd bathing fatality."

"I know, I know, but this was so uncanny. Even the same little beach."

"That's the tide. You could put a log of wood at the mouth of the river and it'd wash up on that little beach nine times out of ten."

"But the face — "

"Look, lots of Japanese are travelling the world now. Many more than in the nineteen-sixties. He was probably a Japanese. They're everywhere. The world's greatest tourists. We'll just have to wait until the coastguard gets any information about a drowning."

"You've told them?"

"The police will."

"Sorry, Frank, I forgot to ask you if you'd like a drink."

"No, thanks, Ellen, I've got people coming. I'd better not."

"People?"

"From London."

"Girls?"

He laughed. "There might be one."

"Don't you think you're getting too old for it?"

"It?"

"This sort of life."

"Oh, I don't know. I'm enjoying it. When I'm not then I'll be too old for it." He rose. "Don't worry about anything. It's disturbing, I know, but that's all."

"Does Gracie know?"

"I doubt it. She doesn't know much these days."

"Poor Gracie."

"I must go." He flicked his hand at a crack in the wall which gaped at them above the drawing room door. "You really must get out of here, Ellen."

53

"Oh, for God's sake, let's not go into that again."

"Why not? You can have the dower. I've always told you so."

"Me in a dower house. You'd like that, wouldn't you!"

He laughed again. "All right, have it your way."

They walked to the front door. The view looked down on the creek. The alien boat was visible. Frank stopped and said, "Doesn't look good, a boat down there, does it?"

"Can't be helped at the moment."

"They'll all come in, every boat owner around here. It'll be like a marine caravan park."

"He's only staying a few days until the police are finished with him."

He turned and kissed her lightly on the cheek. "Look after yourself," he said.

4

"I'M going to have a steak," Mike said. "And you?"

"We're in a fishing village," Alex said. "We should be eating fish. But I'd like a steak too."

"And chips?"

"I shouldn't."

"But you will."

They were in the Lexton Arms having walked along the road from Bill Maitland's cottage. The pub was crowded with Sunday evening drinkers and Mike and Alex had found a table in a corner of the main bar. It was a cheerful place.

"I'll go and order." Mike pushed himself to his feet.

For a long time Alex had taken over such things as ordering food at bars and now she had to restrain herself. There had been a pattern to his recovery. In the early days he had used two aluminium crutches with arm supports. He had been useless without them. The two crutches had eventually given way to one. Then he had removed the arm support from that one and used it as a walking stick. The moment that happened he had resumed his male role of doing and ordering and carrying and had reacted badly when she had offered.

She saw that some of the other drinkers were watching him. It wasn't just because he was the owner of the new boat, for she had seen him attract attention in other places. There was a kind of energy in his frame as though it had been charged, a controlled energy that sometimes switched into controlled aggression. That worried her occasionally but she told herself that as long as he controlled it things were all right. And so far he always had. His anger tended to be quiet.

He came back to the table with a bottle of red wine and glasses and had just sat down when the fisherman, Chris, loomed over them. He leaned towards Mike and said, "I told you once. That's the only time I'm telling you."

His face was shiny with sweat and his voice was slightly blurred.

She put her hand on Mike's arm. She could feel the hard tension in his muscles. He began to push himself to his feet again. She held on. Chris turned and went out of the pub.

Mike did not say anything but looked down at her hand. She removed it. He said, "Please don't do that."

"I'm sorry, but there's some problem between the two of you. I saw it this morning."

"He was the one who told me I couldn't berth in the river."

"Did he say why?"

"Because there were no free moorings. Which I don't believe. Let me deal with it. OK?"

He was angry and his voice had dropped. This was a mood she was always wary of.

He said, "And don't put me down again like you did with Maitland. I'd told you about Lexton and — "

"Oh, come on, darling, I wanted to hear what he had to say. I couldn't just say yes I knew all that. Anyway I didn't."

"You made me look a fool."

"That's not the case. And you're taking out on me your frustration over what's just happened. Please don't. I don't want to start my holiday this way."

His fingers began to fret with the cork of the wine and then he said, "Oh to hell with it. I'm sorry. Let's have a drink."

They ate well and drank well and it was past closing time when they made their way back to the boat over the little bridge further upstream.

It was a clear chilly night and they went along the towpath on the opposite side and cut up the bank of the creek. The moment they turned away from the river they were engulfed in reeds and might have been in another world.

They made love in the big brass bed and it rattled and shook and once or twice banged against the steel hull of the boat making a deep clanging sound. She never quite knew what to expect when they made love. After they had started their affair he had seemed to her to be sexually insatiable. Then she had realized it was a test he was running for his own emotions. Provided he could make love to her he was getting better. That was the ethos. It had changed. He had become more of a normal lover, they had, in fact, started to 'make love'. But there were other times, only occasionally but there nevertheless, when the old uncertainty and the need to prove himself returned. Tonight, she thought, might have been one such. But tonight had also seen a subtle change in his behaviour pattern. He had apologized to her. That was relatively new.

She lay with him in the big bed listening to the night breeze in the reeds and the slop of the tiny waves on the boat's hull. There was a strong smell of the sea. Her mind went back to the body they had found earlier. She had seen dead bodies in the hospitals in which she had trained. But there had been no sense of shock. Hospitals were places one expected to see dead bodies. Not here, not in these innocent waterways.

There was moonlight coming through the porthole and lighting the cabin. Mike was asleep on his side with his back to her. She saw his legs jerk slightly and then bend and flex. She wondered if he was getting cramp. Sometimes she would find him in the middle of the bedroom floor rubbing a foot or raising himself on his toes. He had asked her only once if his legs would ever be normal again and she had said she didn't know, no one knew. Now she was sorry she had sown those doubts. Wouldn't it be better if he had hope?

It wasn't as though he was a pessimist, but you couldn't call him an optimist either. Sometimes she wondered what he had been like before the shooting but she had never been able to ask anyone because the people who had known him then, other Scotland Yard specialists, for instance, were not the people to ask. Nor was his father.

She had met Mike more than two years before on what had started as a typically nasty evening. She had been working then for a north London practice and she was on call. It had been relatively quiet and she had gone to bed. The next thing she knew the phone was ringing.

"Dr Somerville. Oh, Dr Somerville — "

She knew the voice and she knew there was no use telling old Mrs Mathews that

Dr Somerville had been dead these past five years because she had told her three times already.

"It's Dr Kennedy, Mrs Mathews."

"I want Dr Somerville."

"What can I do for you?"

"Isn't Dr Somerville there?"

"No, Mrs Mathews, he's not."

"Oh well, you'll have to do."

Even as she spoke Alex was imagining the scene at the other end of the phone. The untidy flat, the fetor.

"I'm feeling poorly."

Alex went to the computer. Up came Mrs Mathews's name.

"All right, Mrs Mathews, I'll be there as soon as I can."

The Meadowvale Estate lay about a mile away. Alex had been there several times to see patients, including Mrs Mathews, and at no time had the words 'meadow' or 'vale' ever occurred to her. It was a huge estate built in the thrusting 1960s as part of slum clearance in the area. It had become a slum faster than the wretched streets it had replaced. Alex did not like going there in daylight and hated going at night. It was now 1.20 on a misty winter's morning and this was the last place on earth she wanted to be.

As she entered the estate she made sure the car doors were locked. She had to travel slowly because there were humps on the approach roads. These had been put in a year before because the place was becoming a racetrack for stolen cars and people had been injured. She eased her car over the humps and swore to herself that she was never going to come here again.

The area resembled old newsreels she had seen of World War I battlefields. The trees, stripped of leaves, seemed to be in a dying no man's land. Many of the buildings had boarded up windows, and old tyres had been abandoned on verges that had once been grassy but were now mud and stones, and the whole place was enveloped in a mist made yellow by the sodium lights so that it looked like mustard gas.

She parked in front of Honeysuckle House in a group of other cars, some of which were surprisingly expensive, and checked that the medical identification sticker was in the windscreen — not that it did much good these days. She sat for a few moments looking carefully about her before getting out of the car.

Mrs Mathews lived on the second floor and Alex chose the staircase. She did not want to be trapped in a lift — if indeed there was one working — by some addict who wanted her money. At the bottom she stopped and listened. All she could hear were the millions of London sounds that had merged into one continuous hum. She went up to the flat, stood in front of the steel security door, which Mrs Mathews had paid for, and rang the bell.

There was no light visible inside the flat but that didn't surprise her for she had seen the black curtains the last time she had visited the old woman.

"Yes?" The voice came from behind the steel door.

"It's Dr Kennedy, Mrs Mathews."

"Come a little closer."

A light over the door went on. Alex knew she was being studied through the security peephole and thought, as she had on each previous visit, that she would rather be homeless and on the streets than living in the Meadowvale Estate.

"Is there anyone else on the landing?" asked Mrs Mathews.

"No."

"Hang on a sec, then."

Bolts were drawn and chains unhooked and at last the door swung open.

"Quickly," Mrs Mathews said.

Alex entered and the door was locked behind her.

"Go through."

She went into the sitting room. It too was enclosed by black curtains as though Mrs Mathews was seeking to make herself as inconspicuous as possible, indeed to pretend that the flat was empty. The smell of drains and old food was overwhelming in the airless room.

"Sit down, Doctor," Mrs Mathews said. "Make yourself at home."

Once she had been a big woman, now she was a skeleton. She wasn't much more than seventy but looked ninety. That's what living in the Meadowvale Estate did to you, Alex thought.

"I won't sit down, thank you. You said on the phone that you'd had one of your turns. Have you been taking your tablets?"

"Haven't any left. I run out three days ago."

"But you've got a repeat prescription."

"Can't get out. Not with them louts in the building."

"How do you normally get them?"

"Social services got to get them for me. And they say they got too many staff off sick."

This was also a familiar routine and Alex couldn't be sure whether Mrs Mathews was telling the truth or whether she had been unable to sleep and simply wanted company.

"I'll give you some to tide you over, Mrs Mathews, and I'll ring the social services tomorrow. OK?"

"Sit down, Doctor. I'll make us a cup of tea."

"No, thanks. I've got other patients to see. I mustn't be long."

She counted out the tablets and put them on the table. "There you are."

Mrs Mathews looked at them. She was wearing a stained dressing gown and Alex wasn't sure whether this had been put on during the evening or was now her daily wear.

"I got some other things wrong," she said.

Alex knew this was an attempt by a lonely old woman to keep her there. She said, "I'll tell social services to arrange to bring you to the surgery. But I must go now. I'm very busy tonight."

It took her another twenty minutes to get out of the flat and start to descend the staircase. She wondered if anything would be left of her car and hoped that the night was too cold and the hour too late for the kind of vandalism that operated on the Meadowvale Estate. She always thought of vandals as a group out to enjoy itself. You wouldn't go out to enjoy yourself on a night like this, would you?

She was on the first floor when she heard the voices. They were talking, it seemed to her, softly and rapidly. She checked and listened. There was only silence. She walked on. They began again. Did someone have a TV set on?

There had been many times, when she had had to make a call in an estate or in a street known for its danger, when she had considered carrying some defensive weapon in her medical bag: hairspray, a scalpel, some blunt instrument. And each time she had abandoned the idea. What if she faced a man with a scalpel in her hand? Wasn't he more, not less, likely to attack her? And wouldn't the attack be more ferocious? Even a heavy torch would pose a heightened threat to a would-be attacker. So she had decided she would be a doctor and nothing more.

Now she wasn't so sure she had been right.

She did have a torch but it was a small one. On the other hand her bag itself was heavy and she shifted it to her right hand and went on down the staircase to the ground floor.

The voices came again. Whisperings. Sibilants. Soft laughter.

The staircase was set into the building, wrapped around the lift shaft, which meant that every few steps it turned an angle. She arrived in the foyer and saw that one of the lifts was working. As she crossed to the main door it stopped and the doors opened. Two figures emerged.

The interior of the lift had been vandalized and there was no light. The foyer was also in darkness. A voice said, "Where you goin'?"

She knew she could not ignore the question and the door was only a few feet away. "Are you talking to me?" she said, half turning but keeping on walking.

"Who you think we talkin' to?"

Her hand was on the door.

"Hey! We talkin' to you."

The door opened and she was halfway through. She felt a hand on her arm.

"We ain't finished talkin' yet."

"I'm a doctor. I've been to see someone in this house."

"Oh, a doc. You got pills for what we want?"

The other voice said, "You got pills for what we going to do to you?"

The two men laughed and one of them grabbed her. She swung her bag and felt it make hard contact on a face. Then she was through the door and running for her car. Even as she ran she knew she was never going to make it. She ducked behind a car and twisted between it and another but they caught her easily.

They were not big men but powerful. Both were in their twenties and she thought they were high on something.

"You want to run, you run," the taller of the two said. "Go on, run!"

"Don't do this," she said. "I'm a doctor. I have other people to see. People who need treatment badly."

"You hear that?" the other said. "You need treatment?"

"I gonna have treatment!"

Both of them grabbed her. She tried to raise the bag again but one pulled it out of her hand. "What you got in here?"

"We look later," the other said. "Come on."

They dragged her back towards the foyer doors. She began to fight. She screamed and spat and tried to get at their eyes with her nails.

One of them held her around the shoulders while the other forced her against the wall. She could feel his hands under her coat. Then there was a ripping noise as he broke the catch on her trousers. The one who was holding her lifted her off the ground, the other pulled off her trousers and threw them aside. He grabbed the elastic of her pants and as he did so she felt a violent movement from her left side and saw a hand holding something flash past her face and land with a thud on the shoulder of the man who was trying to pull her pants off.

Suddenly she was released, the men turned to run, and then all hell broke loose. Car engines started up, there was the clipped, sharp sound of pistol shots and the squeal of tyres on tarmac.

Then silence.

She stood against the wall in an almost catatonic state. In front of her, on the ground, was a man she had never seen before, but who had saved her from a double rape. He was lying on his side and in the sodium lights she could see his face was contorted with pain. Then she saw the dark liquid on his chest and legs and knew it had to be blood.

She grabbed her trousers and pulled them on then she picked up her bag which was lying in the roadway. She knelt beside the man and said, "I'm going to have a look at you. I'm a doctor." She saw that there were wounds in his chest and in both legs. "We have to get you to a hospital."

She went to her car and phoned for an ambulance but when she told them it was the Meadowvale Estate the dispatcher said, "We'll have to get police protection. They burnt one of our vehicles there last week."

"I'll take him myself," she said.

She went back to him and wiped his face. "What's your name?"

"Mike Harley."

"Mine's Alexandra Kennedy. We're going to have to go in my car. OK?"

She managed to get him to his feet. She put her arm around his waist and he hobbled on one leg. It wasn't a big car and she had to move the seat back. He tried to sit but his weight caused him to fall to one side and he called out in agony.

"I'm sorry. Listen, I've got to put a ligature on that." She tore up a small towel and tied a length around his thigh. "Now I've got to lift your leg."

He closed his eyes and gritted his teeth and she raised his leg into the car and closed the door. She got in beside him and drove slowly over the humps to get to the great world outside the Meadowvale Estate.

"We'll have you there in a few minutes," she said. His head was lying back on the restraint and sweat was dripping down his face. "My name's Alexandra," she said again. "What's yours?"

He did not reply and she said, "It's Mike, isn't it? Mike Harley. How do you spell that?"

"H . . . " he began. She could hardly hear him.

"H . . ." she said. "Then . . . A . . . R . . . L . . . Come on."

" . . . E . . . " he said

"Isn't there a Y?"

He didn't hear her because he had lost consciousness. But the emergency gates of North-East General were coming up on her left so it didn't matter.

She went into casualty and stayed while they examined him. He had been shot in both legs but the wound in his right was a flesh wound. The chest injury was a glancing shot off the ribcage. It was his left knee that was the problem.

72

They pumped him full of pain killer and trolleyed him into a side room.

"Who is he?" they asked her. Name. Age. Occupation. She had to say that all she knew was that his name was Harley. Michael Harley. And that she had paged her answerphone and that there were patients needing her. She'd keep in touch.

She came off duty at eight o'clock and went round to the hospital. Harley was in a private room and there was a beat policeman outside the door who wouldn't let her in. She found the casualty doctor who was still on duty. "He was a copper on a drugs bust," he said. "I think he was undercover. They've got a man guarding him because drug barons operate on a revenge basis and they could try to get him in here. They must have rumbled him just before you came along."

"Yes, they must," she said.

"I'll tell the duty copper you're not on any hit squad."

Mike was drowsy and in pain and she took his hand and held it for a moment and said, "I've come for two reasons. One to find out how you are and the other to say thank you for what you did. If it hadn't been for you I might be dead now."

He said something but she couldn't hear what it was.

"I didn't know you were a policeman until just now," she said. "Is there anything I can get you?"

He whispered something.

She leaned towards his lips. "What?"

"A new knee," he said.

5

THE high street of Lexton faced east-west. It was narrow and in the fourteenth century had not been there. Then there had been a grander street with a market cross, a hospital, two churches, a preceptory and four alehouses. Now they were all under the waves. The modern street dated from the early nineteenth century and there were the usual shops, a chemist, a clothes store, a butcher, a shop selling fishing tackle and bait, a couple of grocers that called themselves supermarkets, a small hotel named the Templars' Rest, and a wine bar called the Rod 'n' Line. Unlike most places of its size Lexton's High Street had no estate agents or insurance companies and looked more of the past than the present. At ten o'clock on a weekday morning the street gave a semblance of busyness but there were a dozen empty parking spaces. Ellen Blackhurst and Dommie claimed one.

They parked outside the fishing tackle shop and the vehicle gave two convulsive heaves after Ellen switched off the engine. She would, she thought, have to do something about the car. She'd had it nearly ten years and it was beginning to cost her a lot in repairs.

They got out and Dommie went to the shop window, which had a display of Penn reels.

"Can I have a reel, Grannie?"

"No, darling. Come on."

"Why can't I have a reel?"

"Dommie, we can't afford one. Please come on."

She pulled at his arm but Dommie was like a rock.

"I want a reel," he said.

"All right. If you're good I'll buy you one."

"Promise?"

"I promise."

He came away from the window and walked by her side to the supermarket. Promises, however valueless, usually worked, she thought.

In the shop he said, "Can I have an ice cream, Grannie?"

"We'll get that last in case it melts."

He followed her with the trolley. "What's that?"

"Ham."

"Is it nice?"

"You've had it often. Anyway, this isn't for us, it's for Gracie."

"Are we going to see Gracie?"

"After I've been to the library."

"Can't we go and see her first?"

"If you want to."

"Are we going to Gracie's now?"

"All right."

Gracie Potter lived in a cottage about a mile out of the village. It stood by itself, small and almost derelict. It was built of red brick and many of the roof slates were missing. An upstairs window was broken and had been covered on the inside with newspaper. One of the downstairs windows was obscured by a holly bush.

"Gracie!" Ellen called at the front door. "Gracie, it's me."

"What you want?"

Ellen and Dommie went into the little front room. Although the day was warm and the sun high, there was a fire in the stove. Gracie, wrapped in a blanket, was sitting on one side of it. She was small and old. She wore spectacles on the end of her nose and her hair was in a net.

"What you want?" she repeated.

"Just to see you, Gracie. That's all. See how you are. See if there's anything you need."

"I don't want to see you."

"Look, Dommie's come too."

"I don't mind seein' the boy. It's you I don't want to see."

"Now, Gracie, that's not a nice way to talk. I've brought you a little ham and a loaf of bread and some butter."

"I don't want your bloody food."

"Of course you do. Food's food. Doesn't matter where it comes from and this came from the supermarket just a few minutes ago so the bread's fresh and I know you like fresh bread."

She put the food down on a small table next to Gracie's chair. The old woman pushed the carrier bag away and it almost fell.

"Don't be silly now," Ellen said. "I've got to go to the library. Dommie can stay with you for a little while."

"Gracie doesn't like you, Grannie."

"Well, she likes you. See that she eats something while I'm away. I'll be back for you in a few minutes."

It was nearly half an hour before she returned. Dommie was holding a plate in front of Gracie and she was picking at the ham with her fingers.

"That's good, Gracie, that's very good," Ellen said. "Has she had any bread, Dommie?"

"One slice. With butter."

"Oh, well done. All right, Dommie, we'll go now."

"Are we going to buy me the reel?"

"Only if you're good. Say goodbye to Gracie."

Often the car wouldn't start if it was hot but this time it did and she drove across the river bridge and onto the marshy side and up the road to her house standing on its cliff.

"There's a man," Dommie said.

"Yes, it's Mr Harley, the man with the boat." She slowed. He was walking through her gate and she pulled up next to him.

Mike bent to the driver's window.

79

"Good morning. I was coming up to see you. I wondered if you'd given any thought to what we talked about?"

"Yes, I have." Ellen got out of the car and leaned against it. "I don't mind you mooring there but it depends how long you want to stay."

"I've got to be here for the winter. In the spring I'll find somewhere else. But right now I've got work to do on the boat. I'm not likely to cause anyone else to come here. Not at the end of the season."

"I suppose not. But I don't know about the whole winter, though. I'll have to think about that."

She got back into the car and drove up to the house. She stopped and switched off. Again the car gave a couple of shudders. The money would come in handy, she thought, not least for a car. She could really do with a new one. Even a new second-hand one.

She watched Dommie go into the house. What money she had in the bank was his. But she knew it wasn't enough to look after him for the rest of his life. As it always did nowadays, her

80

mind became filled with thoughts of what would happen to him after she'd gone. And as always she found she couldn't bear to contemplate it.

★ ★ ★

"That's marvellous," Alex said. "I'm sure she'll let you stay the whole winter. As you say, no one's likely to try to moor in this creek during the bad weather."

They were in the wheelhouse drinking coffee.

"That's what I want," Mike said. "A few months without any hassle." He touched the scuffed bulkhead and ran his fingers along it. "All this . . . and the woodwork . . . I want it looking brand new."

She had first seen the converted MFV on a dismal winter's day in Lowestoft — which wasn't a place to be on a dismal day.

"You bought that?" she had said, looking at the beaten-up vessel riding at anchor in the fishing port.

"Yes, I bought that."

There was a dangerous edge to the way

he replied and she had decided not to get into an argument.

There had been times after they returned from Africa when he had spoken of boats and wrecks and diving and trying to duplicate the diving safaris he had found there. But since leaving the police he had talked about many projects, most of them romantic. The more she had got to know him the more she had realized that beneath the carapace of police reserve and cynicism was a romantic young lad ready to burst out.

What he didn't want to do when he left the police, he had said, was to go into private security. "I don't want to be counting bloody whisky bottles in someone's warehouse and then discover that the manager's been stealing them. I don't want anything like that."

But the boat had come as a shock. She knew he had sold his house and had assumed he would invest the money in some sort of scheme to bring him an income to go on top of the disability pension paid to him by the police.

Instead he had invested in a steel-hulled ex-motor-fishing vessel that had been built in 1978 for cod and haddock and had then been bought by a Dutchman in the Eighties to run drugs. The Dutchman was now in jail and it was through Mike's contacts in the customs that he had heard they were going to auction the boat. He had paid thirty-five thousand pounds for it and had spent another twenty-five on a refit.

And here it was, sixty thousand pounds' worth of metal slopping about in a Suffolk creek waiting for its rust to be scraped off and to be repainted. The best you could say for it was that it was a floating home. And that's how Alex had begun to think of it: as a houseboat. For she assumed that the diving safaris wouldn't work or that Mike would get tired of them. At least if that happened he'd have somewhere to lay his head when he wasn't with her in London.

But her view might change. It had changed before. She had told herself, that dismal day in Lowestoft, that what he did was his problem. But she had known, even before the thought had completely formed, that that was nonsense. His problems were her problems and that was the way it had been from the moment she had come down the stairs of Honeysuckle House on the Meadowvale Estate on the night he had been shot.

She had visited him every day in hospital even when it meant rearranging her own complex schedules. Words like gratitude and sympathy were in her mind, gratitude for being in one piece because of him and sympathy for what had happened to his legs on her behalf. Well, those words had quickly been abandoned. She knew now, of course, that had he even suspected her of harbouring such feelings he would have told the uniformed duty officer not to let her into his room. But pretty soon she realized that they didn't fit into their relationship at all.

It was on her second or third visit that she found him out of bed dressed in nothing but a white T-shirt.

"Look," he said, seemingly quite unaware of his nakedness. He was holding himself up on the metal bar at the end of the bed and was slowly hobbling around it. "Nothing wrong with my right leg at all. Nor my ribs." He pointed to his chest. "It's only this bloody left knee."

"You'd better get into bed before the nurses find you like this," she said. "You'll be up for indecent exposure."

"You're a doctor. You've seen better."

She went to help him and he flung off her arm. "I can manage."

She had stayed with him for half an hour, and then she had gone to see the consultant who was treating him. "He'll never walk properly again," he had said. Knowing Mike as she did now she realized how hollow that sentence had been.

It was on the next visit that she had met his father, Sid. Mike had told her that he was a cab driver who lived in London near the Angel. He was small and thin and combed his sparse hair across the top of his skull in a style Alex had never much liked. But that was the only thing she didn't like about him.

He was very different from Mike. His East End roots were plain to see and hear, unlike Mike's, which had undergone the sea change of a good education. Later Sid was to explain this to Alex.

"I was in Edinburgh years ago and went to a paper seller to get a paper and you know what he was doin'? He was doin' the bleedin' crossword puzzle. A paper seller! You look at the perishers sellin' papers in London and ask yourself if they could do a crossword puzzle. So I says to myself what's the cause of this? It's got to be education."

Alex said, "The Scots always had better education than the English."

"Right. And with his mother being a teacher we knew what to do. It meant working long hours, both of us, but we done it."

Mike had been in hospital for nearly a month and then he had gone to Effingham. That had been Alex's suggestion. She knew of its excellence in orthopaedic work, just as she knew the country around it because it was only ten miles from the Suffolk coast and less from her Aunt Hannah's house. And yes, she admitted to herself, that was one reason for choosing it. It meant that every weekend she could stay with Hannah and spend most of the time with Mike. For by then her visits had nothing to do with gratitude.

She continued to be amazed at his

progress. Each weekend she found him walking more easily. He also seemed to have taken over the orthopaedic unit. The female nurses ate out of his hand, so that when he said he wanted Alex to help him in the pool he got his way.

His wounds had looked very raw in those days and even though she had seen wounds of every sort these were different because they were on the body of someone she was growing to love and had been caused because of her.

What had happened that violent night emerged slowly. Mike never told it to her from A to Z as a story — sometimes she thought it was because he was then still in the semi-secret Special Intelligence Section and had been working undercover. But it came out in bits and pieces.

A consignment of cocaine had arrived at Southampton from Venezuela in a German freighter. Customs, working on a tip from the US drug enforcement administration, knew the drug was in a double-sided container and put on a twenty-four-hour watch. When the target was picked up and delivered to a depot in London they informed Scotland Yard and the job of surveillance was given to the SIS. Eventually the container was claimed, the coke distributed and the middle-sized drug barons went on a buying spree. Each was being targeted in a massive sting. Mike was in a distribution deal at the Meadowvale Estate, waiting with others to buy, when Alex had come down the stairs and the would-be rapists had used the lift.

"I shouldn't have come after you," he had said. "I shouldn't have interfered. Anyway, that's what my boss said. We lost out on that one. But I knew you were a doctor because I saw you park there and I saw you put up your ID in the windscreen. I grew up in a place that was pretty tough and where the doctors were vulnerable on their calls, so I did it without thinking. If I'd thought, I would have sat still."

"Thank you," she had said.

He had smiled and said, "Joke."

She realized then, and it wasn't to change, that she was sometimes not quite sure whether Mike was making jokes or not. This one, she doubted.

When she spoke to the staff at Effingham she heard how obsessive he was about getting well again. If he wasn't on the walking frame he was on the parallel bars and if not on either then in the pool. And he read a lot. That was something that surprised her. With his background she would never have thought he was bookish. Then Sid had told her about Mike's mother who had managed to instil into him a desire to learn, so much so that he had gone to one of the last grammar schools in his area.

At Effingham he raided the library on a daily basis and it was there he discovered books on the topography of the Suffolk coast, and in them descriptions of the drowning of towns like Lexton and Dunwich and Pakefield and Eccles.

He became fascinated. When Alex came to see him at the weekends he would take her to dinner and spend the time telling her of his new finds. Did she know about the great sea battle in Sole Bay? Did she know that half a million ships had gone down on the British coast since the Middle Ages? He said that he'd worked that out on a calculator, and if you took it just from the end of the fourteenth century that came to nearly two shipwrecks a day. Did she know that the Suffolk coast was one of the great smuggling coasts of Britain? Did she know . . . ? The way he told her these facts was the way she had heard detectives give evidence in court: brief, to the point, with little romance. Yet the romance was there in his eyes.

It was during these hospital visits that she got to know Sid better. They would often sit together and watch as Mike went through his exercises and the weekly swimming competitions organized for the disabled. (That was a word she would never utter in his presence.) She learned that Mike had wanted to be a journalist before he had joined the police, that he had spent two years backpacking around Europe and Australia after leaving school, that his mother, a Yorkshire woman who had died a few years ago, had given him every scrap of her love and attention and had hoped for better things from him than joining the police.

"She wanted him to have a profession," Sid said. "To be a doctor like you, or a lawyer. He had the brains for it all right."

One Saturday afternoon Sid had said he had invented something and later in Mike's room he showed him a small treadmill he had made out of wood, leather straps, and roller skate wheels.

"He can do it in his own room if he wants to," he said to Alex. "Doesn't have to wait for the OK."

That was when Alex had learned that Sid was an inventor. He was a member of the East London Inventors' Club and had invented at least one important thing: air-conditioning.

"I was sitting on a bus when I was a kid and it was the middle of a heatwave and I was beginning to melt and I thought if you could use the cooling tubes of a fridge and blow a fan onto them you'd be cool."

"So why aren't you a millionaire?"

"Some other perisher had invented it years before. It was a bit like reinventin' the wheel. But it never put me off."

Mike was pleased with his treadmill

and started his walking exercises as soon as he could.

"His mother would have been proud of him," Sid said. "She always was. Sometimes I wonder how that boy came to be mine."

Alex didn't know it then — she didn't know it for quite some time — but Mike had a brother and neither he nor his father ever mentioned him.

6

"THESE are the best days," Alex said. "Just when you think summer's over you get a spell like this."

They were in the boat about three miles offshore, the sea was calm, and the single diesel was pushing them along at eight knots. It was early afternoon and the sun was warm enough for Alex to be on deck in a light T-shirt and jeans. Mike was in the wheelhouse and all she could hear was the thud thud of the diesel and the cries of the seabirds that followed the boat hoping for fish. They passed the crumbling cliffs of Lexton.

"What d'you think?" Mike called.

"About what?"

"About doing this for a living. Some living, eh?"

She nodded. She still didn't think very much of it, but, and she had to tell herself this over and over, it was his life. They weren't married. And, as things stood, didn't seem likely to be. But did she really want to be?

She said, "There's an oysterage at Orford. Hannah and I go there sometimes. You want to try it?"

"I don't like oysters."

"Have you ever tried them?"

"No, but I wouldn't like them."

"There speaks a man with an open mind."

It was a day for this sort of conversation, she thought. A day for gentle bantering. Followed by an evening of good food and wine. Followed by bed. And not a sore throat or a constipated bowel on the horizon.

Mike made a big sweep out to sea and then brought the boat back on a westerly tack and slowed.

"Watch out for red marker buoys," he said.

"What are you marking?"

"Not mine. Probably put there by that chap who drowned. Remember Bill Maitland telling us about him? The chap who was doing marine archaeology? As far as I can tell the buoys are directly over the old town."

"Aren't you putting your own buoys down?"

"Don't have to." He flicked his finger at something that looked like a car radio. "That gives us our position by satellite so we never need a buoy."

"There they are," she said. "On your left. Sorry, your port side."

He throttled down and brought the boat alongside one of the buoys. "We're over what might have been the old High Street."

"Are you going to dive?"

"Why not? There won't be many more chances until next spring. Just a short one."

She watched as he put on his wetsuit and then the oxygen cylinder and the gloves, mask, and flippers. In a few minutes he was ready and flopped into the water. It was relatively clear in the calm weather and she saw him go down and down and found herself thinking: What if he never comes back? After a few seconds all she could see was a shape and then that moved away and she lost sight of it altogether.

She crossed to the other side and

95

leaned over. She had done a little diving in Africa and had loved it. But there the water had been very clear compared with this and the weather had been hotter. Diving in the North Sea did not have quite the same attraction. Added to that there was something portentous if not indeed ominous about diving on a drowned town. People said, and of course it was ludicrous, that when the storms came at Lexton you could hear the church bells tolling under the waves. But ludicrous or not, thoughts like that were thoughts she did not need.

No, she would not become a diver, at least not here. Instead she would show interest and rally round and be optimistic and generally be a good little pal.

She stared down into the water. It was green and not too cold when she put her hand into it. She decided to take off her T-shirt and get what sun there was, and as she did so she noticed something attached to the second buoy. Their boat was tied to the first buoy, the second was about thirty feet away. At that moment Mike surfaced. He lifted his mask and shouted, "It's lovely down there. Bloody dark but lovely. I need a stronger torch. Why don't you come in?"

"No, thanks. It's not warm enough for me. Mike, there's something on the second buoy. I couldn't see what it was."

"Where?"

"There. They look like little boxes."

Mike was treading water and now he kicked his way to the buoy.

"Can you see it?"

"Yes. There's something tied on. No, not tied, looped. I'll try to get it undone."

She watched as he pulled at whatever it was. His feet in the flippers were working hard under water to keep him afloat.

He shouted, "The things are tied together with nylon line and it's got into a mess."

He worked at the buoy for a few minutes with the big sheath knife he carried then he passed up to her something that looked like a heavy belt. It consisted of a series of eleven packages tied together, each the size of half a brick. They were individually wrapped in plastic and sealed with grey parcel tape. She put them down in the wheelhouse.

He came out of the water, shrugged out of the straps of the oxygen cylinder, and took off his flippers. Then, still in his wet-suit, he crouched down and stared at the packages.

"What d'you think they are?" Alex said.

He didn't reply but went on looking at them and touching them and weighing them in his hands and turning them over. Whatever they contained they had been neatly packaged in plastic and had been tightly wrapped.

"Mike? What're you thinking?"

"I'm thinking drugs," he said.

"Drugs? On a buoy out at sea? Come on."

"I've seen them like this before. We had a case of a yacht off the Isle of Wight that was running heroin from France. The packages were not too dissimilar to these and they were tied together like these except they were joined by thin cord and had cork floats."

"But what for?"

"So if anyone — like the customs for instance — wanted to search the yacht the smugglers could drop them overboard attached to a fishing buoy and come back a little later to pick them up."

"These haven't got any floats."

"No, but they're wrapped the same way and they were attached to a buoy."

"And you really think they're drugs?"

"Why not? This is how a lot of drugs come into the country. Small boats from Europe. They don't all come in big containers, you know."

"What are you going to do? Open them and look?"

"Not bloody likely. I'm going to get them to the nearest copper and get rid of them. I don't want anyone saying, 'He opened one, he might have opened six.'"

"You're being a bit paranoid, aren't you?"

"Listen, it's the police who are paranoid about drug seizures. A lot of drugs have been stolen *after* they've been seized by the police. No, no, we'll take them in like they are — and I've got a respectable London doctor who can attest that we found eleven and we're handing in eleven."

He got out of his wetsuit and dried himself, then dressed. "You OK?" he said.

"For a drug runner I'm fine."

He cast off from the buoy and opened the throttle and they headed back to the little creek at Lexton. During that time Alex could not take her eyes from the packages that lay on the wheelhouse floor. She didn't like them and wished she hadn't spotted them. There was something malevolent about them.

The first thing they saw as they turned out of the river into the creek was a white police car on the gravel road near their mooring. Two men were standing by the beach where the body had been found. As they came to their mooring Alex saw that one of them was Somers, the local police sergeant, the other was someone she had not seen before. Somers was a forgettable figure, the word average came to her mind, but, as they walked towards the boat, the other man gave a different impression. He was of medium height but heavy, with a bald head fringed by grey. His face was square and his eyes set close together. Everything about him was square — face, hands, body. He did not wait for Somers to come aboard first to introduce him but stepped onto the boat and said, "I'm Detective Inspector Brady, East Suffolk Police. I'd like to ask you a few questions."

Mike smiled. "I've been expecting someone like you, Inspector, let's go below."

The four of them went down to the big saloon. It had been furnished with a desk and a chart table and two sofas that converted to bunks, leather swing chairs and cupboards and hanging space, a TV and video recorder, and, as Alex had said when she had first seen it in the shipyard, all the comforts of home. They sat around the table and Mike said, "Coffee? A drink?"

Brady shook his head and put his hands on the table. Alex noticed that the nails were bitten down to the quicks. He lit a cigarette and looked round for an ashtray. She fetched a saucer. He had a notebook and opened it on the table and began to turn the pages slowly.

"Mr Harley? Mr Michael Harley?"

"That's me."

"Mrs Elston?" He looked at Alex.

"That was my married name. I've gone back to my former name. Kennedy."

"Miss Kennedy."

"That's right."

"It's Dr Kennedy," Mike said.

Brady said, "Oh, yes. Doctor. Can't read my own handwriting."

"May I ask how you got my former married name?" Alex said.

"Checked you out. You were the two who found the body." It wasn't a question but a statement. Brady had a habit of looking down at his notebook and then into the air between Mike and Alex, never quite in their faces.

"That's right," Mike said. "On the little beach where you were standing."

Somers, who was sitting on the same side of the table as Brady, said, "I don't think that's — "

Brady held up his hand, then with deliberation unfolded a sheet of paper and looked at it. "Says here you first saw it under your boat. Then you beached it there."

"Sorry. Yes. That's how it happened."

"Let's get it straight. OK?"

Alex saw Mike's hands tighten.

Brady said, "Right, so you saw the body here at the boat. What were you doing then? It was early, wasn't it?"

"Having a cup of coffee."

"Wasn't it a bit cold at that time in the morning to have coffee out on deck?"

"We were having it in the boat. We heard the body scraping on the hull."

Brady flicked the paper. "Doesn't say anything about having coffee in the boat."

Somers said, "Didn't think it was important. Not the bit about having coffee."

"I'll judge what's important. OK?"

Somers looked away in embarrassment.

Alex had been reminded of someone when she looked at Brady — and then she realized it was Miss Piggy of the Muppets, except that Miss Piggy smiled and looked much prettier than Brady.

He said, "I want to know everything. Doesn't matter how inconsequential it might sound."

"Like coffee in the early morning," Mike said.

"That's it. You've got it. Right, let's

get on. What happened then?"

Alex watched Mike as he spoke in short clipped sentences. He gave a detailed and accurate picture of what had occurred.

Brady put up a hand to stop him. "When did you call Dr Kennedy?"

"After I'd tried to revive him."

"Doesn't say that here. Why didn't you ask the doctor to come right at the beginning?"

"Because she was changing."

"Changing?"

"Out of her night — out of her sleeping clothes into day clothes."

"Oh, so the coffee was in night clothes?"

"Yes, we had the coffee in night clothing."

"Doesn't say that. Anyway, you asked the doctor to come and do what?"

"See if she could get any life into him. I'd tried myself. He seemed pretty dead. He'd lost his eyes and — "

"You think you know a dead body from a live one?"

"Yes."

"You an expert?"

"No, but I took a course in first

104

aid when I did my navigation course. Drowning was the most important part."

Brady nodded. He turned to Alex. "OK. So you got changed and came down and . . . what?"

"Gave him a thorough examination. Or as thorough as I could."

"Wasn't it a bit late?"

"How do you mean?"

"I mean what if he had a bit of life in him and you went and changed and wasted that bit of life?"

She found herself having to restrain the anger that was rising inside her.

"I had examined him before that."

"He didn't say that." He pointed to Mike. "Said you went and changed and then examined him."

"I gave him a brief examination first."

"So he got that wrong too."

"It wasn't a thorough examination."

"Still in your night clothes?"

"Still in my night clothes. And I knew he was dead."

"You knew he was dead. OK? How long?"

She thought if he said OK once more she'd scream. But meantime she knew he had her statement in front of him and she could not remember if she had said two or three days. She guessed at it. "I estimated he had been dead for a couple of days at least."

"Right. So you came back once you were dressed and examined him again."

"I had my bag and I was able to do it more thoroughly. But I didn't expect to find any signs of life, and there weren't any."

"You said you thought the man had been dead for at least a couple of days. How did you arrive at that?"

"The distension of his stomach, the elasticity of his skin. Things like that. But I'm no expert."

"So it wouldn't surprise you to know that our pathologist says he wasn't dead much more than a day."

"No, it wouldn't surprise me. I told you, I'm no expert."

"I wish you'd told someone before. We had you down as one, you see."

Mike said, in a soft voice that worried Alex, "That's your problem."

"What is?"

"No one said Dr Kennedy was an

expert in pathology." Mike turned to Somers and said, "You want to get your notes right."

Before Somers could reply Brady turned to Mike and said, "You people from the Met think you know every bloody thing. Anyway, you're not even Met, you're ex-Met. OK? Listen, let me tell you something, the Met always patronized the Regional Crime Squads. The country boys, someone called us. Well, I could have worked for the Met. No bloody doubt about it. But I didn't want to. OK?"

Mike was smiling slightly at this rush of pent-up hatred and Alex wondered whether Brady's hatred of London's Metropolitan Police had not come from being turned down by them.

"You want to say anything?" Brady said.

Mike said, "No, Inspector, nothing more at the moment, thank you."

The way he said it made Brady blink and Alex realized there was a subtext. Mike had reached the rank of Chief Inspector of an élite squad before he resigned and Brady, at least ten years older, was one rank below him and perhaps would not make another.

"Right. OK." He went back to taking them over each point in their statements, sometimes the same point two or three times.

There was something frightening about Brady, Alex thought. There seemed so much pent-up hatred in him that when the volcano burst it would be violent, so she kept her own voice down and allowed him to dominate her and finally he seemed to regain his control.

"Have you found out who he is, Inspector?" Alex asked, and the way she said 'inspector' implied nothing but admiration.

"No, we haven't. But we do know where he came from: Hong Kong. Labels in his clothes, though a lot of clothes are made there these days. But our guess is that that's where he came from." He rose and turned to Mike. "I'll want to see you again."

"If you say so." Mike's voice was well controlled and still soft.

"Yes, I say so. And I'll tell you for why. Our pathologist said those cuts in his chest weren't made by rocks but by a knife. See what I mean?"

"He was murdered?" Alex said.

"That's exactly what I mean. OK?"

The two policemen left the boat. Once he was on the shore Somers called up to Mike, "You let me know where to find you."

"I'm not going anywhere."

"I told you you can't moor here, it's private. And no one's allowed — "

"I've got permission from Mrs Blackhurst. See her about it."

"You've got what? You couldn't have got permission from her. I mean — "

Brady said, "For Christ's sake, leave it. I want to get back."

Somers looked confused. "I'll check," he said.

"You do that," Mike swung round to Brady. "Right?" he said. "OK?"

The police car drove off in a cloud of dust.

"What a bastard," Mike said. "You get them like that sometimes. Not often but sometimes. OK?"

"Don't you start!"

They went back to the wheelhouse

and there, on the floor, was the pile of packages. Alex said, "You didn't do what you said you were going to do."

"And I'm not going to. I wouldn't give that bastard ice in winter. Let's have a look at one."

"I thought you didn't want to take the risk."

"I'll take them back to London. Give them to the people in the Drugs Squad. They know me and they know I wouldn't touch the bloody stuff."

He took his sheath knife and snicked the wrapping of one of the parcels. Beneath it was a plastic box which was also taped. He snicked that and opened the lid. It was filled with what looked like coarsely ground coffee grains. He stared at it for some moments then took a pinch and sniffed. "Ugh," he said. "Smells like a bloody farmyard."

"What on earth are they?" Alex said.

"God knows. But I'll tell you one thing, it's like no drug I've ever seen."

7

DOMMIE was in his 'castle'. This was an outbuilding of flint and stone near the cliff top. It was said to be very old and some experts thought it had been a bakehouse or a brewery or a laundry — no one was certain — to a much older building on the site of what was now Lexton House. It was the size of a large room and the inside had been stripped years ago of whatever had been there. It had a stone-flagged floor, which made it cold in winter, and a couple of windows overlooking what had once been the garden.

In more recent times when there had been a garden this had been the garden shed where the mower and the tools were kept, but since the house had not had a garden for years it had been changed to Dommie's needs. The garden tools had been removed. A table and chairs had been put in and also a fan heater that Dommie could switch on and off but which was installed behind a heavy wire grille so that he could not touch it. Before it had been secured, Ellen had once found him in his 'castle' using the whirling fan heater as a propeller and trying to fly.

But now she felt happy about him being there. It was as safe as she had been able to make it and it gave him a place where he occupied himself for hours. Here he would bring his stamp albums — there were twenty-four of these — and his 'photograph' albums which were filled with pictures he had cut from newspapers and magazines. He kept his fishing gear there and also his collection of walking sticks which ranged from silver-headed canes to thumb sticks and heavy blackthorns. Here he also did his 'art'. He had an easel and waterpaints. Most of his paintings were unfathomable to Ellen or anyone else, but not to him. When asked what a yellow and purple splodge was he would more often than not say, 'Cow.' But precisely the same splodge might be a fish. He only did the two.

Without his castle Dommie would have been inside the house all day and that would have made Ellen's life considerably more difficult.

Dommie was wax polishing one of his walking sticks when a car came up the drive and stopped. He dropped the stick and sprinted towards it. Frank Spender got out of the Bentley and waved at him.

"Aren't you cold?"

"I'm hot." Dommie was in a short-sleeved shirt and his muscles showed. He took Spender's hand and shook it firmly. This was something he did on occasion. Sometimes he would even shake Ellen's hand when she said good morning to him.

"Hot, are you?" Spender was dressed in well-cut salmon-pink corduroy trousers, a heavy dark blue shirt and a cashmere cardigan. The morning was made chilly by the fog that lay out at sea and came in over the cliffs in broken banks. But the day promised well once the fog had gone.

"Grannie in?"

"Yes, Grannie's in. I've been painting.

Then polishing my sticks."

"Painting what?"

"A fish."

They began to walk to the house, both men stepping over the cracks in the drive.

"What sort of fish?"

"A toadfish."

"Don't know that one. There's your grannie."

Ellen stood in the doorway. "Morning, Frank. I heard the car."

"Could I see you for a few minutes?"

"Of course you can. You don't have to ask."

The two went into the drawing room and Dommie returned to his castle. Ellen, dressed as she usually was in creased trousers, scuffed walking shoes, a man's shirt and a big khaki jersey, said, "Come into the kitchen. I'm cleaning the silver."

They went through. The table was covered in candlesticks and chafing dishes and a pair of life-sized silver partridges.

"I hope you've got this stuff well insured," Spender said. "They look like a robbery waiting to happen."

"John had them insured."

"John died a long time ago."

"I'm pretty sure they are. I'll make sure."

He put his hands in his pockets and went to the window. It looked out over the cliff tops to the sea beyond. The fog bank was clearly visible.

"I've come to see you about Gracie," he said.

"Oh, Lord, what's the matter with her now?"

"She's rambling again."

She said, "That's what Alzheimer's is, isn't it? Rambling? Living there by herself has made it worse. She talks to herself because she's got no one else to talk to. I suppose it's the anniversary. She's always remembered the time of year."

"But how would she know? Her mind's a blank about things like that. Except if it was stimulated, of course. You went to see her, didn't you?"

"Yes, I did. Frank, someone's got to keep an eye on her. I know you do and there are one or two others. Bill goes round. But I take her the odd bit of food and Dommie gets her to eat it. She

115

still knows who he is and she's fond of him."

He wandered round the table examining the silver. "Georgian?" He held up a candelabra and she nodded. To hear Frank Spender, the Frank Spender she had known all these years, comment on a piece of silver, even know there was a period called Georgian, never failed to surprise her. He returned to what he'd been saying. "Well, you stimulated her this time. She's been going over it and over it."

"Oh, Frank, there's no one to listen."

"If it's the anniversary that's brought it on why don't you stay away for a bit? I'll see she gets something to eat."

"*You* won't see to that at all!"

"All right, I'll get the food sent round from the pub. Like meals on wheels."

"She gets meals on wheels several times a week. I arranged that."

"On the other days, then."

He went back to the window and there was silence for a while. "Fog's still there," he said, then, in an abrupt change of subject, "I hear you've let him moor the boat in the creek."

116

"I don't really mind him being there and he's paying me."

"I thought you said you'd never let anyone moor there."

"Times change, Frank. What's good one year isn't good the next. You should know that."

"What I do know is that this is a fishing village. You've refused local lads moorings in the past. What are they to think about this?"

"I don't care what they think. It's none of their bloody business."

"That's exactly what it is. Their business. The fish have never been so scarce. In another twenty or thirty years there won't be a cod or a haddock, not even a herring, in the North Sea. But in the meantime it's everything to them."

"Harley's not a fisherman and everyone knows that. He's like that other man, the one who drowned. He wants to dive on the old town."

"That's what he says now. Ellen, you're missing the point. If Lexton is anything it's a fishing village and fishermen are like miners, cliquey. They don't like newcomers. Think about it from the point of view of the village as you've always known it." There was the noise of a diesel starting up and Spender went to the windows at the side of the room. "There he goes."

Ellen went on rubbing the silver and he watched Mike's boat turn out of the creek into the river and head for the sea. Then he said, "I must be off. Think about it."

He stopped at the kitchen door and pointed to a crack on the far wall. "That's got worse, Ellen. You should get out of here before something happens."

She shook her head. "Don't go on about it, Frank. This is our home. Dommie's and mine. And it's been like this for a very long time. Since before John died. It'll see us out."

"You hope it will." He waved his hand and left.

★ ★ ★

"Soft hands, that's what you must have for this boat."

Mike and Alex were in the wheelhouse and she was at the wheel. Both were

118

wearing heavy Guernseys and rubber boots.

"You've got a lot of boat to get to port or starboard and the big thing is not to pull the wheel over like you're turning a corner in the car. Try it again. Port . . . that's left . . . gently . . . gently . . . See how she comes round? And now straighten up . . . that's it . . . See?"

"All this gently, gently stuff sounds like you're talking to a young virgin."

"I am. That's what the boat is. Well, perhaps not all that young — except to me. And they don't like the rough stuff. That's why they're feminine."

"Don't you think she should have a name, not just 'the boat'?"

"I've thought of one. I'll tell you later. Watch it! You've done it again. Gently. And make up your mind early."

He took the wheel and brought the speed down until they were almost wallowing in the calm sea.

"There they are!" Alex said as the buoys came into sight. "I'm still not sure exactly why we've come out. I don't like this fog."

"To make sure there aren't any more

drugs hanging from these buoys."

"I thought you said they weren't drugs."

"I know. They aren't like any I've ever seen but they've got to be. What the hell else could they be? If there are more I've got to have them and if there aren't I've got to know there aren't. That's the first thing Laddie Broakes would ask me: have I got the lot?"

"Who's Laddie Broakes?"

"I've mentioned him before. He was my guv'nor in the SIS. Well, I can't see anything on the buoys but we'll come back and check. We'll make circles."

He took the boat in a series of circles with the buoys as the centre. He went slowly round and round, gradually increasing the size of the circles until they were almost a mile from the buoys. But all they saw were pieces of flotsam. The sea was grey and uninviting and the fog swirled around them.

"Right, let's go back to the buoys and I'll do a short dive. See there's nothing further down those ropes."

"Why not wait until the sun comes out? The radio said the fog would lift."

"Makes no difference in a wet-suit."

He took them back to the red marker buoys. They tied up on one and killed the engine. Again he got into his wetsuit and put on his mask and flippers and oxygen tank and in a few minutes was over the side. This time he did not disappear so quickly into the gloomy sea but spent some time looking at the buoys and the seaweed that had collected just below them. Then he went down each rope.

Alex sat on deck in the misty air. The fog seemed to come in banks. One moment she could hardly see her hand in front of her, the next she could see twenty or thirty yards. It was a ghostly place and she did not like sitting alone above a drowned town. Mike had said something about the buoys being over the old High Street. Was this where the noise of the church bells came from? She listened but all she could hear was the slap of the waves on the boat and, in the distance, the foghorn in the lighthouse on Lexton Point. She knew it was a romantic and totally incorrect view that a town simply slipped under the waves with its churches still standing and its bells ringing. In reality, as Mike and Maitland had explained, the sea would have gnawed at the cliffs and the town would have crumbled and broken up and slid down into the sea in bits and pieces. So there would be no standing buildings and no bells to go on ringing. But knowing that didn't change anything, she still expected to hear the bells.

Suddenly she did hear a noise, not of a bell, but of an engine. It came from starboard and grew quickly in volume. She ran to the side of the boat and then, out of the fog, came another boat. It rose hugely in front of her, water foaming from its bows as if some mad Ahab was driving it forward in search of the White Whale. At the last moment, as she thought it was about to crash into her, it veered away missing Mike's boat by a skin of paint. As it did so she threw herself headlong to the far side of the deck and lay motionless for a moment, her head buried in her arms.

And then it was gone. Just the thump, thump of its engine growing fainter in the fog. Then nothing.

She rose to her feet, shaky and terrified, and in front of her like some ghostly creature himself Mike rose from the depths. He lifted his mask and said, "Not a bloody thing."

"Did you hear the boat?"

"What?"

"I'll tell you when you come aboard."

As he was getting dressed again she told him of the near miss. She thought he might smile and dismiss it but he didn't. He got her to describe the boat but the best she could do was to say it was like the one they were on.

"A fishing boat?"

"Must have been. It was so sudden, so huge . . . I just dived for cover."

When they got back to the creek he took out the dinghy and rowed Alex up the river where the boats were. She looked at them carefully then she shrugged. "They all look the same to me."

"But it was like these?"

"Oh, yes, like these all right."

They rowed back to their boat in the creek. Mike said, "I was going to say let's go to the pub for lunch. How do you feel?"

"I'm fine, but I'd rather cook. I don't get much of a chance in London and pub food is all right as far as it goes but it goes too far on me." She patted her bottom.

"I like it like that," he said.

"I like you to like it but in slightly smaller quantities. I bought some monkfish. How about I poach it in vermouth?"

She was cooking in the galley when Mike came down and said, "Those things we found. The drug things . . . You know what I think? I think they had something to do with that dead bloke. I've been telling myself not to think that because there's no proof but now I'm telling myself he was killed because of them and I'm also thinking that the boat that nearly ran us down had come out to pick them up and then saw us there. What do you think of that scenario?"

"I think everything becomes a police scenario to you. I think you can't help it." She realized how much braver she was feeling now they were tied up to dry land. "There's probably a perfectly simple explanation for everything."

"Such as?"

"I just can't think of one at the moment."

8

"WELL, this is nice," Hannah de Meer said. They were in the living room on the first floor of Hannah's house in Southwold. Its windows overlooked the golf course on the common and on this warm morning people were playing golf and walking their dogs and a couple of kids were trying to fly kites in almost no wind.

"More coffee?"

"No, thanks," Alex said. "That was good. Sometimes it tastes the way it smells."

Hannah helped herself to another cup. She was a tall woman in her sixties with short grey hair and she drank a lot of coffee.

"Hennie taught me what to buy and how to make it," she said. Her husband, Hendryk de Meer, had been a Dutch oilman who had been killed in a helicopter crash in the North Sea before Alex had come to live with Hannah. He

126

had died about the same time as Alex's parents so she and Hannah had needed each other.

"I didn't expect to see you for a couple of weeks," Hannah said.

"I think Mike wanted me to start painting the boat this morning while he went into Bury. So I ran away."

"How is Mike?"

The phrasing was natural enough but the inflexion was careful. There was just that slight emphasis on the word 'is' which gave the question its heightened pulse. Hannah had only met Mike a couple of times. Once she had gone with Alex to see him swim in a patients' gala at Effingham and once he had come to Southwold for lunch. There was a chemistry that didn't seem to work between them. Both had been on their best behaviour, which was probably one of the reasons. Best behaviour, Alex rationalized, didn't make for genuine warmth. She thought it might also have been because they were so alike: direct people who normally said what they thought without giving consideration to how it might sound and how it might offend. When they went into their best behaviour routine, neither was behaving naturally.

"Mike's fine. His knee isn't ever going to be dependable but provided he takes care he should be all right."

"Is he still in pain?"

"He doesn't talk about it."

"Poor boy."

There it was again. The emphasis this time was on the word 'poor'. It sounded almost patronizing yet Alex knew this had never been a characteristic of Hannah's.

To change the subject, she said, "How's the new novel coming along?"

"Slowly. I've had your room done up."

"I saw. It looks lovely."

She always wandered around the house the moment she arrived and went first to 'her' room. The possessive sounded natural, even though she had left Southwold more than ten years before, had been married and divorced and had a home of her own.

Unlike most children's rooms this one had terrible memories as well as good ones. It was the room she had come to after she had been picked up by Hannah at Heathrow when she was twelve years old. Hennie had died three weeks before and Alex's mother and father had died in the same week. They had hardly spoken on the drive from the airport to Suffolk. Hannah had taken her into the house and had said, "This is your room. This is your house. This is your home." Then she had taken her in her arms and they had wept.

So this woman, who had practised as a psychiatrist until her husband was killed and had then started writing impenetrable psychological novels, who had always been referred to by Alex's mother and father as 'your Aunt Hannah', and who had been a remote figure as an aunt; this woman was to become both mother and father to Alex. And Alex knew that had Hannah not been a good psychiatrist, she, Alex, would have been a very different person after what had happened.

"Where's Mike gone?" Hannah said.

"In search of Templar treasure. He's gone into Bury St Edmunds to see what he can find out. The Reverend Maitland's with him."

She recounted Bill's story.

"Is that what he's going to do? Look for treasure? I thought he was going to organize diving trips."

"Oh, this is just a fringe idea. He thinks it's too good to miss. You're looking disapproving."

"Not at all."

"Yes, you are!"

"Well, I suppose I am in a way. I mean it all sounds fun, but — "

"But life's not supposed to be fun?"

"It's not supposed to be anything. It's supposed to be life. It's what you make of it that counts."

"And that's exactly what Mike's doing. He's making something of it."

"Of course you're right, so don't pay any attention to me. I think I've got more security-minded in my old age. About you, anyway."

"You mean after Freddy?"

"Yes, after Freddy."

"But you always liked him."

"He was sweet. He just wasn't a good husband for you."

"He wouldn't make a good husband for anyone."

"That's true enough. Is he still on the *Chronicle*?"

"With an assistant and a secretary. He's empire-building. Anyway, I don't have his problem with Mike, thank God."

"Are you going to marry him?"

"He hasn't asked me."

Hannah lit a cigarette. "I don't usually smoke in front of doctors but I make an exception with you."

"You're a doctor yourself."

"Not a real one. I've booked a table at the Crown. We'll have lunch there. They do marvellous fish."

"That'll make a change. I tried to get some in Lexton and had to go to a supermarket freezer. But they seem to catch other things."

"Oh?"

"Drugs and bodies."

"What?"

She told Hannah about the body.

Hannah said she had read about it in the local paper. "But they didn't say anything about drugs."

"No, they wouldn't. Mike and I are the only ones who know about them, but the trouble is we don't really know if the things *are* drugs. I've worked with drugs and so has he. Neither of us has ever seen anything like them yet he thinks they have to be. So much care had been taken with the packing that they must be valuable and he says this is how drugs are often smuggled from France."

She pulled an envelope from her pocket and emptied some of the brown granules onto the palm of Hannah's hand. "Have you ever seen anything like them?"

Hannah looked at the coffee-like granules for a few moments then smelt them. She turned down her mouth. "Very agricultural." She smelt them again. "There's something . . . the smell reminds me of, something apart from Cold Comfort Farm only I can't think what. And you found them off Lexton! Doesn't sound right, does it?"

"Not the Lexton I remember. Now bodies come ashore there, and drugs, or whatever they are, are found, and people won't let Mike park his boat there. And I can sense a hostile atmosphere."

"The natural hostility to strangers?"

"Yes, I suppose so, but more than that. There's a kind of wrong note about the place. As though it's pretending to be something it isn't. Like being a fishing village and not catching fish."

"That's hardly their fault. The North Sea is fished out — or rapidly becoming fished out."

"I know. It's just that . . . It's difficult to explain . . . "

"You've got to remember that fishing villages are very neurotic places. The fishermen and their families don't know from one day to the next if they're going to have any money in their pockets. A bit like writers."

"You're not neurotic, are you?"

She laughed. "Of course not. Let's walk in the sunshine before we eat."

They walked down to the sea and along the front with its Edwardian houses to the bathing boxes and then turned back towards the town centre. As always, Alex thought it was like putting a penny in a time machine and going back into a more decorous age. Southwold's miracle was that it was still unspoilt; not a kiss-me-quick hat or a holiday souvenir shop in sight.

And that had offended Mike. When

he had come to lunch with Hannah
he had been back in the police for
four or five months, still with a limp
and a pain-drawn face, and when she
had mentioned how much she loved
Southwold for precisely this unspoilt
character he had said, "A lot of people
need to come to places like this for
holidays but they won't come if they're
middle-class morgues."

It was then, Alex thought, that Hannah
might have become disenchanted by him,
for she had cut herself off from the
argument.

Alex remembered how much she herself
had argued with him and it was only by
reminding herself what was happening to
him that she had found a perspective to
live with.

Going back into the police had been
traumatic for him. Before he was shot
he had worked for the highly specialized
SIS. When he went back he was desk-
bound in a back room. People, including
his boss, told him that he was doing an
important job and that it was only a
matter of time before he'd be back in
the front line. But the doctors said that

his knee would probably never be one hundred per cent again. And he knew and they knew and she knew that if it wasn't a hundred per cent, he would have to stay doing this 'very important' job at the desk.

Those had been the worst times. He had been in constant pain and yet he had exercised all the time. She had offered, when she could, to take him to work by car. He had flatly refused. He'd walked to the tube station and down thirty or forty steps to the platform and stood in the train all the way to St James's Park and climbed up from the platform there. Sometimes — and this, to Alex, had seemed almost like the flagellants of the fourteenth century — he would get off a couple of stops before he needed to and force himself to walk the extra distance to Scotland Yard.

He would come to her flat most nights and start drinking. That had worried her. She had found out what painkillers he was using and unethically substituted stronger ones without telling him. It didn't seem to make any difference. Then he began to invite his former colleagues round in the evenings. They would drink heavily and Mike would talk and banter and seem once again to be part of the elite squad. Their visits affected him like amphetamines and the high would last until the following day. Then the reaction would set in.

Everything became worse when the visits tailed off. Fewer old mates came. They were bloody busy, you see. Then none came. Mike became a kind of zombie and it was then she realized that it wasn't so much the pain that was destroying him as the lack of hope that he would return to front-line duty.

When he wasn't drinking with his mates because they no longer wanted to drink with him, and when he wasn't on the phone to one or other of them, and when he wasn't poring over the newspapers to see if any of his cases were coming up in court — then he and Alex argued. It always began in the same way, trivial arguments over what to watch on TV or who had last had the newspaper or what to have for supper — arguments that would suddenly flare into something serious.

It began to get her down. She was working hard all day. When she came back to her flat in the evening Mike would already be there. If he wasn't he'd be at his place and she'd go there. Wherever he was, by the time she got to him he would already have had several drinks. She would get the supper or else they would go out and eat. Normally, she loved eating out, but not when seated across from someone who was angry and silent and half drunk. She would find herself crying at odd times of the day for no reason she could think of; tears would just be there in her eyes and her throat would close. She put it down to exhaustion.

She had wanted their relationship to end then. She had wanted to say, goodbye Mike. And thanks a million for what you did. See you around sometime.

But she couldn't. He was like he was because of her and there was no getting round that.

So she went to Hannah, who listened in silence for a long time and said, "Two things. First you know why he's like he is. You've rationalized that. But there's an extra dimension. You know how it is with some people: they can't retire. They have their retirement party and get their present but then come back to the office on any excuse until the people there start avoiding them. That's what's happened with Mike. He's being metaphorically retired. It may be that he should think about doing it properly. If his knee is never going to work adequately then he's never going to get his job back."

"And the second thing?"

"The second thing is you. Mike has to face his past because his future depends on it. So do you. I've been wanting to say this for a long time and now I think is the moment. You've got to go back to Africa, darling. Just let the memories come back and face them."

Instead she'd gone back to London and Mike had got worse and she had got worse.

* * *

Ellen Blackhurst woke and looked at her watch. It was a little before six o'clock and the evening television news was almost due. She was in her armchair in the drawing room with *The Times* open on her lap. This was a part of the day, when she had finished her chores, when she would read what she had not read of the paper in the morning and frequently have a short nap. These moments of sleepiness were occurring more often these days and she knew it was age and accepted it. But she prided herself that she never slept for much more than ten minutes.

As always she cocked her head and listened for Dommie. He was usually in the house at this time watching the early evening soap in his bedroom. He was never quite sure what was happening but loved it all the same. But she could not hear any sound coming from that. Had he gone fishing?

"Dommie!" she called.

If he was there he would shout, "What?" at the top of his voice. But this evening there was only silence. Ellen pushed herself out of the big chair and went to the bottom of the staircase.

"Dommie, are you there? Are you in your room?"

At other times he would play games with her. He would hide somewhere in the house, behind a door or a cupboard or even in the dark of the half-demolished cellar, and when she came near he would spring out and shout, "I'm here!"

Even though she half expected it she always got a fright.

"Dommie!"

She wandered out of the house to Dommie's castle. The sun was shining through its windows and she looked through the dusty glass. Dommie wasn't there, nor was his fishing tackle. She checked the time. It was nearly six o'clock and she always watched the news. If he wasn't back by the time it finished she would go and fetch him.

He wasn't. The news ended. Ellen put on her jacket and went outside. After the morning fog dispersed the day had been lovely and the air was thick with salt and late sunshine. There were half a dozen fishermen on the beach but she could not make out from the top of the crumbling cliffs whether Dommie was one of them. She went down the zigzag path, slipping and sliding on the sandy soil. Down on the shingle the smell of the sea was strong. She walked along just above the tide mark where the small waves were hissing. She asked one of the fishermen if he knew Dommie.

"The simple man?"

"Well . . . yes, the simple man."

"He was here about an hour ago. I gave him one of my fish and he said he was going to cook it for someone. I didn't get the name."

"Thanks." Ellen went back to the path. At its base she saw what she had not noticed coming down. Lying about a yard away but hidden by reeds and grass were Dommie's fishing rod and fishing bag. She picked them up. The fisherman had said Dommie was going to cook the fish for someone. That was always his way of saying Ellen was going to cook it and that's what she had assumed.

But he wasn't at home and he wasn't on the beach — so where was he?

9

ALEX drove back from Southwold in the late afternoon. The visit had, in a way, been unsettling. She often found this after going back to Hannah's and seeing her old room with the furniture she knew so well. The house had not only memories of that period of school and university but also the memories that came later when she was married to Freddy.

She hadn't thought of Freddy for some time. Soon after they had split up she had thought of him every day, had dreamed of him, but that had become less frequent until now it had almost dried up. She wondered how he was liking the *Chronicle*. It was ironic that he of all people should have gone to her father's old paper. And Medical Correspondent. How respectable it sounded!

Lexton was full of long shadows and the air was beginning to feel sharp as she drove over the small river bridge.

From its raised arch she could see across the marsh to the creek where the boat was moored and, parked near it, Mike's elderly green BMW. She remembered the day he had bought it. It was one of those bad days after the shooting. She wasn't working, and he had wanted to move . . . just move. She had had to drive because he couldn't manage a car with a clutch. As they drove south through Woolwich he had seen a car showroom with this particular used model for sale. It was advertised as being an automatic and he had asked her to stop. Half an hour later he had bought the car even though it was way beyond his means.

"Why the hell not?" he had said. "It's only money."

That was a phrase she would get used to, especially once he had sold his house. But, in the event, it had been a good choice. He loved the car and it had the kind of solid feel about it that gave her confidence to sit in the passenger seat and let him drive her about London even though she hadn't been sure how his legs would react in an emergency.

He was working at his desk in the cabin

when she went aboard. It was covered in papers. Some were photocopies and some had pencilled notes on them. She kissed him and said, "Have you found the treasure? Are you going to be rich beyond your wildest dreams?"

"You being ironic or sarcastic or what?"

There was a fraction of irritation in the question. This often happened when she least expected it.

"Don't be silly, I'm being interested."

"OK. Why don't we go up to the pub and I'll tell you."

She had a shower and came back into the bedroom drying herself. He looked up and half smiled at her. "Don't let anyone ever tell you you haven't got beautiful boobs," he said.

"Right. I won't."

He reached out and cupped one with his hand.

"I thought we were going for a drink." As she said it she saw at the porthole over his shoulder the face of a balding man.

"Christ!" She wrapped herself in the towel. "There's someone at the window!"

Mike whirled and the face disappeared.

He went up on deck. A running figure was disappearing into the reeds. "That was Dommie," he said. "Remember, I told you about him?"

"I'd forgotten we were vulnerable!"

"So had I. Just as well we didn't start something."

"Didn't you say there was something wrong with him?"

"I was told he's got a mental age of six or seven. Did you see his face properly?"

"It didn't look like Down's syndrome. I mean, he looks different but not in that way."

"Different how?"

"I'd have sworn there was some Oriental blood in him."

"You're imagining things. He's Mrs Blackhurst's grandson."

She got dressed and they rowed across the river and moored below the pub. It was empty at this time. He bought a couple of drinks and they sat at a window table in a room overlooking the river.

"OK," she said. "My hunt for the Templars' gold by Michael Harley." As she said it she wondered if she had made another mistake but he didn't react.

Several men came in and went into one of the other rooms. The one called Chris was with them and Mike said sourly, "He's always here. Why doesn't he go fishing sometime?"

"He went this morning, or at least someone did. I was awake about two and I heard a boat go out. Anyway, never mind him, tell me about today. What was Bill Maitland like?"

"Good. Very helpful. You know, he's about seventy but looks as strong as an ox and he walks so fast I could hardly keep up with him." When he said things like that she listened for self-pity but there was none. It was the statement of a perfectly fit man. He went on: "He took me to the library at the old monastery and helped me with the manuscripts. They let us see one called the Bury Manuscript and it was almost impossible to read. He said it was in Middle English but it might have been in Bulgarian for all I could make of it. He read a bit so I could hear the language then he got me a translation I could photocopy."

"I'd like to read it."

"Even the translation is pretty difficult. It was done in Victorian times but I got the general gist."

"About the treasure?"

"Sort of. It starts with the King of France, Philippe le Bel, who put down the Templars."

"I've never really known why. I always thought they were rather splendid."

"According to Bill it's because they were so rich. They owned hundreds of castles and huge tracts of land. The king wanted the land and the castles so he arrested them and executed some and generally screwed up the order."

"I remember the head of the order cursed him, didn't he?"

"De Molay. He was burnt at the stake and he cursed Philippe then. But some Templars managed to flee from France with their valuables and the manuscript tells the story of one group that sailed from Flanders with all their possessions and landed in Lexton where there was already a Temple. So while the Templars were being put down in France the Templars in England and Scotland weren't so badly off. The manuscript

147

says that when Lexton began to be eaten away by the sea and they lost their building they moved back and rebuilt where their old graveyard had been. Bill thinks that's somewhere near Mrs Blackhurst's house. He thinks gold plate might be buried there. He's been looking for any signs of that."

"And has he found any?"

"He found a sarcophagus, or what he thinks is a sarcophagus, on the beach below the Blackhurst house but there was nothing in it."

"Not even any bones?"

"Not a thing except shingle. It was all smashed as though it had fallen from the cliff and whatever was in it could have been washed out to sea."

"Or buried in the shingle."

"He says the East Suffolk Archaeological Society was interested for a time — it's some years back — but after they'd dug for a few months and found nothing they gave up."

"And now you're going to try?"

"What's that supposed to mean?"

"Just exactly what I said. You're going to try to find the treasure, aren't you?"

"No, that's not what you meant. I could hear it in your tone. What you meant was that I was going to go on being a bloody fool."

"No, I didn't, Mike. Really, it was just something to say."

"Balls. You've never been keen on this whole thing. You think what I'm doing here is a waste of time and money. And I know why it's come out now. You've been to see Hannah and she's been talking."

"That's not true, we never discussed your work."

"I don't believe you."

"Oh, damn it, have it your way, then. Yes, I do sometimes think you may be wrong in doing this. I do sometimes think you may be throwing your money away. But — "

"What d'you want me to do, be a bloody cab driver like my dad? Anyhow, they'd never give me a licence with this leg."

"Let me finish. I was about to say that after what happened to you just being able to throw your money around like this is marvellous. And that's what I've

149

always said to Hannah. You might have ended up in a wheelchair."

"Well, what are you complaining about?"

"Nothing. Not a damn thing."

They were silent, both feeling they were near the edge of an emotional precipice.

Alex was the first to speak. "If you're going to argue I'm going to need another drink."

"No, I'm not. I'm sorry. It's just that I . . . well, I don't bloody know what I really want to do either."

She covered his hand with one of her own. "You can walk. You've got some money in the bank. You've got somewhere to sleep. And we're together. What more is there?"

* * *

It was dusk when Ellen drove down the little lane that wound along the river. This short cut was a route she had seldom taken in recent years and her mind went back to that time at the end of the war when she had driven it

150

regularly. There had been more fishing boats then than now and she would watch them swing round in the turning basin and head back downstream to their moorings.

The turning basin was an indication of how much things had changed in the centuries since Lexton had been a major port. Then the river had been wide and navigable, with docks. Now it was so narrow the boats could not comfortably turn at the village and had to come a mile upstream where there was a natural pool.

She stopped the car and stared across the reeds to the basin. This was where she used to wait for Frank. Coming in after a night's fishing he would jump onto the bank as the boat turned and run over to the car. Sometimes his need was so great he would want her right then and he would take her in the car, but mostly they would go deeper into the reeds and put down a rug. Until then she had only ever been bedded by John and that rarely and unpleasantly. Frank had been a revelation and she had wanted him as much as he had wanted her.

But that was all over long ago. She revved up the car and drove on to Gracie's. Dommie had gone there once or twice before on his walkabouts. It was now almost dark and she could not see whether there was a light on in the house. She knocked, opened the door, and went in. Gracie was sitting in her usual place near the stove. There was a dim forty-watt bulb burning in a socket near her but that was the only light there was. A newspaper was strewn round the chair. Gracie's glasses were on her nose but her head had fallen forward in sleep. She woke when Ellen came into the room.

"Oh, it's you."

"Yes, it's me, Gracie. How are you?"

Gracie sniffed. "What d'you want?"

"I've come to ask if you've seen Dommie, if — "

"Who's that?"

"You know very well who Dommie is." This was one of Gracie's games, pretending ignorance when she was asked a question. "I want to know if he's been here to see you."

"He's one of 'em."

"Who's them?"

"The little men."

"Oh dear, you're not on about them again, are you? Anyway, Dommie's not little."

"What you sayin' — that I can't see proper?" There was a sudden harshness in her tone.

"Not at all, Gracie. Listen, I'm looking for Dommie and — "

"Because I 'ave seen 'em. Out there. And eat."

"What's eat? Who's eating? The little men?"

"Ah, what's the use. What d'you want?"

"I told you. I'm looking for Dommie. He's not at home. He was given a fish by a man on the beach and I thought he might have come here to give it to you."

"I don't want your fish."

"It's not my fish. It's Dommie's. And it's not very nice talking like that. Dommie likes to look after you and you always loved him. He was like your own baby."

"He warn't my baby. Nor yours. He

153

was Gilly's. That's whose he was."

"Yes, I know that. Of course I know that. You're rambling again and there's no talking to you. I'm going to look for Dommie in the village. You go to bed and when you wake the little men will have gone."

"Aaah, I don't want your fish. I don't want anything from you."

Ellen turned at the doorway. "Just remember, Gracie, you got the cottage. That's quite a lot. I can always take it away." There was a sudden look of fear on the old woman's face. "But I won't," Ellen said. "Not if you're good. Will you be good?"

After a long moment Gracie said, "Aye."

"Say it properly. Say, 'I'll be good.'"

"I'll be good."

"That's all right, then. If Dommie comes, send him home, you hear?"

"Aye. I'll send him home."

Ellen closed the door and went to her car. The engine turned over half a dozen times before it caught. She drove into the village and up the High Street. It was dark now and there weren't many people about. Sometimes Dommie came and stood in front of the shop windows, especially the one showing the fishing tackle, but tonight he wasn't there. She drove on towards the sea. On a point of land near the mouth of the river, with its own private beach, stood Frank Spender's house. She opened the heavy black wrought-iron gates and drove up the gravel drive to the front door.

This was the finest house in Lexton. A big rambling place built in the 1920s with great double-glazed windows looking out at the sea. It had been owned originally by a peer who had made his money in brewing — 'the bloody beerage' her husband John had said contemptuously — but the house was the most luxurious place around and unlike her own wasn't threatened by the hungry sea.

A manservant answered the door and said Frank Spender was working.

"Who is it?" Frank's voice came across the hall.

"Me, Frank."

He put his head out of a door and said, "Come on in."

She went into his study. It was a

155

beautiful room with a large partners' desk and a world globe by Merzbach & Falk on a stand by the windows. The desk was piled with letters and papers.

"Have I caught you at a bad time?" she said.

"Not at all." The heavy East Coast accent was all in the nose. He was dressed, as he often was, in denim, but it wasn't like any denim she had seen in local shops. This was designer denim at its most costly. It was faded and gave his grey hair and sunburnt, lined face the colour tone in Remington's paintings of the old West. She wondered if there were any of his young London women in the house and decided to get away as quickly as possible.

"I'm looking for Dommie and I wondered if he'd been here."

He shook his head. "I haven't seen him. Gone walkabout again?"

"He went down to the beach and I haven't seen him since. He's usually watching television at this time."

"Have you tried Gracie's?"

"She was the first. But she's rambling. Her mind's full of strange people and past history. She started on me again. But no matter now. When I left her I went down the High Street. Nothing."

"Give me a second and I'll come with you."

"No, no, don't worry. I'll go round the pubs. Sometimes he goes to the hotel."

"Of course I'll come." At that moment the phone rang. "Hello?" he said. "Oh, hello, Phil." He listened for a few moments and his face darkened. "Did she call you? Aye. Well . . . All right. Look, I've got Mrs Blackhurst here. She's looking for him. Yes. I think I'd better. I'll meet you there. And Phil, thanks." He put down the phone and said to Ellen, "That was Phil Somers. He's had a call from Betty Smith. Dommie was there and he's hurt her."

"Oh, God! How badly?"

"Phil hasn't seen her. He's on his way. I said I'd meet him at her place."

"I'll come with you."

They got into Frank's big Bentley and drove up the High Street and stopped at a block of shops with flats above them. Sergeant Somers was already there in a small police car.

"I thought I'd ring you first," Somers said. "You said I should always — "

"Yes. Right. Good. Let's go and see." Ellen said, "Where's Dommie?"

Somers said, "I don't know, she didn't say. Only that he'd been here. Something about a fish."

They went up the stairs to the flat above. A woman came to the door and let them in. The light was dim. She had been crying and looked uncomprehendingly at the three of them. Ellen said by way of explanation, "I was at Mr Spender's house looking for Dommie."

It was then she saw the blood.

10

THERE was blood on Betty's face and hands, and as they went into the one-roomed flat with its low lighting and its red satin hangings Ellen could see that the bed was rumpled and that there was blood on the pillow. There were several cuts near Betty's mouth and she stood in the midst of the ring of new arrivals and dabbed at them with a towel.

Ellen knew Betty. Most of the inhabitants of Lexton, certainly the men, also knew her. She was a middle-aged woman, of medium height with a head of light blonde hair through which grey roots were growing. She was plump with full breasts and once she must have been attractive. It was her breasts that had started her off on her career. Ellen remembered her when she was a young girl. Even then she had had a big bust and one day a photographer had taken her down to the beach and shot a series for a magazine showing Betty as naked as a jay. It had been her fifteen minutes of fame and thereafter she had capitalized on those breasts and become the local tart. She was about seventeen then without a mother or father so no one, including the social services and the police, had given a damn. As long as she wasn't doing it in the streets and frightening the pedestrians it was all right by them.

"What happened?" Frank said.

She dabbed at her mouth and said, "I'll tell you what bloody happened. He come in and said he had this present for me, a fish he'd caught, and wanted to swap it."

"Swap it?" Somers said. "What for?"

"What d'you think, Phil?"

"Sex?"

"Course it was sex."

Ellen said, "What?"

"Oh, Christ," Betty said. "He wanted to have relations with me, to fuck me."

Ellen said, "Are you telling me — "

"Hang on," Frank said. "Did he do this?" He pointed to the cuts on her face.

"Course he did. When I said I didn't

160

want his bloody present and that if he wanted me he had to come here with money like he usually did, then he tried to stuff the fish down my throat. That's why I'm all cut."

"You mean he's been here before?" Ellen said.

They ignored her.

"He didn't rape you?" Somers asked. He began to take down notes.

"No, he come too soon, like he does sometimes."

Somers said, "Can you give me a time he arrived?"

Frank said, "Just a minute, Phil. You don't need to make a case out of it, do you?"

"What d'you mean?" Betty dabbed again at her mouth. "You think I'm just — "

Frank said, "I know this must have been frightening but you've handled him well before. And he didn't hurt you badly. Why does this have to go any further?"

"Because he's a bloody danger, that's why! What about that woman on the beach a couple of years ago? And the fisherman who told him to sod off. He hurt them. And she," she pointed at Ellen, "she give them money."

"All right," Frank said. "But they were isolated cases."

"Isolated? You must be joking. He was always a rough little bastard when he was a kid. And when you first asked me to take him on I told you then."

Ellen said, "Frank, what's she talking about?"

"I'll tell you in a minute. Betty, we don't want a big thing made of this."

Ellen said, "Frank, I'm trying not to believe what I'm hearing. Dommie's been here with Betty before; that's what I'm supposed to understand, is it?"

Frank looked suddenly annoyed. "Of course he's been here. He's a grown man with a man's urges. What do you want to happen, do you want him to start raping girls on the beach like — "

"Don't say that!"

"Well, it's true. He occasionally comes round to my place when he's on walk-about and sometimes the . . . the female guests have to put up with a lot. If you want to know, he's exposed himself. Isn't it better that he comes round here to Betty and gets it off his chest?"

"Will you two stop bloody arguing!" Betty said loudly. "What about me?"

"You?" Ellen's voice too had risen. "Don't you talk to — "

"Hang on," Frank said. "Let's — "

But Ellen said, "God Almighty, we're talking about a child and you — "

"A child!" Betty said. "That's what you think! That's what you've always thought. You treat him like a little boy but he's not a little boy. He's a man."

"All right, Betty," Frank said. "Listen, if you're sure you're all right, why don't you come down to the house tomorrow and we'll sort this out."

"You think you can just put your hand in your pocket and that's that?"

"Betty, let's — "

"No, you listen to me!"

Spender turned to the policeman and said, "I'll take care of her, Phil." Then he turned back to Betty. "I'll see you tomorrow. Come in the morning." He took Ellen's elbow and eased her from the room. In the street outside he said, "I'm sorry you had to be involved in that but it was for his own good. Come on, let's find him before he hurts himself."

★ ★ ★

Bill Maitland said, "I hoped you'd be here." He had joined Alex and Mike in the pub. "I went to the boat and it was dark but your cars were there so I assumed you'd walked." He turned to Alex. "Has he been telling you about the treasure?"

"A bit."

"She always says I tell it like I'm giving evidence in court," Mike said. "That I lack romance."

Maitland was dressed in his rough walking gear and leaned forward at the table so that he could hear what Mike was saying. The noise in the pub had increased. Chris and the fishermen were playing dominoes in the other room, slapping down the pieces and shouting the plays.

Bill said, "In a way there's too much romance about the Templars. People talk about the present age being money orientated but in the fourteenth century they were very materialistic. None more so than the Templars. They were really the first bankers. Say you wanted to go to the Holy Land, they would mortgage your property, sell you the boat tickets, and their agents in Jerusalem would advance you money for accommodation once you arrived. If you couldn't pay back the loan you lost your house much as you would to a building society today. It's no wonder the French king envied them. I found something today that might interest Mike . . . Good Lord, there's Dommie."

Dommie came in the door of the pub and stood for a moment as if undecided what to do. Bill Maitland half rose and called him, but he had already turned towards the group of fishermen in the other room.

Chris said, "Look who's arrived. Dommie, come over here."

Dommie went over and stuck out his hand. Chris rose to his feet and gave a mock bow as he took it. "You want a drink, Dommie?"

"A drink."

"Course you do and you'll have one.

Jerry" — he called to the barman — "a nice lemonade shandy for Dommie."

"Shandy," Dommie said, forming the word as he heard it.

Alex saw Chris wink at the barman who filled a pint tankard almost to the top with strong ale and added the merest touch of lemonade to it.

Chris took it over to their table. Dommie put his hand out for it and Chris moved the drink away. "What do you do first; before you get the shandy?"

"Shandy," Dommie said.

"What do you do to earn the shandy? You've got to do something. Remember how to dance? You remember! Dance and . . . ?"

"Dance and . . . dance and . . . sing!"

"That's it! Give us a dance and a song. You remember 'John Peel', don't you? I taught it to you last time. 'D'ye ken John Peel . . . ' Come on."

"Deeken John Peel . . . "

"Come on, Dommie, dance."

Dommie began to throw out his legs and move his pelvis backwards and forwards in an obscene dance and all the time Chris was singing his version of 'John Peel'. The other fishermen were clapping their hands to keep the time.

Chris sang, "D'ye ken John Peel with his prick of steel?"

Dommie repeated the line as he gyrated across the room.

"And his balls of brass," sang Chris.

Dommie repeated that.

Bill Maitland was on his feet. "I've got to stop this." He went into the other room.

Mike rose with him. Alex said, "It's not your business, Mike." He ignored her and followed Maitland.

" . . . And a carrot up his arse . . . " Chris went on. Dommie sang it after him and swung his arms and danced and in the small room his strange flat face was shining with sweat and effort.

"That's enough, Dommie," Bill Maitland said.

Dommie didn't hear him and went on dancing.

"Oh, leave him, Bill," Chris said.

"No, I'm not going to leave him. Dommie!"

Chris said, "Dommie, you go on

dancing if you want your shandy!"

Alex watched Mike. He was standing just to the rear of Bill Maitland, rising slowly on his toes as he did when he was exercising his legs.

"I want you to stop this," Maitland said as much to Chris as to Dommie.

But Chris had half a dozen fishermen, all half drunk, as his claque, and he was confident.

"You ain't the preacher now, Bill, and it doesn't matter a toss if you was. This is our bit of fun and Dommie likes it. He's going to sing and dance and then he's going to get his shandy."

"That's no shandy," Mike said. "It's a pint of the strongest. I saw the barman pull it."

"Who asked you?" Chris said.

Suddenly the quality of the tension changed from a retired vicar trying to keep the peace to a stranger not minding his own business. The pub went suddenly quiet and Alex saw that several of the fishermen, young tough men sitting behind Chris, were half smiling in anticipation.

"No one asked me." Mike's voice was

low and filled with what Alex had once described as sweet reasonableness. It was this that worried her. He was at his most frightening when sweet reasonableness overcame him. He went on, "I just wouldn't want to see him get hurt. I heard you order a shandy and I watched a pint get pulled. Just thought you mightn't know. I'm sure you wouldn't want Dommie hurt."

Chris, a big swarthy figure with his shiny black hair caught in the usual ponytail, looked momentarily nonplussed.

"You what?" he said.

"Is that so, Jerry?" Bill Maitland said to the barman. "Did you pull a whole pint for Dommie?"

"Not I, Bill. God, no, you want me to lose my job?" He was smiling as he spoke.

Faces turned to Mike. All had questions in their eyes including Maitland. Mike went forward and picked up the mug of ale. Chris's hand went out and held Mike's wrist. "That ain't yours," he said.

"Take your hand off me."

"Leave it."

"I said take your hand off me. If you don't I'll break your arm."

Mike was holding the tankard in his left hand and now Alex saw his right hand flatten as though he was about to use its edge in a downward cut. She rose and went forward. "Mike!" she said.

He didn't react but stood quite still waiting instead for a reaction from Chris.

A voice behind them said, "Dommie! For God's sake! So this is where you are!"

Ellen and Frank Spender came into the pub. In a matter of seconds the whole picture changed. Dommie ran forward and put his hand out for his grandmother to shake. "I've got a shandy," he said.

Chris dropped his arm and Mike jerked forward and in doing so knocked the pint from the table and spilled it on the floor.

"God, I'm sorry, Dommie," he said. "Let me get you another."

But Ellen said, "Dommie doesn't drink. Come on, Dommie."

Spender said, "Come on, lad, we'll go to my house and you can have a Coke. How about that?"

"Coke."

"That's it. A Coke."

"I like Cokes."

"Right, you can have two."

Dommie, smiling, followed Ellen out of the pub. Spender paused at the door. He said, "I don't want to see anyone buying drinks for Dommie, not now, not in the future."

There was a sudden silence as he went out into the night, then an equally sudden rush of talk.

Bill Maitland shepherded Mike back to the table. "Let me get us another," he said. "I think we need it."

The fishermen began to leave. Chris came over to Mike while Maitland was at the bar. "You want to play, we can play any time, mate."

Mike said, "I don't want to play, all I wanted was to let you know what was in Dommie's glass."

"It's got nothing to do with you what's in Dommie's glass. You understand me? You're a bloody nobody here. Oh, I know you was a copper. We all knows that. Well you ain't one now and you better bloody watch yourself."

Bill Maitland came back to the table carrying glasses and Mike said to Chris, "Right. I'll remember that. Thank you."

"What's he going on about?" Maitland said as Chris went out of the pub.

"I think he just wants me to learn their ways," Mike said.

Alex leaned back in her chair, stretched and felt the tension begin to leave her body. She was proud of Mike. He seemed to have changed recently and the last half-hour was proof of that. There was a time when he would have said something brutal that would have sent the situation spinning over the top. Had he begun to realize that his leg would never cope with the rough stuff? Then she remembered he had threatened to break Chris's arm so maybe he hadn't.

"Here's to Dommie," Bill said, raising his glass. Then to Mike, "Did you really see the barman pulling a pint?"

"A pint of best bitter with a dash of lemonade."

"Thank goodness Ellen arrived before he drank it."

"Oh, he wouldn't have drunk it," Mike said in a tone that Alex recognized as left over from his earlier mood. "I suppose you've known him since he was a child?"

"Since the day he was born. I also baptized him. Odd to think of the Blackhursts coming to the end of their line with Dommie but that's what it looks like. They've been here for generations. Hundreds of years. Now it's all coming to an end."

"Like the house," Mike said. "I've never seen a place like that. It's coming apart at the seams."

"It's been like that for years," Bill said. "Ellen says it'll see them out and I suppose she's right. Her real problem is Dommie. What she's always thinking about is what will happen to him when she goes."

"Wouldn't he have been better in some sort of institution?" Alex said.

"Don't ever say that in front of Ellen."

"Just to obviate exactly what she's worried about."

"You may be right, but it's too late. You couldn't simply take him away from her now and put him somewhere. He'd never get used to it."

"What happened to his parents?"

"Dead. His father was drowned here, or at least that's what we think happened. His body was never found. His mother, Gilly, died later. Ellen brought him up. She did all the work. Still does. Frank helps. We all do for that matter. I mean we always watch out for him and see that when he goes what we call walkabout he gets back to the house in good order. That's why I interfered this evening. I don't like to see him made fun of. It doesn't happen often and I'm surprised at Chris and the lads doing it. They watch out for him too. Probably had too much to drink and wanted a little game. But giving him liquor isn't a game I approve of. Goodness, that makes me sound holier than thou. Sorry about that."

"What about that man Chris?" Alex said. "He seems a pretty rough customer."

"I've also known Chris Cottis since he was a baby. I'm afraid he is on the rough side. He didn't have much upbringing. Never knew who his father was. Brushes with the police when he was a juvenile, then a prison sentence for assault. I've watched him turn into what he is and it's been depressing." He stood up. "Anyway, I must go. When you've got a moment, Mike, I'd like to show you something."

"I'm going to be in London tomorrow."

"No hurry. It's about Lexton in the old days. You might find it interesting." He said goodnight and left.

"London?" Alex said. "You never said anything about London."

"I want to get those drugs looked at. You want to come? It'll be pretty dreary for you."

"Where are you going?"

"There's a laboratory in Kensington we used sometimes if we wanted an analysis done in a hurry."

"I could go to Harvey Nichols. Haven't been there for years. Not to buy, I don't have that kind of money. But I'd like to walk around and see what I'm missing. We could stay at my flat."

"I was hoping you'd say that. I don't fancy the drive back."

They had a sandwich and then walked back to the boat. Alex said, "You told me you had a name for it."

"Her. Yes, I have, but we haven't got a bottle of champagne to break."

"Well, let's pretend we have. What's the name?"

"I thought of *Sea Eagle* but that's too long so then I thought *Osprey*. That's a sea eagle but it's shorter."

"It's a lovely name."

They crossed the bridge and walked through the reeds. She scooped a handful of water from the creek and splashed it over the boat's prow. "I name this boat the *Osprey*," she said. "God bless all who sail in her."

"Listen," he said.

In the distance they could hear engines throbbing and voices shouting orders. The boats in the river were putting to sea.

11

"SEE that desk?" Laddie Broakes said. "Yew. Over two thousand quid. And that chair? Swedish. Bloody nearly eight hundred. Money means damn all to them."

Mike Harley was sitting in Broakes's office in the five-storey building near London Airport that had the name Premier Transport International emblazoned on its side.

Commander Broakes was pacing up and down the room like the lion he so much reminded Mike of, a grizzled lion with a heavy head of hair and wrinkles round the mouth; a big man with big broad shoulders and wide-spaced blue eyes that had seen everything there was to see.

He had been something of a legend in the Metropolitan Police: youngest head of the Murder Squad, head of the Flying Squad, in charge of the Anti-terrorist Squad at the worst time of the IRA bombings, head of the SIS when Mike had worked for him. Now he was a security guru in civvy street.

He went on, "It's your office, they said. Spend what you like, they said. So I did. I spent a bloody fortune, so would you if you had to look out at that all day."

Mike went to the window and the two men stood staring down at the big yard from which the container lorries came and went.

"And there's not a decent restaurant for miles. I have to eat in the bloody canteen."

Premier Transport was in what used to be called an industrial zone and was now called a business park and the view of the other business park buildings was not inspiring.

Broakes sighed. "There's something about early retirement that buggers you. It's certainly buggered me." Then he remembered who he was talking to and said hastily, "Well, not you, of course. I mean you're young so you've got your working life ahead of you. But I'd give anything to go back to the Yard. Christ Almighty, d'you know what I do here? I spend my days checking up on consignments of bloody bathroom fittings and mild steel rods that have gone missing. And I'm always on the phone to some bloody depot manager who's not only lost the container but sometimes the bloody truck itself. You've got no idea how often our drivers go into a caff for sausages and chips and leave the keys in the truck. Course some are doing it for hard cash. Bloody marvellous, isn't it!"

He began to pace again, but more slowly. "Yes, I'd go back tomorrow to that small room at the Yard and a quarter of the salary. But madam wouldn't have it. Madam wanted a place in France and now we've got one — well, not in France, in Corsica. But by Christ I'd rather be doing the old job." He paused and collected himself and said, "What about you? How the hell are you getting on? How's the leg?"

He stopped pacing and lowered his leonine frame into his eight hundred pound Swedish chair.

"The leg's fine, thanks, guv'nor. I can't run like I used to, but fine."

"Guv'nor." Broakes tasted the word

with pleasure. "Here they call me Commander Broakes. I won't have them calling me Laddie. They're just a bunch of bloody suits always talking about the 'corporate image'. Anyway, go on."

"Well, I'm living up on the Suffolk coast now in a boat." Mike told him about his plans and then filled him in about what had happened recently. Broakes nodded and fiddled with a brass letter opener on his desk. He became, as Mike's story progressed, an entirely different personality. His face changed from self-pitying frustration to an expression which combined interest with judgement and when Mike reached the finding of the drugs he threw down the letter opener, leaned back in his chair and put his feet up on the two thousand pound desk. It was a gesture that brought a flash of memory to Mike. Laddie Broakes had always had his feet up on his desk when he listened to his boys and his desk had been the most battered in the building. The yew wasn't going to last.

"What drugs?" he said.

"That's the problem. I've never seen

any like them. I've wondered if they're some new compound from Thailand or Cambodia. There must be stuff they've got out there we don't know about here in the West."

"Bloody unlikely, I'd have thought. We've had teams there for years. Anyway you said this dead gent was a Chinese from Hong Kong."

"That's what that bastard from the regional crime squad said."

"Is that why you didn't give him the stuff to analyse?"

"What do you mean, guv'nor?"

"Well, why not?"

"Oh, sorry, I thought you were still talking about the body. No . . . I mean yes. He was a shit. One of those bastards who hate the Met because he thinks we look down on them."

"Well, we do."

"Course we do. But there was another reason. If he wanted to score he could have made things a bit rough for us. And with me not being able to moor the boat it would have been tricky. But the first reason is the real one. That's why I thought I'd come and see you. See what you think about it."

"So where's the stuff?"

"I took it to Garroway's in Kensington. They've promised to let me have an analysis by tomorrow at the latest."

"I could have got Forensic to do that for you. I've still got influence, you know."

"I know, but it could take weeks." He took an envelope from his pocket. "This is what was in one of the packages."

Broakes spilled some of the brown coffee-like grains into his hand and smelt it. "Ripe," he said. "Bloody ripe." He placed a little on his tongue. "Ugh!" He rubbed some of the grains back and forth between his fingers and looked at the fine powder. "No. Never seen anything like this." He gave Mike back the envelope. "Wrapped up . . . sealed against the water . . . tied round a buoy cable . . . Got to be something valuable."

"That's what I thought. And what else is there? Has to be drugs."

"You think this stuff belonged to the gent from Hong Kong? And that he put it round the buoy cable? And then what? Died?"

"Could be."

"Could also be he had nothing to do with it. I grant you that would be coincidental. But where the hell did he come from?"

"I checked the shipping lists for that part of the North Sea two days on either side and the only possibility was a Dutch freighter called the *Wilhelmina* making for Rotterdam. She'd been to Jakarta and Manila and Taiwan and she'd also called at Hong Kong."

"She could have picked him up in any of those places but he'd have to be a crew member, ships like that don't have passenger accommodation."

"I asked about that too," Mike said. "There are still some freighters that take passengers. Not many. But no one knew whether the *Wilhelmina* did. Apparently she was carrying timber."

"Where'd you get all this stuff?"

"Remember a chap called Manners? Customs at Felixstowe? I got on to him and he came back to me."

"Good boy."

It was as though the months had dropped away. The phrase 'good boy' was Broakes's accolade and the one his 'boys' had most wanted to hear.

Now he said, "OK, let's say there's some argy-bargy going on. How do we find out what it — Hang on." He pulled out a small organizer from his desk drawer and began to hit the keys with his big spatulate fingers. "Never thought I'd use these names again." Mike could hear a sudden rush of interest in his tone. "Aaah, here we are." He picked up the phone and dialled. As he waited for a connection he switched on the desk speaker and they heard the phone ringing at the other end.

"*Staats polisie*," a woman's voice said.

"Is that the Amsterdam police head-quarters?" Broakes slowed his delivery.

"*Ja*."

"Could I speak to Inspector Van Hoogstraten, please."

"Who wishes, please?"

"Commander Broakes, Scotland Yard."

In a moment Mike heard another voice. "Laddie? Is dit you?"

"Willie? How the hell are you?"

"Oh, niet so bad."

They talked generalities for a few

moments and then Broakes said, "I'm helping a colleague with something you may be able to advise us on. He's got involved in a case where a dead body was washed up on the Suffolk coast. A post-mortem gives the cause of death as stabbing. The body was of a Chinese male in his thirties and the local police say he came from Hong Kong. The only ship in the area at the time was the *Wilhelmina* making for Rotterdam. I was wondering if you could come up with anything."

"What sort of thing?"

"Well, the guy was murdered and there might have been witnesses in the ship. We think he was running drugs."

"You got a name?"

"No name."

"Listen, I got something going here right now," Van Hoogstraten said, "but I ring Rotterdam port police later. I come back to you. OK?"

"Right. Fine." He gave him his number. "Many thanks, Willie."

Broakes put the phone down. His face had lost its pinched look. He rose to his feet and rubbed his hands and said, "Let's go and have a bloody good lunch.

It's all on PTI. That's what the suits call this bloody place! And we're not eating in the canteen. I know a good place on the river."

★ ★ ★

Alex unlocked the door of her Camden flat and eased herself out of her shoes. "Oh, God, thank you for small mercies," she said as she flexed her toes and dropped the two carrier bags she was carrying. She looked at her image in the hall mirror and said, "I'm getting past this." She had spent the afternoon walking round Harvey Nichols and Harrods. She had gone with the unashamed purpose of spending money but the only thing she had lusted after was an olive-green suede jacket that would have placed her deeply in debt. She was tempted but resisted and had then gone to Marks & Spencer at Marble Arch and bought underwear. The good weather was holding and the day had been hot and London filled with backpackers. The lonely marshes of Suffolk began to assume new attractions.

She made herself a cup of tea and stood by the window. The street was leafy and the houses had all been done up long before. They were painted cream and the doors mostly black and the whole area looked attractive.

She wondered when Mike would get back and what state he'd be in when he did. This was where she had waited for him many a night when he had decided to go out with his mates, and at the back of her mind she associated her flat with that time. She told herself to forget it; it was all past; Mike was a different person. But he hadn't really become a different person until she had literally followed Hannah's advice. She had said to him, one hungover morning, "Mike, why don't you retire?"

"And do what?"

"Let's have a holiday and think about it."

So they had gone to Africa. They had taken a direct flight to Cape Town because that was the city Alex knew, the place that was deeply and tragically inside her. It was also the place where she hoped that Mike would recover not only the use of his legs but his ability for self-analysis and self-criticism and also the optimism he had shown at Effingham.

They had flown out at the beginning of December when the weather was settling into the heat of summer and taken a holiday apartment in the beach suburb of Clifton where the water was colder than on the southern beaches, but where the sun was hot and the weather calmer.

At the back of her mind was the knowledge that one day she would have to face what she had come out for but she decided she would soak up the sun and the sea until she felt stronger. In wet, wintry London, this had seemed the ultimate objective but after they had moved into the block of beach flats, with the blue water only a hundred yards away across a brilliant white beach, the dreams of sun and sea and indolence faded.

Neither she nor Mike, she realized, were people content simply to lie in the sun. Mike was too restless, and as far as she was concerned she knew she could not settle into lethargy and hedonism until she had exorcized, or tried to exorcize, the demons that lived in her subconscious.

The apartment was simple but good. It came with everything including air-conditioning and a black housemaid. This was her first experience of the new South Africa — and she found that it wasn't much different from the old South Africa except in two fundamental ways. The first was that the feeling of guilt, the kind of pervasive guilt that she had heard her father and mother talking about, no longer existed. That had vanished with freedom. The second was the danger from robbery. In their apartment there were three panic buttons and the telephone numbers of the security company that guarded the block and its occupants. There was also a notice to tenants telling them the danger areas and where not to go after dark.

For the first few days they drove their hired car round the sights. She also went to look at her old school and the house they had lived in when her father was the southern Africa correspondent of the London *Chronicle*.

And then came a morning when Mike

said, "What are we going to do today?" And she said, "What would you like to do?" He had looked restless and irritated and she had been irritated herself because they had come a long way to do nothing and now nothing wasn't what they wanted to do. He had wandered down to the beach by himself. She found she did not want to swim much. Did not want to lie on the beach. Did not want to drive around by herself. Did not even want to go shopping.

One afternoon a couple of days later Mike came up from the beach and said he had met someone and they had been invited to a barbecue — here called a *braai* — that evening. It was at a lovely wooden house built out on a low reef of rocks at the far end of the beach. The owner a small, neat South African, was a professional diver and had bought the house because about a mile out to sea from the end of the reef was the wreck of the East Indiaman *The Duke of Hampshire* which he had discovered the previous year. She had been returning from the Far East, had been wrecked by a north-westerly gale and had lain on the bottom for more than two hundred years. He was now organizing diving safaris for tourists and making a good living out of it. So far they had found two brass cannons and a mass of broken china.

The following day Mike joined his little company as unpaid dogsbody. He would go off in the morning and sometimes would not be back before dark. Alex could actually see the change for the better taking place in him. He was being asked to do menial tasks like helping tourists with their wet-suits and flippers, like running errands for the boss and his other two divers, and, of course, learning to dive himself. And he was loving it. It was a great training place for anyone interested in diving, and Mike absorbed everything like a sponge.

But for Alex things were different. She spent a good deal of her time reading. One day, in one of the local papers, the name Athlone appeared in a headline as a place of suburban violence where a robbery had taken place. Athlone was where she had to go. She got into their rented car and made sure every door was locked — this was stressed in the security brochure in the apartment — and drove out to the southern suburbs.

She came off the throughway in Rondebosch and cut down past the Common. This was where they had lived, right here under the mountain called Devil's Peak. She became momentarily confused then consulted her map, picked the road to Athlone, and drove on. The comfortable middle-class suburbs gave way to poor quality housing and then to streets of even poorer housing and battered stores and in the side streets wheelless cars like beached whales.

She reached a wider street where the word Athlone appeared in shop names, and stopped outside a crumbling fruit and grocery store. Was this where it had happened? It all looked different. In her mind was a pile of burning tyres, a couple of wrecked cars, and in her ears screams and shouts. Now people walked into the store to shop for ordinary, mundane things. Men stood in small groups on the street corners. A woman pushed a baby in a pram. None of these people were white but they did not convey menace. Not only did they not seem to mind her presence, they appeared to ignore her completely.

The last time she had been here the day had been cold and wet and she and her mother had driven out to the airport to fetch her father who had been covering a story in Johannesburg. In those days Cape Town, like most of South Africa, was in political turmoil and there was violence everywhere. The freeway from the City to the airport had been particularly vulnerable so they had come back through Athlone and in the dusk had failed to see the smoke of the burning tyres in the middle of the road. There was no way past. Alex's father braked and tried to turn, but before he had got halfway round the car was being attacked by a dozen men with clubs and chains.

The windscreen was smashed and the car rammed into the pillars supporting a shop. Then side windows were smashed, the doors opened, and the two adults were pulled out. Alex, in the back, dropped to the floor. She heard her parents screaming and the men shouting. The back door was opened and she was pulled out. Then a strange thing happened. A group of about fifty black women with their own clubs attacked the men. They shouted and yelled and hit about them and were able to get to Alex and carry her away to one of their houses. That was how she was still alive, saved by women who were sick of the violence all around them and had decided to act.

And now, here she was, in the street where she thought it had happened. Was this where the tyres had been burning? Was that the shop whose pillars their car had hit? She recognized nothing. It was a different world. An alien world certainly, but it contained nothing belonging to her; no memory; nothing. If there was a malignancy in the air it had nothing to do with her.

She turned the car and began the drive back to Clifton. She felt no better, no worse, she felt nothing at all. And perhaps this was the best she could hope for. She remembered one thing that had haunted her. The people who had killed her parents were seen by the rest of the world to be part of a violent movement that had right on its side. That had been hard to live with. For a while those violent men had been her demons. But she was over that too now. They had just been people. Ordinary people pushed to the end of their tether.

Now, in her London flat, her memories were broken by the ringing of the phone. It was Mike. He was at Garroway's. They hadn't been able to identify what drugs they were yet but they were working late and he would wait until they had finished. Even though she was in her own flat, she felt suddenly lonely.

12

"MUSK?" Alex said.

"That was my question too."

"No drugs at all?"

"No drugs at all; just this stuff musk."

"Hasn't it got something to do with perfume?"

"You know more than I did. That's what Garroway said. I don't think he'd ever seen it before but he wasn't going to admit it. Anyway, it's a bloody bore. I thought we really had something there. A dead body. Drugs. Just like the old days."

They were in the sitting room of Alex's flat. It was a little short of eight o'clock and Mike had only just got back, sober and in his right mind.

She said, "Not too much like the old days, I hope. I don't want you yearning for police work, not after all that's happened. Though I can see why you might be."

196

She had been experiencing diametrically opposed sensations. On the one hand she had hated the thought of having found and being in possession of narcotics, but now, on the other, she shared with Mike a sense of anticlimax.

He shook his head. "I'm not yearning to go back into the Force. Not the way that Laddie Broakes is. It's just that I like finding out things. I'm programmed that way."

"They checked all the packages?"

"Yeah. And this is what they found in several."

He showed her what looked, at first glance, like a handful of tiny coconuts.

"What on earth are they?" she said.

"Garroway opened one and that's where the coffee grains come from."

She took one gingerly and examined it. It reminded her of a large plant pod except it had what looked like animal hair on it.

"Ugh." She handed it back to him. "What's the next step?"

"Nothing, I suppose." Again she heard the disappointment in his tone. "And I had Laddie really going. Just like — "

197

"The old days?"

"Sorry."

"I wondered if you were going to make a day of it."

"He wanted to. Took me to some expensive place on the Thames full of expense-account porkers. And he sank a couple of bottles of expensive burgundy. I helped, but not much. He doesn't like private security, wants to be back at the Yard. Anyway, he got interested in what I told him, especially when I gave him the name of the ship and he phoned some contact in the Dutch police and — " The phone rang and he said, "That could be him now." It was.

"Mike? Sorry I've been so long but Willie van Hoogstraten's just called me back."

"No problem, guv'nor. Look, the thing's come a bit unglued. Garroway's said the stuff isn't a drug at all but something called musk — "

"What the hell's that?"

"It's used in perfume manufacture. So it's not what we thought."

"You've still got a murdered Chinese."

"The regional boys can have him."

"Right, well I don't feel so bad, then. I've got nothing for you. Willie found the *Wilhelmina*. She's off some place ... hang on, I wrote it down. Too much of a mouthful to remember otherwise. Hellevoetsluis. See what I mean? She's anchored there and the Rotterdam harbour police say they'll go and have a look at her. But that's all."

"Fine, guv'nor."

"You sound as though someone's pinched the cream."

"I just thought the stuff might be valuable."

"Listen, I've had a thought. If you want to check up on something like this musk and you think it might have come from Hong Kong, there's a chap I used to work with when I was much younger. He left the Met to join the Hong Kong Police. He's retired now but he's younger than I am. Lives like a bloody king in Chelsea. If you want his name give me a buzz."

"OK, guv'nor, and thanks."

Mike put down the phone and said, "Well, that's that."

"What do we do with the rest of

tonight?" she said.

"Drink. Dinner. Sex."

"In that order?"

"In any order you like."

"Given a choice, I'd say let's go out and combine one and two and come back for three."

* * *

The following morning they drove back to Suffolk. When they reached Lexton and were approaching the little road bridge, Alex said, "Where's the boat?"

"What do you mean?" Mike said.

"I mean I can't see her."

"Of course you can. She's over there. Beyond the reeds."

He stopped on the bridge. From there they had a view of the river where the fishing boats moored — they were at sea now — and if they looked to the right they could see the opening of the creek and then, normally, over the tops of the reeds they would have been able to see *Osprey*'s wheelhouse. They couldn't.

"Oh, shit!" Mike drove the big BMW down onto the far side of the river and along the gravel road that finally came out into the little parking area where Alex's car stood.

"There she is," he said.

He stopped the car and they walked along the creek, past where *Osprey* had been tied up, past the little beach where Mike had pulled the body ashore and went on for about two hundred yards. The creek narrowed and became much more overgrown, and there was *Osprey* lying athwart the creek, her prow buried in one bank and her stern pushing backwards into the reeds of the other. She was wedged across the waterway at an angle.

From her far side there was a splashing noise as though a dog was swimming in the water, then Bill Maitland waded ashore and saw them.

"I've just seen her," he said. "I was trying to find out how far the bow's gone into the mud."

"What happened?" Mike said.

"Happened?"

"Yeah, how the hell did she get here?"

"She slipped her moorings. Have you seen the ropes?"

Mike went back to the area of bank where she had been moored. He had tied her fore and aft to small trees. The trees were still there.

Bill came up behind him. "The ropes are in the water."

"Listen, I checked them before I left yesterday. Double-checked them. They couldn't have come loose by themselves. Someone's been playing bloody games. Someone in this village."

Bill said, "It might have been an accident."

"And it might not. It might have been done on purpose."

Alex had caught up with them. "Come on, Mike. You're sounding as though the whole village had something to do with it — if indeed anything was done."

"I've told you I checked the ropes before I left!"

"OK. OK. But kids could have done it."

Bill shook his head. "The kids here are mainly fishermen's children. That sort of thing would be anathema to them."

"Not to Dommie, though."

Mike looked at her sharply but Bill

said, "I don't think so. There's no real harm in Dommie. He does childlike things but he's not harmful."

"Well, there's no use arguing," Mike said. "Let's see what we can do about getting her back to where she was."

He walked into the water fully clothed and began to check the far bank. She had swung round on the tide as it carried her along the creek and her prow was pointing the correct way. The problem was that he couldn't try to start her because her stern was in the reeds and her propeller probably in the mud.

"What you need is a tow," Bill said. "If we can get her bows off the mud she'll swing back into the middle of the stream. When the boys get back I'll ask — "

"No!" Mike said, "I'm not asking those bastards for anything. I'll bring my car down, we'll pull her off with that."

He backed his car along the bumpy bank, ploughing down stands of reeds and almost going into the water twice. Then he fixed the bow rope to the towing bar at the back of the car and revved up the engine. The wheels spun.

"Did she move?" he shouted.

"I don't think so," Alex said.

"Can't you look?"

"I am looking." She felt a knot of anger in her stomach and then told herself this was Mike's home stuck on the far bank, and was able to control herself.

He revved up the car again but the wheels gouged into the soft leafmould and spun fast enough to send up clouds of smoke.

"Hang on," Bill said. "Tell you what. Why don't we wait until high tide? That should help."

Mike rubbed his cheek. "I should have thought of that."

"You're not quite the old sea dog you thought you were," Alex said. She wondered for a moment if she had gone too far. It had been a calculated gamble to make him lighten up.

It worked. He laughed, more of a bark than a laugh. "OK, we wait." He looked at his watch. "It should be high water in about four hours. We'll get your car down too and use two ropes."

It was the middle of the afternoon

before the tide was right and slowly they warped *Osprey* back into the main channel. Mike got into his wetsuit and went down aft but the water was too cloudy to see the propellers clearly so he used his hands. He brought up gouts of mud and grass and in about half an hour he said, "She's clear now."

He came aboard and started the engine and she sounded as though nothing untoward had ever happened. By sunset she was tied up where she had been earlier, Bill had left and Alex and Mike were having a drink in the saloon.

Mike said, "It was that bastard Chris."

"How do you know?"

"Got to be. I think I'll have a word with him."

"Just for interest's sake, what will you say?"

"What do you mean?"

"'Listen here, Chris, did you . . . ?' et cetera, et cetera . . . And if he says no?"

"I'll tell him I don't believe him and I'll . . . "

He paused.

She said, "Kill him? Prosecute him?

Bash him? What?"

"Don't be so bloody bitchy."

"Listen, my love, you haven't got Scotland Yard behind you now. You haven't got a team of detectives or police or whatever. It's only you. It probably was Chris. But you don't know. And if you start something with him — how shall I put it, untoward? — he'll get Somers and Somers will call in the regional crime squad and that man Brady will come down on you like a ton of bricks. You said yourself he'd love to do you for something."

"What you're saying is that I just have to put up with whatever people want to do to me."

"Not at all. What I'm saying is that you've been in an elect and powerful group for a long time. You've got used to that as your base. What's happened is that you've been forced to join the rest of the human race and you have to act like an ordinary human being."

"To hell with that!" he said.

★ ★ ★

Ellen and Dommie were in the living room of Lexton House watching television. Dommie had wanted to watch in his own room but Ellen had unplugged the set and said it was broken. She didn't want him out of her sight at the moment. He was watching one of the soaps he liked and she was watching him.

Was it true what Betty had said? Did she think of him as a child still? A boy? He was sitting on the chair, legs outstretched, head leaning back, mouth slightly open, and his eyes, those strange un-English eyes, staring fixedly at the screen. She tried to see him as others might see him for the first time. She saw the brow, wrinkled in concentration, the balding head, the powerful jaw with the stubble of early evening on it, the square hands, the heavy arm and shoulder muscles visible under his shirt. No, he wasn't a boy. And yet, in many ways he wasn't a man. Frank said he was a man but he meant only in that one particular, physical way. She had never faced up to that and she knew damn well why. The problem was, what did she do about it? You want a woman, Dommie? Was that how she was supposed to think? Well, it was unthinkable. Perhaps that's why she thought of him as a child — because it was just too dangerous and complex to think otherwise.

Frank hadn't. And according to him, his had been the only way to deal with Dommie.

They had gone back to his house from the pub and he had given Dommie two Cokes as he had promised he would. Ellen had still been feeling humiliated and angry and confused. They'd left Dommie in the billiard room and had gone into Frank's study but had left the door open so Ellen could hear the click of the balls as he rolled them on the table.

Frank had handed her a large malt whisky and said, "I'm sorry you had to see all that."

"So am I."

"I could probably have saved you from it but it would only have been temporary. He'd hurt her, and I didn't know how badly."

"It was unnecessary."

"No, it wasn't. You must have known that from what happened to the woman on the beach."

"She was teasing him. We were told that by one of the bathers."

"Rubbish. He grabbed her bathing costume and tried to pull it off. By the time anyone got to them he'd ripped the top."

"She was leading him on."

"Ellen, you're doing what you've always done, you're making excuses for him. I can tell you from first-hand experience that Dommie wants women. He's been after the ones here. He's opened his flies and pulled out his — "

"Oh, Frank, I can't believe it was that! He must have wanted to go to the loo or — "

"That's not true. He knows all about loos. This was a sex urge just like anyone has a sex urge but unlike normal people he wanted to relieve it right there and then. That's why I thought it best to let him — "

"For God's sake! The local tart!"

"What the hell do you expect? The vicar's wife? Ellen, Dommie's not a child, he has powerful drives and you can't just have him neutered like a dog or a cat. I suppose what you could do is take him to a doctor and see if he can give him something to take away the drive."

"I'm not going to do anything of the sort. I'll look after him like I always have."

And that had been that as far as last night was concerned. Now, sitting in the same room with Dommie, she wondered whether there were pills that would damp down his urges. She was damned if she was even going to contemplate an operation. No, she'd always looked after him and she always would and perhaps . . . and she had thought of this more and more lately . . . perhaps when the time came, when she knew she herself had only a little left — then would be the moment to end it. She already had the pills for that. Enough for both of them.

Pills! My God, what would Gilly have said to that if she had been alive? After all the pills she had taken. And what would John have said? Not that his opinion mattered much. Usually when memories came crowding in she thought of them separately for the simple reason that it was too sad to think of them together. She didn't like to remember how father had treated daughter, especially towards the end.

Gilly had been such a lovely young child but that, of course, was when her father had been away at the war and when Ellen had had her all to herself. Then John had come back and his relationship with Gilly had begun, a relationship that had ended in her death.

So she didn't think of them together if she could help it, but the pills had now brought them both into focus and she could hear her husband's voice saying to Gilly, "Walk, damn you! Walk!" He had walked her up and down the drawing room. Up . . . and . . . down . . . And every now and then he had shaken her and shouted at her and poured more coffee down her throat.

Ellen remembered how she herself had

begged him to go and get a doctor and John had said, "No bloody doctors. I don't want this round the district. We'll get her over it."

And they had. They'd walked her up and down the room and then up and along the beach in the early dawn until she had cried out for mercy. But by then she was safe from the pills and John had slapped her face and said if she ever did it again he'd throw her out of the house. Of course, neither she nor Gilly believed him. He wouldn't want the neighbours to know he'd done that.

Poor Gilly, what would she say now if she could see into her mother's mind, where the future was predicated on more pills?

"I'm tired," Dommie said, breaking into her thoughts.

"All right, darling. Off you go to bed."

She switched off the TV and began to lock up the house. After a few moments she went to Dommie's room. He was in bed lying on his back with his eyes closed. It never took him long to go to

212

sleep. She kissed him on his forehead and said, "Done your teeth?"

He nodded.

"That's a good boy. Sleep tight."

★ ★ ★

"Hannah says it's very valuable."

Alex came into the galley where Mike was preparing their supper. Every now and then he would decide to cook something. He liked Chinese food and had developed a dish of noodles with bean sprouts and spring onions, garlic and ginger and chopped bacon, which they both loved. He was now cutting up ginger root.

"How valuable?"

"She didn't know how valuable, she just said very valuable. It's apparently the basis of the really expensive perfumes. But that's about all she knew."

He put down the sharp knife and rubbed his chin. "I wonder . . . "

"What?"

"Well, what if someone thought like I did, that the stuff was drugs and killed him for them."

213

"If Hannah's right and it is very valuable then he might have been killed because it was musk. Doesn't have to be drugs at all. You're programmed to think drugs. There are other things that people kill for."

"Who the hell would know anything about musk?"

"Another Chinese from Hong Kong?"

"Well . . . maybe . . . Listen, Laddie Broakes said he knew a retired Hong Kong copper. I could have a word with him."

"You might as well, you're never going to rest until you get this off your chest and then I'd like to have you to myself."

"This gent lives in Chelsea. I'll go up tomorrow. Laddie says he lives like a king. The only coppers who can live like kings after they retire are bent coppers and in Hong Kong they were as bent as safety pins a couple of years back."

"Mike, I really don't want to go to London again. Do you want to stay at my flat?"

He shook his head. "In, out. I'll be back by night."

"I'll go to Hannah. I don't fancy

being here on the boat alone. Not with Dommie popping up in the reeds."

"He's harmless enough."

"We don't know that. We don't know anything about him."

13

AS Mike looked at Grenville Street he thought that just because this was Chelsea it didn't mean the whole area was trendy heaven. This street was on the north side of the King's Road and bore little resemblance to those around it. It had clearly been bombed during the war and now it had a garage at one end, a municipal depot for road-sweeping equipment at the other, and in between was a small block of flats of liver-coloured brick built cheaply in the 1950s. Was this where Laddie Broakes's friend Rawlings lived like a king? Perhaps Broakes had done what Mike had done: used the name Chelsea as a metaphor for fashionable living. He went up to the first floor. There was no name next to number four and he rang the bell.

A voice came out of the intercom. "Yes?"

"It's Mike Harley, Mr Rawlings."

"Who?"

"Laddie Broakes phoned you about me."

"Oh?"

"He told me he did."

"Well, yes, he did."

The door, which had a peephole, opened on a chain. All Mike could see was a shadow in a darkened hallway.

"He said you'd see me."

"Listen, at first I said yes and then when I thought about it I changed my mind. So I called him back and left a message on his machine."

"About me?"

"Saying I didn't want to talk."

"I never got a call from Laddie, so maybe he didn't get your message."

Silence.

"Mr Rawlings, I've driven all the way from Suffolk. I honestly thought we had a meeting lined up."

"Yes, well . . ."

"You're not going to make me drive all the way back without a talk, are you?"

A pause, then Rawlings said, "Did anyone follow you?"

Mike opened his mouth to say, "Who

the hell would follow me?" and then decided that wasn't the way to deal with Rawlings and said instead, "Absolutely not. No way. It's second nature."

"I mean did you see anyone here, in the flats? Was there anyone on the stairs?"

"Not that I could see. The whole place is deserted."

"OK, come in." The chain was slipped, and Mike found himself inside the apartment with Superintendent Leslie Rawlings, Hong Kong Police (Retd.). A memory came to him of the night he had been shot. This, Alex had told him, was how the old woman on the Meadowvale Estate had lived. It was how frightened people lived.

Rawlings went to the window and looked out into the street and seemed to satisfy himself that no one was watching the building. While he did this Mike studied him. He was a plump man in his middle fifties with a small moustache and thin greying hair. He was dressed dapperly in white trousers, a blue sports shirt and espadrilles. The apartment was neat, functional. Mike could see through into the bedroom which had a double bed covered in a Chinese embroidered silk quilt.

Rawlings came away from the window and said, "So you worked with Laddie Broakes. So did I in the early days."

"He's a great guv'nor."

"Yes, I suppose so."

He indicated a chair for Mike but did not sit down himself. He went back to the window and looked through the net curtain, then said, "I don't usually have a drink until the sun goes down, but" — he looked at his watch — "it's nearly noon. So I'll make an exception. What'll you have?"

Mike didn't want anything except coffee but said, "I'll have a white wine, if you've got any."

"I've got the lot."

He went into the small kitchen, came back with a glass of wine and said, "I think I'll have a sherry." Mike watched, idly expecting to see a small copita, but instead Rawlings poured himself a full wineglass of sherry from which he took a long pull.

"To tell you the truth I do sometimes

have a drop of something before lunch. Improves the old appetite."

For the third time he went to the window and glanced out.

Mike said, "I wasn't followed, if that's what's worrying you."

"Can't be too careful."

Mike began to get irritated. "Just between one ex-copper and another, what the hell are you expecting out there?"

Rawlings suddenly sat down in the other easy chair, shook his head, then waved his hand. "Oh, to hell with it. Tell me what you want to know. Laddie Broakes said you'd found something to do with perfume. He couldn't remember the name but he said it came from Hong Kong."

Mike said, "Musk."

Rawlings frowned. "Musk? Ah. That's a bit different."

"You know about musk?"

"Every Hong Kong copper knows about musk." Another change took place. He got up, poured himself a second generous sherry, sat down, brushed up the ends of his moustache, and said, "Tell me about it." He had become what Mike had often seen Laddie Broakes become — an attentive copper.

Mike told him. He mentioned just the bare elements and left Alex out.

"You found musk?" The tone was disbelieving.

"That's what the lab said it was."

He took out a small packet and emptied a little onto Rawlings's hand. He rubbed it and smelt it.

"I'm no expert but it smells like the stuff to me. That smell of farmyard piss. And you just found it?"

"Wrapped up like the drugs that come in by sea. That's what I thought the stuff was until I looked at it and smelt it. And it comes in these things." He took from his pocket one of the pods.

Rawlings nodded. "That's a musk pod, all right. I've seen a lot of those. You can buy them in any Chinese medicine shop in Hong Kong if you've got the cash."

"But where the hell do they come from? It's animals, isn't it?"

"It's produced by a deer. Some sort of gland. It's illegal to ship the stuff but you'd never know that, so much goes through Hong Kong." He held up the musk pod and said, "You know how much one of these bloody things cost? Two thousand Hong Kong dollars. Hang on, I'll show you what's what." He went into the kitchen and came back with a small pointed knife and opened the pod slightly, then lifted out some of the coffee-like grains on the tip of the knife. "Dealers have been killed for pods like this, especially in the New Territories — that's where the stuff comes in from China."

"Murdered?"

"Oh, sure. I've investigated at least three that had to do with smuggled musk and I've known of a couple more."

"How much is two thousand Hong Kong dollars in real money?"

"It varies, but it's over two hundred pounds."

"Not much to get killed for."

"Listen, this powder is worth more than gold. The last time I priced the stuff gold was running at about two hundred and fifty pounds an ounce; musk was about four hundred an ounce. How much did you find?"

Mike had been waiting for the question and said in the same flat tones with which he gave evidence in court, "Oh, not much. Couple of ounces, if that."

"And all wrapped up and floating out to sea from this place Lexton?"

"Yeah, after the Chinese guy was washed ashore."

"It was his, all right. He was probably going to sell it."

"Who the hell would he sell it to?"

"Perfume houses. They use it to 'fix' perfumes. Indian or Chinese folk-medicine dealers. I remember them advertising that with musk they could cure syphilis and gonorrhoea and diabetes and rheumatism and God knows what. That's the point about musk, it's everything you want it to be. Japan can't get enough of the stuff. Over there it's an aphrodisiac and it's also a kid's tonic. I looked into this when I was investigating a man who'd had his throat cut. Japan takes eighty per cent of all the world's musk and most of it comes through Hong Kong. There's a hell of a lot of it floating around in China, and people from Hong Kong go and see their relatives for Sunday lunch or whatever and take over Sony Walkmans and Canon cameras and come back with musk pods. I'm told if you want a night out in Tokyo with the geishas you have a musk drink to start with. You can get it at any chemist's shop."

"If it's so valuable and there's so much violence why the hell have we never heard of the stuff?" Mike said.

"Because heroin and firearms are the really big deals in Hong Kong. But the Triads have got into musk and are trying to control the supply. The less there is around, the higher the price. Law of supply and demand. Those gents who got their throats cut in Hong Kong thought they could buck the Triads. Can't buck the Triads. They've even got the customs sewn up. We know that in one year over a thousand kilos of fresh musk got into Japan and less than three hundred was legal."

"I thought you said trading in the stuff was illegal."

"Not all of it. Same as whaling. It's OK if you're using it for scientific purposes. Anyway, we know around seven hundred kilos got into Japan illegally but the

224

bloody Hong Kong customs only ever found three kilos being smuggled on an aircraft. Three kilos!"

"I can't think in kilos," Mike said. "What's it in our old weights?"

"Don't know. But if you're thinking of the total in money terms it's about fifteen million pounds sterling."

"Christ! I had no idea — "

At that moment the front door chimes went and Rawlings looked up in alarm. A woman's voice said, "It's me, Leslie."

"Hang on." Rawlings turned to Mike. "Just a sec."

He opened the front door and Mike had a brief glimpse of a woman going into the bedroom ahead of him. The door was closed and their voices were rapid and low.

Bang! Bang! Bang!

A thunderous knocking came from the front door. The bedroom door jerked open and Rawlings stood just inside it. Behind him was a young and attractive Chinese woman. Their faces were etched with lines of confusion and apprehension.

The banging came again and then a woman's voice said, "Les, I know you're in there, you bastard!"

Rawlings was sweating with embarrassment.

"Open this bloody door!"

Rawlings came up close to Mike and whispered, "It's my old woman. She thinks we . . . well, you know." He indicated the Chinese woman who had gone to the dressing table and was emptying small objects into her handbag. Mike saw earrings and a brooch disappear.

Bang! Bang!

"Les, if you don't open this door you're going to be sorry."

"You go," Rawlings said to Mike.

The Chinese girl was stuffing expensive underwear into a shoulder bag.

"Me?"

Mrs Rawlings's voice came again. "Listen to me, you bastard! I know you're in there with that bloody Hong Kong tart! If you don't let me in I'm going to pour petrol through the letter box and throw in a match."

Rawlings whispered, "Tell her she's made a mistake."

"For Christ's sake, I don't want — "

"You hear her? She's got a terrible temper. She'll do it. You owe me."

Mike went towards the door.

"Les, this is your last chance. You let me in or I'll — "

Mike heard the bedroom door close as he opened the front door. "What the bloody hell's going on?" he said.

The woman, stout, grey-haired, and with a dark downy growth on her upper lip, had been trying to look through the letter box. She straightened up.

"Who are you?" She had a bottle in her right hand and looked as though she would use it on his head.

"I own this flat, that's who I am. And why are you shouting and carrying on and threatening me with arson? Do you know what the sentence for arson is?"

Rawlings's wife looked momentarily confused then she said, "Where's that sodding husband of mine?"

"I don't know what the hell you're talking about. But if you don't go I'm going to call the police and tell them you threatened to burn down the building."

"No, I never said that. Not the building."

"You said you'd pour petrol into the flat and light it. Do you think the fire would stay in one place?"

"Isn't Les inside?" The voice was uncertain now.

"I don't even know who Les is."

"Oh, Lord. Look, I'm very sorry for disturbing you. And it isn't petrol." She held the bottle in front of her. "It's only lemonade."

"I don't want lemonade poured into my flat either."

"No. Right. Of course not. Can I ask you a question?"

"It depends."

"I'm looking for my husband. I know he lives around here. I thought he lived in these flats. You haven't seen him, have you? Portly bastard with a young Chinese girl."

Mike was tempted, just for a second, but then it passed. "No. I haven't seen a soul. I was getting dressed when you started banging."

"Oh. OK. Thanks." She turned and walked slowly away.

Mike went back into the flat. The bedroom door opened.

"She's gone," he said. "And it wasn't petrol, it was lemonade."

"Well, you can never tell with Moira. Listen, I don't want you getting the wrong idea." He half turned to the Chinese girl who had come up behind him. "Shirley comes to do my back. She's my physiotherapist." The Chinese girl looked at Mike indifferently. "Yeah, that's what she is, a physio. But Moira, she thinks it's the other thing."

There were more questions Mike wanted to ask about the musk, but he decided the time wasn't right.

★ ★ ★

It was late by the time he reached Lexton and the night was chilly and clear. He had gone to see his father and had had a fish-and-chip supper with him. Then he had pushed the old BMW up the M11, swung right past Bury St Edmunds and it was nearly midnight when he came to the village.

Everything was still, the pubs were closed, the restaurant too. In the High Street the shop-window lights were out and the fishing boats were no longer at their moorings. He had the strange feeling that while he had been away the village had been left unoccupied.

He drove down to the hardstanding in the reeds where they parked their cars. From there he could see the boat clearly and it was, thank God, still moored as he had left it. But a feeling of depression came over him and he realized it was because Alex's car wasn't parked next to his and she was not in the boat. He had known she was going to spend the time with Hannah and had simply accepted it as the best arrangement. But now he reacted differently. It was the fact that she was not going to be in the boat that was important and he had never thought her presence there was going to be important. Indeed, when he had known she was coming to Lexton for her holiday he had wondered what his reaction was going to be since he had made the boat his very personal territory. Now he knew that was all wrong. The fact of the matter was that she had only been there a few days and he was already missing her.

His mind dwelt briefly on their future,

briefly because he had no real idea of what it might be. She was a doctor in London, he was a . . . what? Explorer? Diver? Archaeologist? Those were nice words but too grand and didn't describe him at all. Anyway, she wasn't going to give up what she had for what he didn't have, so there was no point in thinking about it. Of course if the diving safaris worked . . . well, that was another thing . . .

He left the car and went up the gangplank. The water lapped and gurgled against *Osprey*'s sides and he knew that the tide must be running. If the day was fair he'd go out in the morning and dive on the old town. He went up the gangplank and switched the lights on in the wheelhouse and then went down the companionway to the saloon. He switched on the light there and saw immediately that something was wrong. The charts that were usually on the table had been swept onto the floor and . . . he heard a movement behind him and turned. He was struck savagely on the side of his head.

" . . . Michael . . . Michael . . . "

The voice echoed faintly in great caves. It was soft and lulling.

" . . . Michael . . . "

It seemed to come from a great distance and slowly got nearer.

"Mike!"

He opened his eyes and found his head was being cradled by Bill Maitland.

"Mike, are you awake?"

He tried to speak but only heard a jumble of disconnected words.

"It's all right, old chap. I've got you. Goodness, you must have come down hard." He had been wiping Mike's face and head and now he dabbed the cloth softly onto an area above his right ear which sent a shooting pain through his skull.

"Ow!"

"Sorry," Bill said. "Just getting a little of the blood off. Let me help you. D'you think you can get into that chair?"

For a moment, as Mike struggled onto his knees, he thought his head might explode.

"That's better," Bill said. "Do you remember what happened?"

"No." He touched the bump. "That hurts!"

"You must have fallen off the companionway. Tripped and fallen and banged your head. Can't have happened too long ago because I looked out of my window just as I was going to bed and saw the lights on in the boat and thought I'd come down and check after what happened the last time you were away."

Mike looked at the charts on the floor. "Help me up," he said. Bill helped him into the big sleeping cabin. The blanket and mattress had been pulled to one side, drawers had been emptied onto the floor. There were papers everywhere. Mike went into the next cabin. He felt dizzy and balanced himself by leaning against the bulkheads. Here too drawers had been emptied onto the floor and mattresses pulled out from the bunks.

"What's happened?" Maitland said.

"I've been bloody burgled, that's what's happened. And I didn't fall. I was clobbered when I came in and disturbed them."

233

"I'll go and wake Phil Somers," Bill said.

"No, no. I'll do it in the morning. Coppers don't like getting out of bed at this time and there's nothing much he can do."

"I don't want you sleeping here."

"No. All right. I'll lock up and go to the hotel."

"No, you won't. I've got an extra bed in the cottage."

Mike didn't want to go to Bill's cottage. Nor did he want to go to the hotel. He wanted Alex but there was no way he was going to phone her now.

"That's good of you," he said. "I'll get my pyjamas."

14

IT was dark when Ellen woke. She lay in bed with her eyes closed not looking at her bedside clock because she didn't want it to be three o'clock in the morning. Then she opened her eyes and looked at the clock and found to her delight that it was six thirty. She'd had a good, long sleep and would not have to lie in her bed thinking gloomy thoughts.

Waking early and having gloomy thoughts went back a long way; first was during the war when John was fighting in North Africa. Then they were wartime gloomy thoughts: she had worried about John and what might happen to him, and worried about her baby Gilly, and worried about money. Then John had come home from the prisoner of war camp and he wasn't the same John who had gone away or the same man she remembered and the gloomy thoughts changed. She remembered once wishing that the war was still on and he was still away. It wasn't something she was proud of but it was a fact.

She had sometimes had to lie in the big double bed in the mornings because he did not like being woken, especially after a heavy night on the gin — which was most nights — and he complained if she got up that she disturbed him. But Gilly was little then and she had to get up to look after her and that led to rows.

She lay now remembering John in those days when he would have his breakfast and then put on his old combat jacket and a pair of old tweed trousers and a heavy scarf and go down to the beach and try to walk off his hangover. In her mind's eye she could see him going out through the conservatory — still undamaged in those days — and sliding down the soft sand of the cliff path. She would stand at the upstairs windows and hold Gilly in her arms and watch as he hunched his shoulders against the wind, and walked along the hard shingle just above the waterline. And would wonder how long it would be before Frank was back and how long before she would be in his arms again.

Who would have thought that she would ever have been unfaithful to one of the Blackhurst men? John had been one of three brothers all as handsome as each other. People thought she was bloody lucky to have nabbed one. But the war had changed things both for her and for John and for a lot of people. She'd hardly known him before he'd left on a troopship for Egypt. They'd been married just before war had broken out. She'd been far too young for all that marriage entailed but people were doing crazy things in those days. You felt you had to do whatever it was because you might never have another chance. So when John's regiment left to fight Rommel she was already pregnant with Gilly. She'd given birth to her in the first year of the war in one of the coldest winters for years. That hadn't been much fun. She'd had her in the big house where she'd lived alone. Other houses were taking in evacuees from London but even then Lexton House was thought to be too isolated for young city kids. In those days there was no proper ford over the creek and sometimes, when the tides were high and the wind blew, the house was cut off.

When Gilly grew up they'd had a small bridge built over the creek, but even so she was lonely too. There was no one of her own age and social class in the village so it was no wonder she took up with the local boys. And Ellen couldn't really complain after what had happened between her and Frank.

Most of the arguments with John had been over Gilly and her friends. They had been what had filled his days, there hadn't been much else. What was shattering was how much he had changed. The young good-looking and arrogant man had come back as someone who had slipped into early middle age and was no longer good-looking — though he was still arrogant; even more than she remembered. And he'd developed habits that grated on her. He always had to be right, even about small things. He had a compulsive need to write things down. He spent most of his days writing what he called his 'war memoirs'. She was never allowed to see any of this but she would hear him muttering in his study as he wrote and he spent much of his time on the telephone and ordering books from London bookshops as part of his research. "They've got to bloody know," he said to her one day, referring to the memoirs, "those bastards don't really know." She knew that 'those bastards' meant the army high command.

He also made lists. He made them about saving money, about things in the village he wasn't happy with, he made them about people he thought had been rude to him or ill-used him in some way. He wrote lists of things for Ellen and commands for Gracie and later on, when she could read, for Gilly. It was as though he had never given up being an army officer. Yet he was no longer in the army. He would, of course, have stayed on except for the fact that the army hadn't wanted him to stay on. He'd never talked to her about that and she had never had the courage to ask him why. Oh, she'd suspected there had to be something that had gone wrong when he had been captured in Libya, but he didn't like people prying.

She remembered one day not long after the war ended — it had to be before Sylvia had killed herself — a man had come to the house and stood outside and shouted for John to come outside. She even remembered him calling John a 'cowardly bastard'. But John had stayed in his study and had not allowed either Gracie or Ellen to answer the door. "Bloody lower-class lout!" he had called him. Later that evening he had mentioned him again, calling him a drunk, a mentally unbalanced corporal in his old regiment. That was all he had said. He was a secretive man and someone who did not like being pried into. And when someone has been a prisoner of war and suffered as John had, one didn't pry.

So Lieutenant Colonel John Blackhurst had been sent home and pensioned off and forgotten. The war had claimed both his brothers which meant that with John the line of Blackhursts that had started in the army before Waterloo finally came to an end.

Grey morning light began to fill the room and Ellen got up and went along the passage to look in at Dommie. As she got nearer his room she could hear a kind of rubbing noise and knew exactly what was causing it. Dommie was sitting on his bed in his pyjamas polishing one of his walking sticks with beeswax.

"Morning, darling."

He went on polishing and said, "I like the smell." He held the stick to his nose and breathed in deeply.

"Yes, it's a nice smell. What are you going to do today?"

"Paint something."

"What?"

"Fish."

"That's good. You enjoy painting fishes."

"A whole fish. A person eating a whole fish." He used his hand and indicated a fish going into someone's mouth.

"Do you think you should? Won't it be difficult?"

"I can paint fish."

"Of course you can. What about painting a cow?"

"I want to paint a fish."

She watched him go on rubbing the stick. The room was filled with the smell of polish. She had hoped he had forgotten the fish and the act of forcing Betty to try to swallow it. Perhaps only a tiny part of his mind was holding the thought. Perhaps it would vanish in the next few days as other strange thoughts had done. For instance, there had been the problem with the woman on the beach and what had come afterwards. God, she would never forget that. The woman had been terrified, of course, though if you wear skimpy costumes and have most of your bosom sticking out you're asking for something. Still, it shouldn't have happened. Ellen hadn't seen exactly what did happen because Dommie had been on the beach alone, but she had had several first-hand accounts.

So, what she had paid the woman for was her silence. It came down to that. It wasn't that she was badly hurt. She'd had the top of her bikini pulled off and there were fingernail scratches on one of her breasts and that was all. Unpleasant, of course, but not too bad. No, it was her silence. For Phil Somers had come to Ellen and said there was nothing he could do if the woman wanted to press charges. Ellen had gone to Frank. Frank had phoned Phil. But the facts were the facts. The woman who was in her thirties was talking about attempted rape and that was a word that scared everybody in Lexton — the older generation, anyway.

And so Ellen had paid up. It had cost her a thousand pounds when she could ill afford it but at least that's where the matter had ended. And she could thank Frank for that. He'd done the talking and the arranging and had got the woman to make a signed statement in which she said she thought the whole thing had been exaggerated and that she would not be pressing charges.

But what happened later had worried her more than the event itself. Dommie's behaviour pattern had changed. He had been introverted and secretive and twice, once when she was in her bedroom and once in the bathroom, he had suddenly opened the door and looked at her naked body.

It was not as if there was any mistake about that, it wasn't as if he had entered the rooms in error. He had opened the door and looked at her, his face alight, and she had been angry with him as much as she could be angry. But that had passed. Or at least she had thought so. Now Frank was telling her it hadn't and that he was handling it by taking Dommie to Betty for servicing.

My God, she thought, as she looked at his powerful shoulders, Betty had been fortunate. What would have happened if Dommie had gone on with what he started and forced the fish down her gullet?

History was repeating itself. Frank was fixing things. He was paying off Betty and today she must refund the money to him. She knew that he would say she wasn't to bother but she wanted to bother. She didn't want to be in anyone's debt. Especially not Frank's.

★ ★ ★

"For God's sake," Alex said to Mike. "You've got to report it to someone. I mean look at it."

She waved her hand at the chaos in the saloon.

"To hell with that Brady bastard. I'm

244

not having him here again."

"It doesn't have to be him," she said crossly. "He's not the only policeman around."

Mike threw a book down on the chart table and turned to her. "Look, you've been bloody angry ever since you got back. So let me spell it out again. I was OK. I'd had a bang on the head but I was standing and walking and rational and Bill was looking after me. All right, maybe I should have phoned you but it was well after midnight and you were probably in your bed in Hannah's house and I thought why the hell should you be bothered with this?"

"Bothered! My God, what a word! You really are something. All right, I'm touched you were thinking of me like that but I'm also damn annoyed that you thought you could leave everything until I got back. I mean, what about your knee? We haven't even talked about that."

"My knee's fine."

"Well, that's something anyway."

"I've got a sore head and it's getting worse with you arguing." She waved a dismissive hand at that. "And the only problem is that I can't really remember what the hell happened. I can remember coming aboard and I can remember being in a kind of cave and hearing voices and then I can remember Bill Maitland bending over me and holding my head."

She took his head in her hands again and looked at the contusion for the third time. When she had first come aboard and heard what had happened she had given him a careful examination and had been as satisfied as she could without a brain scan that he was suffering from nothing more serious than concussion.

"That's normal," she said. "Retrograde amnesia. You'll probably never remember what happened." She still had his face between her hands and said, "You're grumpy. You're also dotty. Here you've got a straightforward burglary and — "

He said, "Listen, you might be a bloody good doctor but you don't go much as a copper. Let's leave this tidying up and have some coffee and then just listen to me for a bit."

He made her a cup of instant in the galley and she was too relieved that he was all right to reject it. They went out on deck and drank it. The weather was still warm though the sky had now grown hazy and some of the brightness had gone.

"A straightforward burglary, you said. Have you noticed anything of yours missing?"

She shook her head. "I haven't looked carefully, though."

"No, but you've had a fast check — and nothing. Same as me. Well, you don't come and burglarize a boat and take nothing."

"They could have been surprised. You surprised them, remember."

"You've seen the state of the boat. It means they'd had enough time to find something. Don't forget, these villains would bring a suitcase or a holdall and if they didn't have one that's the first thing they'd steal. Then they'd stuff things into it as they went along."

"You keep on saying 'they'. Perhaps it was a single man and perhaps we didn't have anything he fancied. Maybe he hated the whole lot. Said to himself, 'My God, what a terrible lot of stuff to steal. I'll just leave it.'"

"Very funny."

"So what are you saying?"

"I'm saying they came here for one thing only."

"What's that?"

"The musk."

"The musk? Oh, come on, Mike, you want to know who I think did this? I think it was Dommie. You saw all my underwear on the floor. That's what people like Dommie do. And he's a voyeur. He looked through the window at us, not once but twice. He's a loner and he's got the instincts of an adult male with the brain of a — "

"Listen, Hannah said she thought musk was valuable, didn't she?"

"Hannah's no expert."

"Hang on. Just listen. Hannah may not be an expert but Rawlings is and I think what we've got here is worth a fortune and I've been waiting for you to get back so I can find out."

"Why wait for me if you're so sure?"

"Just in case I need you as a witness for what I'm about to do. In the wheelhouse there's a scale that I bought this morning. We'll see."

He went to the flagpole at the stern of *Osprey* and unfurled the blue ensign. Underneath it and hidden by its folds was the belt of wrapped packages. He took it into the wheelhouse and began to open the packages and pour the brown grains into the scale. He worked for about fifteen minutes, weighing and then pouring the weighed grains into plastic food bags and tying the ends tightly. Each time he did this he entered the amount in a small notebook.

"Right. That's it. You want to know how much I think we've got?"

"Of course I want to know."

"Rawlings said musk was worth just under four hundred pounds an ounce."

"Oh, my God, that's more expensive than — "

"Gold. Right."

"So, let's call it three hundred and ninety pounds sterling an ounce. And we've got . . . " He looked at his notebook. "We've got two hundred and seventy-two ounces. And that's . . . " He used his calculator. "Christ, I make that just over a hundred and six thousand pounds."

They looked at each other in uneasy silence for a moment and then he said, "Enough to get burglarized for, enough to get killed for."

"God, Mike, what are you going to do?"

"I don't know."

"You really do have to get hold of the police."

"Who? Phil Somers, the local village bobby? And tell him what? That we found some musk in the sea? What the hell would he know about musk? You knew damn all and so did I. So the local bobby's not going to know much."

"So who do you go to?"

"Why go to anyone?"

"Mike — "

"Listen, a Chinese man washes up ashore here. He's been stabbed a couple of times in the stomach. That's one thing. We go out to the old drowned city and we find packages of something around a marker buoy. That's another. We don't know what it is but take the trouble to find out. It's not drugs. It's not harmful to anyone. No one's reported it missing and if they did it's illegal. OK?"

"Illegal?"

"Rawlings was vague about that but I'm going to find out and I'm also going to find out who would buy it in this country and why it's here."

"But why don't you just let the police find out? Why get embroiled in something like this?"

"You just don't understand, do you! That's what I am, a bloody copper. And I get embroiled in things. Do you think something like this is ever going to come my way again? And what the hell am I going to do here day after day, and night after night when I've finished painting the boat and you've gone back to London? I've got a whole winter to live. And apart from anything else people are burglarizing my boat and untying it and generally being out of order. So if it's got anything to do with musk then I want to know. OK?"

"Stop saying OK. You're sounding like Brady."

"That's how us coppers sound."

There was an excitement in his voice she hadn't heard for a long time and she didn't like what she was hearing.

15

THEY cleaned up *Osprey* and it took them a couple of hours before both were satisfied. As she worked Alex became more convinced that the 'break-in', as Mike was now calling it, had been the work of Dommie. It had all the characteristics of the kind of attack a child might have made. Things had been spilled everywhere. Even food. It had the hallmarks of juvenile vandalism and not what she imagined professional burglars would have done. She especially hated the thought of her underwear being handled.

Mike would have none of it. "You've never seen a break-in like this before," he said. "I've seen a dozen. This is how it looks. We're just lucky they didn't shit on the bed. I've seen that too."

"You're not being logical," she said. "Either they were professionals who came for the musk — that's your idea — or they weren't. Professionals wouldn't take

252

the time to make messes. It isn't logical. You can't have it both ways."

"You can if you want someone to think their boat was broken into by vandals. Look, say you were a professional and you wanted to search for the musk. Why not make it look like vandals? The police don't have a hope — even if they wanted to — of solving what looks like a random break-in with nothing pinched. And musk isn't even mentioned so there's no publicity about it."

"So who would be after the musk?"

"What about the Triads?"

She laughed. "My God, Mike, you talk about my imagination!"

"It's not so far-fetched. Who would know someone was carrying musk from the Far East? Who would kill him for it? Rawlings says the Hong Kong Triads have moved into the musk trade just as they were moving into every possible money-making area before Hong Kong was due to be handed back to China. Things may be different then for the Triads. They may be better; they may be worse; no one knows yet. But there's one thing for certain: it's best not to take any chances. Get what you can while you can. That's been the motto of every criminal organization since the year dot and the Triads are no different. I know. I've come in contact with them because they're expanding in London."

"But, Mike — "

"Let's not argue any more. This weather doesn't look as though it's going to hold much longer and I want to do as many dives as I can before the autumn storms arrive." He paused then said, "You expecting someone?"

They were in the wheelhouse and he was looking over her shoulder. She turned and saw an old woman walk towards the gangplank. For a moment Alex thought she was coming aboard but she walked past the boat and stopped at the little sandy beach where Mike had brought the drowned Chinese man ashore. She stood there for some minutes and in the still morning air they could hear her voice. She was talking to herself. Then Alex saw that she had a bunch of flowers in her hand and she began pulling off the petals and scattering them in the still water of the creek. She did this for a

254

few moments then threw the bare stalks after them and began to walk back the way she had come.

As she drew level with the boat she stopped and shouted, "You rotten buggers!" She waved her arm angrily at *Osprey* then set off again. She had not gone more than a few paces when she seemed to catch her foot in the roots of a clump of reeds and she fell. All this was seen clearly by Alex and Mike who had not been able to take their eyes off her. She lay on her face and they ran down to her.

Between them they got her on her back and then sitting up.

"How do you feel?" Alex said.

She was small and light and after a moment she said, "Help me up."

Mike looked at Alex who nodded, and they lifted her to her feet. Even though the day was warm she was wearing an old dark blue coat over a dress and apron. She had solid walking shoes on her feet. Alex noticed her hands were twisted with arthritis.

"What you want?" she said angrily.

"You fell," Alex said.

"Oh, yes. I fell." She suddenly smiled at them. "It's a grand day."

"Yes, it is."

"Is that your boat?"

"It's mine," Mike said.

"You can't moor here. This is private land."

"Yes, I know. I have permission."

"Never. He'd never give permission. Never has, never will."

Mike smiled. "Well, I have permission."

"The Colonel give you leave? I don't think." Then she smiled again. "Do as you please."

She started on her way again but her steps were weak. Alex took her arm and said, "Wouldn't you like a cup of tea?"

She thought about that for a moment. "It's more like coffee time."

"Coffee, then."

They helped her aboard and sat her down in a chair on deck and Alex fetched a cup of coffee.

"I'm Gracie," she said. "Do you know me?"

"I'm Mike. This is Alexandra."

"I found him." She waved her old twisted hand towards the beach.

"Dead . . . washed up by the seas. Drowned . . . that's what they said. And I found him on that little beach . . . poor boy." She sipped her coffee. "That's good. I don't get much nowadays. Yes. Just this time of year . . . on a day like this . . . end of summer . . . I found him in the early morning. That's why I come down today . . . can't get away early no more . . . too much to do . . . but I come down to remember him . . . He being a foreigner without people in this land . . . he needs to be remembered. So I brought him flowers . . ."

"Who did you find?" Mike said as her voice ran out of steam.

"Him . . . him what died here. Drowned. That's what they said. They said he'd been scraped on the rocks. But there ain't no rocks around here, its all flat sand and mud."

"Here?" Mike said. "You found him here?"

"Aye. Down there by that spit of sand. That's where he ended up. But nobody was to know. That's what the Colonel said. 'Do you understand that, Gracie? Nobody!' Afterwards he said he'd found him." She looked into the cup. "We always drank the best coffee." Then she said, "I see lots of things. I see small people and eat."

"Would you like something?" Alex said. "Are you hungry?"

"No, no, that's what I *seen*. Eat." She put down her cup and rose. "Thank you. I'm going now."

"Will you be all right?" Alex said.

"Oh, yes. That coffee's made me feel quite fit, thank you."

They helped her down the gangplank and watched her walk towards the bridge over the river.

"What'd you make of her?" Mike said.

"I don't know. She's confused, of course, but — "

"You can say that again. She found the body? This place gets stranger and stranger."

"You were the one who wanted to come here."

"For the diving. And that's what we're going to do now."

"Not me. It's far too cold."

"You'll have to some time."

258

"When I'm good and ready. Maybe next year, if we have a good summer."

They went out to the drowned city and tied up at one of the old marker buoys. The day was calm and the midday sun warm though not as warm as it had been. The sky was hazy and the breeze was cool.

"I can feel autumn," Alex said.

Mike got into his wetsuit and went in. The water was calm and clearer than it had been some days before and she could watch him go down and down. It was too chilly to be on deck so she went into the saloon and put on the stereo. She found it difficult to comprehend where she was and what she was doing, it was so different from her normal busy life.

She lay back in one of the swivel chairs and half listened to the music and thought of Mike's role-playing earlier in the day. What he couldn't seem to realize was that his police days were finished. At some point he was going to get a terrible shock when he discovered they were gone for ever.

Mike and the police had always seemed strange bedfellows to her. When she had first got to know him he was simply a charged personality trying to walk again. It was only once he had got himself as right as he would ever be that she began to see other facets of his character.

She had wondered why he had joined the police in the first place and one day near the end of his stay at Effingham his father, Sid, had told her about his other son, Mike's brother, Neil. It was a story with which she as a doctor in a mixed area of London was only too familiar. He had started on drugs when he was at school and had gone from marijuana to amphetamines and then on to the hard stuff. By the time he was seventeen he was hooked on heroin and was stealing from his parents to support his habit. Then he was kicked out of school and began stealing from just about anyone.

"It nearly killed his mum," Sid said. "She had two heart attacks during the time he was still living at home. They was brought on by Neil doing drugs. Then he began to deal and he'd keep the stuff in the house and once she found it and put it down the toilet and he hit her. Slapped her around the face until he broke her nose. Mike was much younger and smaller than Neil but even so he went for him. Course Neil gave him a terrible hiding. I think that's when Mike decided that one day he would join the police. His mother never wanted him to. He never wanted to neither, but I think he thought it was one way he could stop his brother from harming his mum. Not that he needed to. A few years later Neil was caught dealing and was sent to jail. And that's where he died. Overdose, they said. By that time his mother was dead too."

★ ★ ★

Mike splashed to the surface after about twenty minutes. He pulled off his mask. "I saw something! Bloody great block of stone. Has to be part of the sunken town because it's cut square. But I couldn't see it clearly. That's what I'm going to get next — proper lights. They'll make a hell of a difference."

They returned to Lexton in the early afternoon and they hadn't been back on their moorings for more than a couple of minutes when they heard a woman's voice shouting, "Hello! Anyone there?"

Mike looked out of a porthole and said, "It's Mrs Blackhurst. I'll go and see what she wants."

She wanted Alex and she wanted to see her in private.

"I hope Mr Harley doesn't mind," she said.

Alex took her into the saloon. "No, not at all."

"Well, this is very nice." She sat in one of the swivel chairs. "Bill Maitland tells me you've come to look for the Templar treasure."

"Well, not really. We only heard about it from him."

"He's been looking for it for years. You know what they say about it? They say it'll be found on Friday the thirteenth and the person who finds it will suffer."

"They say that about all buried treasure, don't they? That bad luck attaches to the finder. I've always thought it was simply a way to stop people searching. But why Friday the thirteenth?"

"That was the day Jacques de Molay,

the Grand Master, was burnt at the stake by the French king. That's why it's gone into the mythology as an unlucky day. Anyway, I haven't come to talk about the Templars."

"The moorings? You'll need to talk to Mike."

"No, not at all. It's about my grandson, Dommie. You haven't come across him, have you? He's down here sometimes."

Alex thought of the strange face peering through the porthole but said, "I think I've seen him. In his thirties? Carries a stick?"

"Yes, that's Dommie. I hope he hasn't been getting in your way down here."

"Not at all."

"He sometimes likes to talk to strangers and they don't quite know what to make of him."

"Mr Maitland has mentioned him so I know a little."

"I thought I'd come and talk to you because you're a doctor and you're not a local. I need advice, confidential advice."

Alex looked at the woman in her old shoes, battered cords and thick shirt. This was how people often talked to doctors at cocktail parties. Alex's ex-husband Freddy had had a formula for it. The moment anyone said, "Doctor, I think I've got X and wondered if you could tell me what to do," he would say, "Of course, but I'd need to examine you so why don't you just go into the next room and take off your clothes." That had always stopped them.

She said, "Mrs Blackhurst, I'm on holiday and — "

"I realize that, Doctor, and I hope I'm not keeping you from anything. This won't take long and the reason I've come to you is that you're a stranger here and I don't want the whole village to know."

Alex sighed inwardly, thought about Mike's moorings and said, "All right. Go ahead."

"Well, as Bill Maitland must have told you, Dommie's mentally retarded. I know you've all got other phrases for these conditions nowadays but I can never remember them. He was brain damaged as a baby and he doesn't think as we do. And I'm afraid . . . " She paused and Alex was aware that she was having difficulty in expressing herself. "I'm afraid that . . . that I've probably been treating him in the wrong way. You see he's a man, and I've always treated him as a child."

"It's easily done."

"Yes, it is, especially if you've brought him up from babyhood as I have. The point is, he isn't a baby, he's a man with all the instincts that a man has. Am I making myself clear?"

"Yes, of course you are."

"So you can see why I've come to you and why this needs to be so confidential."

"I think I can."

"Good, because something has happened which could create a problem. I'm not going into it any further but you'll be able to guess what has led up to my next question. Is there any way that a man's natural instinct can be . . . well, damped down?"

"Do you mean his sex drive?"

"Yes, I do."

"Has he been showing a sexual interest in women?"

"Yes, he has."

"I think if you want my advice about

265

Dommie you're going to have to be more explicit."

Ellen looked irritated. "Do you have to know everything? I thought we could have a civilized discussion."

"This is how civilization began, Mrs Blackhurst, with man wanting woman."

Ellen suddenly laughed. "That's very true, Doctor. Yes. All right. Well, Dommie's got to the stage where he wants sexual contact with women and I'm afraid of his reactions if he's frustrated. We've had trouble once or twice and I'm terrified of him being placed in an institution. He's never been away from home in his life and I think it would kill him."

"You talked of damping down the sex drive."

"Is there something that can be done? I don't want him . . . well, operated on. God, no! And I don't want him to have any side effects. I did read up on this once a long time ago and the article talked about men growing breasts or having heart attacks."

There was much more Alex wanted to know but she found herself sympathizing with Mrs Blackhurst and said, "I had a case like this not so long ago and I did my own reading. The difference was that the man in question was not someone with learning difficulties."

"That's the phrase!"

"There are two approaches which are relevant to someone like Dommie. There's a drug called benperidol which acts on the brain as a tranquilliser. It acts on the parts of the brain that have to do with sexual arousal. It's like putting that bit of your brain to sleep."

"That sounds good. Just those little bits go to sleep."

"That's not the end of the story. The problem is that it could affect his thought processes which, if I've got this right, aren't dynamic."

"Dynamic? Anything but."

"And there are other possibilities. His facial expressions will slow down too, and his legs will be restless and so he'll need another pill to counteract these."

"I don't like the sound of that at all. I mean . . . well . . . I just don't."

"There's another drug called androcur which depresses the body's manufacture of testosterone; that's the stuff which heightens sexual desire. That would mean Dommie's sexual drive would be lessened. You were probably reading about this method when you came across heart problems and men growing breasts."

"Horrible."

"They've solved that now so we don't have to worry about those two conditions any longer. But what I would say to you is that with someone of Dommie's mental state the use of drugs, especially the first one I mentioned, benperidol, is often unpredictable."

Ellen nodded her head slowly. "So what you're really saying is you pays your money and takes your choice — and you don't know what could happen."

"That's fair."

Ellen rose. "Neither sounds much good but one or the other may be better than what lies in store for him if he goes on as he is. Thank you, Doctor, you've been very kind. I think you realize how much I needed someone who isn't of the town." She moved to the bottom of the companionway, stopped, and said,

"Was that Gracie I saw down here this morning?"

"That's how she introduced herself."

"Dear old thing. She used to work for our family, you know, when my husband was alive. Even after he died. Oh, yes, she worked for us for many years. But she's all alone now. And not all there."

"Really? She seemed — "

"She's confused most of the time. Did you have her on board?"

Alex was aware of a change in Ellen's tone. It was more than a casual interest.

"She came up for a cup of coffee. She'd slipped and fallen in the reeds."

"Poor old Gracie! Was she lucid?"

"Oh, yes, perfectly."

"I'm surprised. Did she say anything? I mean, did she tell you why she was here?"

The picture of the old woman dropping the petals into the still water was clear in Alex's mind but she said, "No, she was a bit shaken. She talked about the coffee. Said she didn't get any nowadays."

Ellen nodded. "We used to drink the best Jamaican Blue Mountain when she was with us. Perhaps she was remembering that." She began to climb up the companionway. "I wouldn't pay too much attention to Gracie, if I were you. She doesn't know what she's talking about half the time. She suffers from Alzheimer's."

16

MIKE pushed the BMW along as fast as he could — which wasn't very fast. When he had looked at a map and found the village of Sheepwalk in the Cotswolds he had quickly traced a route and estimated a journey time of between two and three hours. It was now three hours since he had left Lexton and he wasn't there yet. He had forgotten how difficult it was to travel east-west in England. Most of the motorways ran north-south. So he was not in the best of tempers when he arrived at the village and found Peter Grieve's house. It was on the outskirts, a big old former rectory with ivy growing up the walls and a long outbuilding that might once have been stables.

A small boy, dressed only in a pair of short pants on this sultry day, was standing at the gate.

"I've come to see Mr Grieve," Mike said.

The boy had an urchin face and long fair hair, the kind of face, Mike thought, that choirboys had, and which he mistrusted. He had seen too many people with innocent faces holding guns or knives.

Mike waited, the boy said nothing.

"He lives here, doesn't he?"

"Yes."

"Well, I've come to see him."

"He's busy."

"I've got an appointment."

"What time?"

"Look, I've come a long way and I don't want to waste any more time."

Mike pushed the gate open. The small boy took a few steps back. There was a rustle in the grass at Mike's foot. He looked down and his heart almost stopped. A few inches from his leg was the head of a huge snake.

"Don't move," the boy said. "Hamish is hungry."

There was no way Mike could move. He had never seen a snake as large as this. Indeed he had never seen a snake except in the London Zoo when he was a child.

The snake's head rose on thick patterned coils. It reached Mike's knees, then his waist. Its tongue was darting in and out, as though tasting the air around him.

"Hamish doesn't like you," the boy said.

"For God's sake," Mike whispered, "get him away from me."

"Not if you don't say please."

A woman's voice called, "Oscar! What are you doing?"

A handsome woman in her thirties, dressed in trousers and a T-shirt, her face devoid of make-up, was coming down the path.

"Oh, Oscar!" she said to the small boy. "You're doing it again." Then she turned to the snake. "Stop it, Hamish! Behave yourself!" She tapped it on the head and it dropped, almost sheepishly, to the grass. She looked up at Mike. "Sorry about that. It's only a reticulated python. Quite tame, really."

Mike introduced himself and Mrs Grieve said, "Peter waited for you."

"I'm sorry I'm late, the traffic was bad."

"Well, he's milking the pit vipers at the

moment." She waved at the outbuilding. "You can talk to him in there if you like. Come with me."

Mike walked past Oscar, who was standing beside the big python. Oscar smiled at him just the way choirboys smile.

Mrs Grieve opened the outbuilding door and Mike followed her in. He was hit by the heat. Then he saw the glass cages and the snakes and felt almost weak with apprehension.

"Peter, here's Chief Inspector Harley."

At the end of the room with its walls of cages stood a man dressed only in a pair of short khaki pants. In front of him on a long table was a short and heavy snake.

He turned and said, "Won't be a sec." In his hand he held a steel rod with a curved end like a miniature walking stick. He had it clamped just at the back of the snake's head and now, with his thumb and index finger, he gripped the snake in the same place and took the rod away. The snake blew like a steam valve. Its mouth was wide open and its long powerful fangs were on display. With his other hand Grieve took a small glass jar, fitted it under the fangs and pressed the head slightly. Mike could see venom drip down the sides of the jar forming a pool at the bottom. After a moment Grieve dropped the snake into a ceramic bath in which there was a coiling ball of similarly patterned snakes, and from a second bath lifted out another snake with the hook of his steel rod and milked this one, too, of its venom.

Mike heard the door close behind him and he was alone in the snake house with a man who hardly seemed aware of his presence.

Grieve dropped the snake into the ceramic basin and picked up another. "Last one," he said. "You want to try it?"

"God, no."

Grieve was about Mike's height but thinner. His body was lean and wiry and he had light hair like his son's. He also wore a beard. His arms and chest were covered in small scars.

"*Bitis arietans*," he said, holding up the yellow and brown snake, part of whose body was nearly as thick as Mike's

275

forearm but almost wraithlike compared to Hamish. "The noble puff-adder. They kill more people in Africa than all the other poisonous snakes put together. Lazy beggars always lying around on bush paths sunning themselves and getting trodden on or else getting into your blankets at night for warmth. When we send our chaps out there as part of the International Wildlife team we like them to have enough anti-venom to cope with any problems. Hence all this."

"You make anti-venom from real venom?"

"That's it. Let's go into my office, it's cooler there. Puff-adders like heat."

They went into an office at the end of the building and Mike looked around carefully in case there were any further surprises of a reptilian nature. He found none and sat down opposite Grieve, who dropped into a hard chair behind his desk.

"You're the chap who wants to talk about musk."

"That's me."

"What do the police want to know about that for and by the way, how do I know you're from the police? Shouldn't you identify yourself?"

Mike had been waiting for this and said, "My jacket's in the car. I'll go and get it if you like."

"Oh, don't worry. I believe you. It's just an odd subject, that's all."

"Let me fill you in briefly. We had a report from the Suffolk police that they had found a consignment of drugs but when they had them checked it was discovered to be musk. A man had been killed and since then I've spoken to an expert from Hong Kong who told me what he knew about musk but because we now have a murder inquiry we want to know a great deal more. He'd mentioned the fact that the trade was illegal but didn't know why. As I told you, I phoned your organization in London and they said you were the man to talk to because you'd spent time out in the Far East working on the problem."

Grieve picked up a battered pipe and lit it. "Hope you don't mind," he said. "I think better with a pipe. So what is it exactly you want to know?"

"Why the stuff is illegal. I've found out its price and was staggered."

"Yes, it's pretty expensive. It would need to be when you consider you've got to kill the musk deer to get it. You've got to find the deer first and they're as shy as anything. And when I say you've got to find them, you've got to look in the Himalayas because that's where they live." He opened the top drawer of his desk and pulled out a box file. "This is some of the work I did. I looked it out after you phoned." He pushed several photographs across the desk and Mike found himself looking at an attractive small deer against a background of giant mountains and forests. "I was lucky to get those. You don't often get pictures of them." He went to his desk drawer again. "This is what the poachers are after." He pushed over a musk pod the same as those in Mike's collection.

"You could say the modern story of the musk deer starts with the Washington Agreement in 1973, when it was classed as an endangered species and dealing in musk was made illegal. In some places there's a five-year jail sentence if you're caught smuggling musk without a certificate from the country of origin. The pod only comes from the male deer, it's part of his sexual equipment, and you've got to cut it out. So you have to kill him first.

"My wife and I spent two years up in Uttar Pradesh studying the musk deer and it's a pathetic story, really. The poachers only want that" — he flicked the pod — "and you can find the remains of the deer after the kites have had their fill. It's like the destruction of the American buffalo, the hunters only wanted the tongue so they left the dead bodies to rot."

Mike said, "My Hong Kong expert said most of the musk goes to Japan. Why would the murdered man have musk with him in the West?"

"Currency. Same reason as people carry diamonds. It goes back a long way. Marco Polo used it as currency. It can be sold easily enough if you know where to go."

"That's what I'm after. The place where you'd go to sell it."

"Musk isn't only wanted in Japan.

It's got a long history in other places, French tarts used to wear sachets of it between their breasts. And there's a huge market in Chinese and Hindu medicine." He looked in the box file again and pulled out a pamphlet. "Yes, here it is. Something I picked up in India from one of these Hindu healers." He read: "'Do you have a problem shamefully affecting your married life? Tila musk wala will restore the male organ to its full potential.'" He smiled into his beard. "You can see now why it costs so much. Then there's the perfume business. I met a chap in Nepal who had come out from England to buy musk but after I showed him what had happened to the deer he decided to use one of the many artificial musks instead."

"So the perfume business would be the one most interested here?"

"Not here. In France. Some of the top houses there still buy illegal musk for their most expensive lines. I went over but no one in the business would talk to me. I had to find scientists and 'noses' on the fringe."

Mike said, "The stuff smells like a farmyard. Hard to think of it in perfume."

"Once it's prepared that changes. It has three main advantages: it makes the scent last longer, it blends the ingredients well, and it makes the finished product radiate off the skin. There are dozens of artificial musks but people say they're not as good as the genuine article."

"So all the musk in the West is smuggled."

"Most of it. Some comes from musk farms in China. Of course we're not allowed to see these but I've been to them, even photographed them. Bloody places. The male deer are kept in wooden crates just about their own size and the musk is removed without killing them. But they might as well be dead because the crates are so small they can't even turn round and they stay in them for life. I think if I was a musk deer I'd rather be dead. And anyway the musk is of low quality. There are musk deer in the Chinese mountains and they shoot these and take the pods which are smuggled into Hong Kong too.

When I was there the trade was being taken over by the Triads and . . . don't move!"

Mike heard a faint rustle behind him and then felt as though someone had put a hand on his left shoulder.

"Oh, for God's sake, Hamish, get down!" Grieve rose and came round the desk. The python's head had now settled firmly on Mike's shoulder. "Just loves people, does Hamish . . . Come on down . . . But people don't altogether love him . . . That's better . . . Come on. This way. Come on, Hamish! Outside . . . "

Grieve lifted the head from Mike's shoulder, put his hand in his pocket, and held something in front of the python's nose. "Toy mouse," he said. "Hamish knows it isn't edible but I think he follows it to please me."

Mike watched the sixteen-foot reticulated python follow Peter Grieve down the passageway between the puff-adder cages and decided he had been there long enough.

★ ★ ★

Alex didn't like being alone on the boat. So far the weather still held so that she could sprawl out in a deckchair under an awning Mike had rigged. But even so she didn't like being alone. She had thought of staying with Hannah but only that morning Hannah had phoned and said she was going to London for a few days on publishing business and was there anything Alex wanted from Harrods? So she couldn't go to Southwold.

She got a book and went up to her chair and flopped. So far it had not been a good day. Mike had left very early for the Cotswolds and she had stayed in bed, unwilling, after a row they had had the evening before, to get up and see him off. Now she thought that was childish and regretted her behaviour.

She tried to pinpoint exactly what had started the row. Logically one thing led to another down a long trail all the way back to the original shooting on the Meadowvale Estate. But last night's row came after she had heard him lying on the telephone to Grieve, the ecologist. He had lied about still being in the police — or at least had allowed Grieve to make the assumption that he was still a policeman, which amounted to the same thing.

When she taxed him with a lie of omission he had rounded on her on the basis that it had been a private conversation and listening to it was like opening someone's mail. Alex wasn't sure about that but what she was sure about was that she hadn't liked what she'd heard and had told him so. There was a bitter aftertaste to the row that brought up memories of those months when he had worked at the 'important job' in the back room at Scotland Yard and had spent all his free time drinking with his mates and bringing them back to the flat and generally clinging on to what he had once had.

Now he was doing it again just when she had thought it was all over and had been replaced by his plans for a new kind of life.

"Isn't there a crime called impersonating a policeman?" she had said at one point.

"And isn't there a phrase called minding your own business?" he had countered.

"But it is my business! I found the bloody stuff."

"I can't argue with that." And he had stopped arguing and gone to bed and done his leg exercises.

Thinking about it she found herself partly, but only partly, in sympathy with him. He'd always been a policeman and now she knew just enough about the police to know that part of the work was boring and the other part was like shooting yourself up with pure adrenalin. That part was addictive.

What was disappointing was that she had thought him cured. But at the first opportunity he had he'd gone back to the addiction.

And what for? A break-in which had inspired a crazy notion about musk smuggling and Triads, when any sensible person would place Dommie at the head of a list of suspects. The more she thought about it the more she was convinced it had been Dommie. Not only the vandalizing of the boat's contents but also the blow on the head fitted what she had begun to think of as his behaviour pattern. He was powerful, he carried a heavy stick most of the time. Striking Mike was the obvious thing for him to do and since he would have had no natural inhibiting factor it was fortunate he hadn't killed him. And now Mike was committing an illegal act. She thought of what Inspector Brady would do to him if he found out. He would enjoy nothing more than going after Mike.

The phone rang and she thought instantly that it was Mike, ringing to say he regretted their row.

It was Laddie Broakes. "Who's that?" he had said irritably when she told him Mike wasn't there.

"This is Alexandra Kennedy."

"Oh, yes, of course. It's Dr Kennedy, isn't it? We've never met. But he told me about you. You're staying up on the boat with him?"

"That's right. Can I get him to ring you?"

"Tell him I've got a couple of interesting things for him."

It was on the tip of her tongue to say: 'Interesting things for someone who's pretending to be a policeman or interesting to an ordinary citizen?' But she remembered what Mike had told her about Broakes and his new job and she realized that he was another ex-policemen who didn't want to be out of the Force and who probably thought as Mike did. So she said nothing.

17

"OLORD, we ask Thee to look after us and bring us closer to Thee. We're all sinners, Lord, and we need Thy help . . . "

Alex paused and looked at the figure standing at a corner of the small square in Lexton. He was an elderly man in a threadbare grey suit with a collar and tie and brown boots. His thin head was bald and what hair he had was white and was blowing in the light sea breeze. In his hands he held a Bible and his eyes were on the heavens as he prayed for the folk of Lexton.

" . . . through a glass darkly, Lord, but what Thou seest we cannot know . . . "

He was talking to no one. People passed him on the pavement without looking up. Alex felt sorry for him in his loneliness but comforted herself with the thought that the Lord would be on his side, and she crossed over to the Lexton supermarket. She had decided that she had been unnecessarily hard on Mike and was going to buy him something he particularly liked for his supper. When the idea had come to her on the boat earlier that morning she had thought it was a female cliché — but at the same time she knew that the boat was too small a space for two people to recover easily from a row. A plate of something nice might help.

The problem was that the supermarket did not seem to go in for treats. As she drifted along the shelves looking at labels she became aware of a low conversation going on in the next aisle. She absorbed the sense of what was being said for a second or two without positively listening. Then she stopped and listened unashamedly.

A woman's voice was saying, "And then he says to me that he caught it and I says I don't give a toss how you got it I'm not cooking it in here, it'll stink the place out . . ."

A man's voice said, "But what'd he bring it to you for?"

"Wanted to swap it, didn't he?"

"What for?"

"What you think?"

"Oh, yeah. I see. Rotten little bastard."

"I've always been scared of Dommie. Even when I was a kid. It was like that woman on the beach. You remember when he grabbed her costume?"

"Yeah."

"Well, he grabs me and tries to push the fish down my throat. That's how I got these bruises . . ."

Alex moved slightly and looked through a gap in the tea and coffee shelves. A woman she had never seen before was talking to Chris Cottis. Still talking they moved to the checkout.

Alex brooded on what she had heard. She had no idea what had happened or why but the pieces of the conversation stuck in her mind and seemed to underline what she had been thinking earlier. On impulse she went to the liquor shelves and picked up a bottle of Old Snorter and one of white wine. The young women at the checkout were talking to each other across the tills and staring after the other two who had just left. Alex paid then walked back through the square. The old evangelist had now collected a crowd of about eight people. Three of them, she thought, were Japanese tourists and they started taking pictures of him. He seemed to notice them then for the first time and paused. When he spoke again his voice had risen.

"We have strangers in our midst, Lord, strangers who have come from a far land to seek us out. To pillory us!"

He began to shake his fist at the tourists who did not know what was happening, but thought whatever it was was funny, so began to laugh and pass remarks to each other.

This seemed to inflame the speaker more and he shouted, "O Lord, we beseech Thee to bring down vengeance upon them!"

The other members of the crowd looked embarrassed and a woman said, "No call for rudeness."

The evangelist was standing outside a butcher's shop and the butcher, in a striped apron and white boater, came out of the shop and put his arm around the old man's shoulders. "Come on, Harold," he said. "Enough's enough."

The old man allowed himself to be led

into the shop and the crowd dispersed. The tourists were still laughing.

Alex went on her way, turned right at the church, and went into the gate of Bill Maitland's cottage. Now that she had arrived she regretted slightly the impulse that had brought her there but at the same time knew she might be on the fringe of finding out something that could change Mike's attitude.

"You're a mind reader," Bill said, as he came to the door. "It's just about time for a pre-lunch pint. Let's sit outside." He fetched glasses and they sat on the battered garden chairs. "I was coming down to see you. I've found something Mike will be interested in. It's a manuscript I've not looked at before and it mentions a grand burial in what it calls the 'west preceptory'. I'd never heard of one before. I thought there was only one preceptory, which of course went into the sea with the rest of the town. But I suppose if one is accurate then any building the Templars lived in could be called a preceptory. It's defined as 'a Templar's estate or buildings'. Now if I've got it right that could mean that the burial took place somewhere that hasn't vanished in the waves and Mike and I can have a damned good look for it. It has to be a sarcophagus, you see."

She enjoyed his enthusiasm about his favourite subject and then, when he drew breath, she said casually, "I must say Lexton has had its share of violent times."

"Hasn't it, though!"

"And more right now."

"How's that?"

She mentioned the old man in the square and Bill said, "Oh that's poor old Harold Potter. He sometimes says things he shouldn't."

"And the Dommie business."

He looked pained for a moment and said, "So you've heard."

"I could hardly not have heard. It's all round the village." She kept it casual. "Even the checkout girls were talking about it in the supermarket."

He paused and then said, "That's the trouble with a village. Poor old Dommie. He deserves better."

"You mean an institution?"

"Well, the problem with a word like

institution is that one shies away from it. But there are some times . . . Well . . . maybe not . . . Maybe he's better off here where Ellen can keep an eye on him."

"But she can't all the time, can she? And I know the village itself watches out for him. But again, not all the time. Like this business with the fish."

"Yes, one has to feel sorry for Betty. She's not the most respectable woman in the village but she shouldn't be threatened with that kind of violence."

"She's apparently got bruising on the neck."

"So I believe. A couple of people — former parishioners of mine — have come to me about it. One old woman wanted me to have Dommie arrested. But then there would be an attempted rape charge and goodness knows what else. What do you think, as a doctor?"

"Purely as a doctor I'd find it hard to dismiss hospitalization. But that's only a medical point of view, it's not the view of someone close to him. I'm told there've been problems before, with a woman on the beach."

He looked surprised. "You're well informed."

She did not reply.

He went on, "And the fisherman, of course."

"I hadn't heard about that."

It was an invitation to tell her but he didn't take it up. Then he said, "She's worried sick about what will happen to him when she goes."

"I think you mentioned yourself that the Blackhursts were once the big landed family here."

"Yes, that's true." He paused. "And he's the last of the line."

"I hadn't realized that."

"Oh, yes. It's all part of our history now and there can't be any harm in your knowing what the whole village knows already. Poor old Dommie's illegitimate. That adds to his problems. Both father and mother dead. It's a sad story really and it all happened a long time ago, in the early Sixties I suppose. Yes, must be, Dommie's thirty-four. I baptized him. Not in church, of course, but in the house. That was before it started falling to pieces."

★ ★ ★

In the early Sixties a stranger came to Lexton. He came one summer day carrying a pack on his back and a map in his hand. He was in his twenties, wasn't much above middle height, and was slender with dark hair. He got off the bus and walked through the village and people noticed him straight away because of his looks. He wasn't a normal tourist. In those days there were few overseas tourists in Lexton. Those that came were mainly British and there were few enough of those. Lexton lived by its fishing. There were no yachts in the river, there was no Rod 'n' Line wine bar or any supermarkets. But the place was busy. There were two dozen fishing boats moored just below the pub and the catches of cod, haddock, and mackerel were good. People weren't wealthy but they were in work and felt secure.

The young stranger, whose name was Tommy Lee, was a Chinese American and came to Lexton at a seminal time for Gillian Blackhurst. She had recently finished school and was considering what to do next. So were her mother and father for she had been a handful ever since she had learned to walk.

By one of those odd quirks of English village life there was no other family of the same social background as the Blackhursts in Lexton. The 'beerage' living in the big house on the front was devoid of children so there were no socially correct young people for Gilly to mix with. The war was supposed to have wiped out all such divisions but here on this lonely and forgotten part of the English coastline they were as strong as ever.

Gilly was good-looking, not brilliant but bright enough. She'd gone to boarding school and had hated it. She had done no work, had experimented with marijuana, had been caught and expelled with three other girls. She had not taken her final exams and was now kicking her heels at home. Her isolation made things worse. She had nothing to do and only the small allowance her father gave her. She tried to get work, but it would have meant the simplest of jobs and no one in the village would have hired a Blackhurst to work in a shop or at the petrol pumps. She begged for a car so she could look for work in Bury. Her father turned this down flatly and told her to take the bus if she wanted to go anywhere. This didn't help matters so eventually her mother bought her a small skiff to give her something to interest her. It quickly developed into something else for she learned to sail it expertly and used it to go far into the marshes and also into the river. For the first time she became mobile.

It was said she had an affair with a local fisherman and another with a man who sold sports cars in a neighbouring village. Her father got to hear of the men in her life and one windy afternoon he went down to her boat, moored just a few yards from where Mike's boat was presently moored, and set it alight. A couple of hours later there were only a few bits of charred wood floating in the creek.

Gilly's relationship with her father had never been good. Even when she was a child he had tried to dominate her and she had reacted badly. Ellen had often pleaded with John not to be harsh with her and indeed had gone to talk to Bill Maitland in his role as her parish priest on several occasions just to release the pent-up tension inside her. After the burning of the boat she had even considered divorce.

All this while she tried to act as buffer between her husband and Gilly. She also desperately tried to arrange parties and dances at the house where Gilly could meet young men of her own class. But Lexton was isolated and Lexton House even more so. At last, after much nagging and cajoling Ellen talked John into giving their daughter a 'season' in London. They rented a flat in Bayswater and held a ball at a small London hotel for Gilly. For a while she seemed to enjoy herself in the London social scene, but then the season was over and back she came to the isolation of Lexton and back inevitably to the men who lived and worked there. Her father ordered her to have nothing to do with them. She flatly refused.

John Blackhurst, according to Maitland, was the real problem. He had come back from the prisoner-of-war camp surrounded by rumour and innuendo. It was said that he had been threatened with a court martial for cowardice and would have been cashiered had he not been taken prisoner. That was only one of several stories that survived the end of the war. But Maitland was one of the few people in Suffolk who knew, if not all the facts, then some of them.

Blackhurst's men had been surrounded by Rommel's armour at Wadi Bereh in the Western Desert and, after fighting a rearguard action for four days and sustaining a high casualty rate, he had surrendered nearly five hundred men. That was the official line. But some officers said it was only packaged like that because to have told the truth would have been bad for morale at that stage in the war.

But Bill Maitland's armoured unit had been less than fifty miles from Wadi Bereh at the time of the surrender. They had known that Rommel was down to his reserve fuel supplies and that he was beginning to withdraw on the northern edge of the pincer. They also knew Blackhurst had been promised reinforcements within seventy-two hours. Maitland was quite sure of that because his unit was part of the reinforcements. But even so Blackhurst had surrendered.

In the POW camp he was treated with contempt and disdain and, for his own sake, was moved to another camp. When he came home he was an embittered man.

So this was the situation when Tommy Lee walked into Lexton one summer's day and set up camp on the beach below Lexton House.

That was when Gilly met Tommy Lee, near the bottom of the path that led from her house to the beach. The first thing that Ellen knew about their affair, and this she was to tell Bill Maitland later, was after she discovered that food was going missing from the house. Not just a few pieces of bread but a whole loaf at a time and a pound of butter and, if they'd had a joint of meat, what was left over.

John Blackhurst did not take much interest in food. He spent most of his time in his study writing his war memoirs, but Ellen became concerned. At first she thought Gracie was taking the food, something that had never happened before, and set about watching her. But it wasn't Gracie and at last she discovered Gilly taking half a leg of roast lamb from the fridge and wrapping it in a piece of newspaper. When she asked her what she was doing Gilly said she was taking it to a poor homeless person.

Then her father learned about this new friendship. As usual he forbade it and as usual Gilly ignored him. He went to the parish council, then to the police, and put in formal complaints about the camper on the beach. Both said they could do nothing, the beach was public domain. He said the fire was dangerous. They said there was nothing near the tent which could catch fire except the tent itself and that was the owner's problem.

The friendship between Gilly and Tommy Lee developed rapidly. Within a week she was spending most of her time with him. She helped him to build a wall of rocks to keep the tent sheltered from the north-easterlies that came off the sea and they seemed to be settling

302

down for the autumn.

It was a situation that was tearing the family to pieces. Ellen tried to bring Gilly back to her senses, John was beside himself with frustration and rage; the village looked on with disapproval.

And then suddenly it was all over. Ellen prevailed on Gilly to go to London with her. She thought that a change of scene might also change her attitude, as it had partly done before. They were going to buy clothes; spend some money.

While they were away Tommy Lee hired a rowing boat to go out fishing. Later the boat floated back upside-down to the river mouth. No trace was ever found of Tommy.

But he had left his legacy. Deep inside Gilly's womb the embryo which would ultimately become his posthumous son Dominic was already forming.

18

"**R**IGHT on my shoulder!" Mike said. "Can you think of anything worse? And then he says, 'Get down, Hamish!' as though he's talking to a Skye terrier. He shows it a toy mouse and it follows him out of the place."

"Follows him where?" Alex asked.

"God knows. Maybe Hamish hangs around in the house with them. He's too big to sleep on their laps but I told you he was with the kid at the gate."

"I would have been petrified. Especially when he was milking those puff-adders of their venom. We saw one on the road in South Africa once. Someone had run over it and we stopped to look at it."

Mike had come back in the late afternoon and she had bought, instead of a foodie treat, a couple of bottles of Carlsberg Elephant lager which he loved. But he was now talking with such intensity she wasn't sure he knew what he was drinking.

"Anyway, that's when he told me all about this deer that's on the endangered species list and the pods . . . "

He had told her this in detail when he had first arrived back: the deer, the perfume business, the sexual tonics, the Chinese breeding . . . everything. She had rarely seen him as excited. It was the kind of mood she had so wanted when he had sat in her flat evening after evening as he tried to come to terms with the fact that his life — or at least the one he wanted — was irrecoverable.

Before she could stop herself she said, "Did he believe you to be a chief inspector?"

The moment she said it she regretted it. He looked down at his glass then picked it up and drank a mouthful and said, "Why do you ask that?" His voice had gone quiet.

"I was worried in case he asked you to prove it."

"Well, he didn't. And why shouldn't I call myself a chief inspector? That was my rank. People who leave the navy and the army still keep their ranks in Civvy Street. I've come across all sorts of half-baked people who call themselves lieutenant commanders or majors even though they left the services years before. Why can't ex-coppers do the same?"

"I don't know why the army and navy people keep their ranks. It's probably something out of the dim past and it's harmless enough, but you can see it wouldn't really do for policemen."

"Why not?"

"Because it allows people to think you have a power you don't have."

"You know something? I like to have you explaining things to me. You do it so well."

There was a cutting edge to his tone and she flinched. She said, "The lager was a welcome home. There's another one if you want it."

He shook his head, then he said, "What have you been doing?"

She knew it was a purely formal enquiry to change the subject but she was pleased. A year ago he wouldn't have bothered with the niceties but would have disappeared until he felt better.

She told him she had seen Maitland but did not tell him what had provoked it. She did not want him to know that she was asking questions — the territorial imperative was strong in Mike. He listened but she could see he had made up his mind that Dommie wasn't to blame.

"What about Chris, then?" she said, taking a new tack.

"He was the first person I thought of but when I checked his boat it was out both times."

"So what now?"

"Now? What do you want me to say? Just forget it? Forget the musk?"

Suddenly she felt her heart drop down like a stone. "Mike? Is that it? The musk? Is that what you're thinking of?"

"Of course I'm thinking of that. I'm thinking of the whole thing."

"No, I don't mean the whole thing, I mean just the one thing. That the musk is worth a lot of money and — "

"Christ, what do you take me for? Listen, someone's tried to wreck the boat. I've taken a beating. All I'm trying to do is avoid anything more."

It was what she wanted to hear and yet the way he said it made it sound just the opposite. He poured the last of the lager into his glass.

"Mike, you're not thinking of selling the musk, are you?"

"I've already told you that's not the reason. But what if I was? It's not drugs. It's not doing anyone any harm. And it doesn't belong to anyone. So why not?"

"Because it's illegal."

"So is parking on a yellow line but we do it."

"Mike . . . "

"It's true! Not selling the stuff isn't going to bring back the deer that were killed, is it?"

"That's not the point. We live by the rule of law and in this case the law says dealing in musk is illegal."

"Oh, shit, let's leave it. I told you I wasn't going to sell it, you'll just have to believe me." He finished his beer and said, "Did anyone call?"

"Oh, yes, sorry. There was a call from Mr Broakes."

"What did he want?"

"He wants you to phone him."

He looked at his watch. "I might just catch him."

He went into the saloon and she could hear the murmur of his voice. She was troubled. She was seeing a side of Mike she had never thought to see. And she was suddenly reminded of something that had happened when she and her ex-husband had gone on holiday to America some years before. It was when he was in the midst of his worst gambling phase and they were driving out to the track at Hialeah when they were stopped for speeding.

"That'll be a hundred bucks," the traffic cop had said.

Freddy had paid and then said, "Do I get a receipt?"

And the cop had said, "The receipt costs another hundred."

Had Mike been that sort of cop? And had she simply not known or not wanted to know?

He came back frowning. "Laddie Broakes is being very mysterious. He's heard from Holland and wants to see me. I'll use the flat tomorrow night. You won't be coming, will you?"

"No," she said.

Gracie was in her little living room kitchen when Ellen arrived. The stove was alight and the room was boiling hot.

"What're you doing, Gracie?"

"Oh, it's you."

"Yes, it's me. I've brought you some veal and ham pie. You'll like it. What are you doing?"

"I don't have to tell you what I'm doing."

"Of course you don't. I just wondered — "

"It's my house. I can do what I like."

"We don't want to argue about whose house it is, Gracie. Not on a nice day like this, now do we? And I only asked in case you needed any help."

"I don't need no help. I'm only cleaning the window." She was wiping it with the palm of her hand to remove the condensation and went on for a few moments longer.

"You'll smudge it that way. Why don't I get a cloth?" Ellen fetched a cloth and cleaned away the moisture. "That's better," she said. "You'll be able to see out now."

"I can see the little people."

"Oh, dear, Gracie. Not the hobgoblins again. Well, never mind. Now come and sit down and I'll get you this nice piece of veal and ham and we can talk."

Gracie eased herself down into the chair by the stove where she spent most of her days.

"You're not sleeping down here in the chair, are you, Gracie?"

"I can sleep anywhere I want."

"Well, I suppose it's warmer by the stove. Here you are." Ellen brought her a slice of pie on a plate with a knife and fork.

"You ain't got Dommie," Gracie said.

"Not today. Dommie's fishing today."

"You shouldn't leave the boy."

"I can't watch him all the time and they take good care of him on the beach. Anyway, he's a man, not a boy."

"I used to watch him."

"I know you did."

"I got good eyes."

"Yes, you always had good eyes."

"I seen the man in the water. The

Colonel said he seen him but it was me. I told the Colonel." She paused and said, "Do you know what day it is, what time of year?"

"Yes, I do, Gracie. Is that why you went to the creek?"

"You don't care, but I seen him and he was not in his own land."

"That's true. Have a little of the pie."

Gracie took a small mouthful and crunched the pastry in her front teeth like a rabbit.

"I took him flowers like I take every year."

"That's a very nice thing to do."

"I sprinkle 'em. Where he lay in the water. I seen him! He lay on his face and I seen his back."

"Yes, Gracie, all right. Have some more."

But Gracie pushed the plate away.

Ellen said, "I'll leave it on the table, you might fancy some later." Then she reverted to what they had been talking about. "And when you'd finished sprinkling the flowers did you go to the boat?"

312

"What boat?"

"The boat moored in the creek?"

Gracie twisted in her chair, her little wizened face frowned down at her hands.

"Is that where you went?"

"I fell."

"On the boat?"

"In the reeds."

"But you went to the boat, didn't you, Gracie?"

"I didn't do nothing wrong."

"Of course not. I know you wouldn't do anything wrong. What happened after you fell? Did they see you?"

"They come to help."

"And did they take you aboard?"

"They helped me."

"That's only what they should have done."

"They give me coffee. It was like when the Colonel was alive. He liked his coffee."

"What did you talk about, Gracie? Did you tell them about the man?"

"What man?"

"You know very well what man. The man you say you found."

Gracie began to cry.

313

"Oh, come on, dear, no one's accusing you of anything. I just want to know, that's all."

"I didn't tell them nothing!"

"Not even about the flowers? How did you explain those?"

"Explain?"

"Gracie, you're pretending now! You're not really crying. I just want to know what you said to them. You must have said something."

"I never said nothing."

Ellen cut up the pie slice into small pieces and put the plate in the food cupboard. It smelt of more than a hundred years of stale food and she held her breath. "There you are," she said. "It'll keep a couple of days but I hope you eat it sooner. By the way, one of the social workers came to see me about you. She was worried about you not eating. She says you're not eating much of the meals on wheels food either."

"It smells of them metal things it comes in," Gracie said.

"You must eat something otherwise they'll take you off to Bridmoor House."

Gracie's face grew tense. "I'm not

going to Bridmoor."

"Now, now, Gracie, don't take on like that. It's not a bad place."

"I'd rather die," Gracie said.

★ ★ ★

The *Lexton Advertiser* was situated in a small alley off the main street. There was a picture of an old-fashioned hot-metal printing press on its window. It had a counter with piles of that week's papers on it and a notice on the wall giving the advertising space rates. There was a bell push on the counter with a small white notice below it saying *Editorial*. Alex rang. Nothing happened for some moments then a door opened on the far side of the counter and a balding head appeared.

"Yes?"

Alex said, "I'm sorry to bother you but I wondered if I could look something up in your library."

"My what?"

"Your library. Is there someone who could show me?"

The head was followed by a neck and

a body and in a moment an elderly man in a white apron was standing in front of her. The apron was covered in black marks and so were the man's hands. His hands were so blackened by handling lead slugs that he stood with them held slightly out in front of him so they wouldn't dirty anything else.

"No, there isn't anyone who could show you except me. I'm it. The one and only. I'm making up a page at the moment that's why I'm so filthy. I thought for a moment you were the lady with the results."

"Results?"

"The vegetable show results. I'm supposed to get the paper out by this time tomorrow. The results were supposed to be in yesterday afternoon. People want to know who grew the biggest marrow, the heaviest tomatoes. Vital."

He had a thin and irritated face and Alex was conscious of the fact that he thought she was wasting his time.

"Results . . . results . . . results . . . " he said. "That's what people want to see. Results of football matches, results of golf matches, results of darts matches. Give them results and the weather, and they die happy."

"I just want to look up something."

"All we've got is back copies." His brow was covered in sweat and he used his arm to dry himself but managed to keep his hand away from his skin. "They go back a month. Cost you fifty pence a copy."

"I wanted to look up something in 1961."

"You what? Sixty-one? Good God. That's archives. Cost you a pound if you want to look up archives."

"All right."

"Follow me, then."

Alex went round the counter and followed the editor into the rear of the building. She found herself in the operating rooms of the newspaper, one leading into the next. In the first there was a desk, chair, telephone, and typewriter, in the second a Linotype machine and a mass of old page proofs on the floor, and in the third an old-fashioned printing press. The place smelt of ink and hot metal.

She followed him through the rooms and down a narrow staircase into an area that might once have been a large passage. It was lined on either side by rows of newspapers all held in wooden grips. There seemed to Alex that there might be thousands of newspapers there.

"Sixty-one . . . sixty-one . . . let's see . . . " He stood on a small stool and looked at several piles on a high shelf.

"Any particular month?"

She remembered what Bill Maitland had said. "From August onwards."

He brought down several bundles to a table at the end of the room. "That's August to December," he said. "I'll leave you to it."

Here the smell of old paper was very strong. The piles he had brought down, each held by its wooden frame, were yellow with age.

She started skimming the pages and quickly saw how the paper was arranged. The local hard news — car accidents, burglaries, magistrate's court hearings — was on pages one and two, the rest of the paper being given over to results, sport, building applications, and a column called Town Crier. She concentrated on pages one and two and found what she was looking for in the first week of September. It was the lead story on page one. It read:

AMERICAN VISITOR DROWNS — OLD
LEXTON CLAIMS ANOTHER VICTIM

Thomas Lee, 22, an American tourist, is feared drowned this week fishing off Lexton Point over the old town. He hired a fishing dinghy from a local fisherman for a day's sport on Tuesday. The empty dinghy was found yesterday drifting at the mouth of the Lexton River.

Mr. Lee, who had been camping on the beach for a number of weeks, had told local villagers that his father had served at Lister Air Force Base during the war and he had come to see the area.

Mr. Frank Spender, a local fisherman, told the *Advertiser*, 'Mr. Lee said he wanted to have a go after mackerel so I hired him a dinghy and fishing tackle. I told him where to go. It was a calm day without much wind but there was fog over the old town and I said he shouldn't go there.

'He said he had fished in Chesapeake Bay in America and that he knew how to handle a rowing dinghy. He talked about the old town and that he was interested in diving there one day.'

Harold Potter, another fisherman, said he was coming back to Lexton that day and he had seen the dinghy in the distance through gaps in the fog. He said it was directly over Old Lexton but he could not see whether there was anyone in it.

The coastguard has carried out a major search of the coast near Lexton but has so far found nothing.

It is understood that Mr. Lee was a university student. Police have been trying to contact relatives in America.

At the bottom of the story was a cross-reference which said 'See Town Crier page eight.'

Alex turned to page eight. The Town Crier's column was illustrated with a small figure wearing a tricorne hat and ringing a bell. From its mouth were coming the words *Oyez! Oyez!*

The text read:

DOWN SAD, BAD, MEMORY LANE

So we have another tragedy over Old Lexton. People will say that there's nothing under the waves but a load of old bricks and stones long since buried in the mud of Lexton Bay.

Well, that's as maybe. But this isn't a story of ghosties and ghoulies but of things that really do go bump in the night, a story of sad times and bad times in the not so long ago.

Mr. Lee apparently came to look at a part of the country where his father had spent the war years — at Lister Air Force Base. Someone should have told him not to bother since it's just another of those grisly housing developments now. Someone should also have told him that Americans were not universally welcome in Lexton or Lister or anywhere around here after what happened sixteen years ago.

Many of you won't know what I'm

talking about or won't care. But there are a lot of others who will. I'm talking about the death of a young woman I knew as Sylvie. Her father worked on the farm for my father and we grew up together.

In those days, at the end of the war, Lexton was full of Americans from the base. They'd come here for a drink and a meal and often for a woman.

All right, they were servicemen. So why not? But there was a saying about the Yanks then, that they were 'overpaid, over-sexed and over here'. And that was true of Lister.

I'll never forget the cars. A lot of them had MGs and Rileys and even Jaguars and they seemed able to get petrol when we couldn't. They'd come into town with money in their pockets. The girls loved it.

But we men didn't. We saw our girls scooped up and taken for rides and given meals and drinks which we couldn't afford. The US airmen gave them nylon stockings and chocolates and even bananas, things we hadn't seen for five years.

Of course they expected payment of a sort. And they got it.

Sylvie wasn't one of those girls. She was good and she was religious and she was engaged to be married to a local man. But she was the one they picked, those three men who came into Lexton one night.

They got drunk down at a beach party to celebrate the end of the war and when Sylvie was on her way home they grabbed her and they raped her one after the other.

Sylvie couldn't live with what had happened to her and it was I who found her two months later. She'd taken her dressing-gown cord and hanged herself in my father's barn. She was nineteen years old.

So here's another American come to Lexton. Someone with links to the old airbase.

Is the Drowned Town exacting its revenge? I wonder.

19

THE weather had changed and the wide Suffolk skies were covered in dark racing clouds. The wind was from the north-east and the air had lost its warmth. Summer was over.

Alex was walking. She had rejected the beach because the tide was high, the shingle wet with spray, and the gaunt cliffs oppressive. So she had decided to go inland instead and walk along the dykes that wound through the marshes. The village was away to her right, the sea behind her, and she was alone in a world of salt marsh and blowing reeds.

According to Bill Maitland this marsh had changed over the years. Originally it had been true wetland, then it had been drained by the Templars, who had built the dykes and split up the area into fields for sheep, but at the beginning of the last war the fields had been flooded to stop a German invasion and never drained again.

Alex could not see another person on this wet and reedy landscape, the only living things being the birds. There were hundreds of them: ducks, plovers, oystercatchers, redshanks, avocets, and the first of the migrant geese coming south for the winter.

She was dressed in cords and a heavy jersey and wondered if she had brought enough warm clothing, for she knew what the winds could do on the Suffolk coast.

The weather had changed when she was in the newspaper office. She had spent much longer there than expected because there was no way of copying the stories she had read other than by writing them out. As she did so she had begun to sense that there was a whole world here that she knew nothing about, that no one had mentioned. It seemed to her a kind of shadowland through which she could dimly see figures and actions — and motives . . . But motives for what?

She wondered what Mike was doing. There had been a message on the answer machine saying that he was having difficulty getting hold of Rawlings and that he would probably spend the night in her flat.

The problem with Mike, she thought, was that he was allowing his romantic fantasies full rein and she wondered if this was what detective work was like: that you created a scenario and then worked towards it. As far as her own job was concerned, if a patient came to you with a sore throat you looked at it and you listened to the patient and you said to yourself, "This is a sore throat until it proves not to be a sore throat." That was the clinical approach. If you translated Mike's approach into general medical practice every sore throat would be the beginning of Lassa fever.

And so it was with the Chinese man. A murdered Chinese washes up in a remote English marsh. No name. No means of identification. One day, perhaps, there might be a name for him and a background. One day it might be established that the musk was his. On the other hand nothing might be established. The point was he had nothing to do with Lexton. Unlike the death — and the short and hopefully happy life — of Tommy Lee. That whole incident came out of real and understandable human behaviour patterns and had happened right here.

She had looked in the old yellowing papers for further stories but all she had been able to find was one a month later which described how Tommy Lee's mother had come to Lexton from Philadelphia and had been taken out in a fishing boat to where her son was thought to have drowned. There a short memorial service had been conducted by the local priest, the Revd William Maitland. The fishing boat owner was named as Mr Frank Spender and other names of those attending the service were given as Mrs Ellen Blackhurst and Miss Gillian Blackhurst.

In her mind's eye she could see the boat drifting over Old Lexton as the prayers were said and the wreath thrown into the water. She could see the big figure of Maitland with the prayer book open in his hands. Was it a sunny day? Was it windy? Rainy? The story didn't tell her.

And why hadn't Bill Maitland told her about the ceremony? It should have been one of his clearest memories of the whole event, after all he'd been with the drowned man's mother. So why hadn't he mentioned it? Were there other facts he hadn't mentioned? And who was the dead man Gracie had seen? Or was Gracie simply as mad as a hatter?

My God, she thought, this is what Mike does! Questions everything, dissects everything.

She heard the throb of a marine diesel on the wind and saw, away to her right in the narrow river, a fishing boat come slowly upstream. From her position it seemed to be sailing along on the tops of the reeds. It had that almost surreal quality she had sometimes seen in Holland when a boat sailed across the landscape in a canal you didn't know was there.

She watched the boat slow down almost to a stop and then it began to make a reasonably wide turn, which surprised her since she did not think there was enough room in the stream for such a manoeuvre. Then the boat came on back downstream making for its moorings near the sea.

She walked in the direction of where it had turned and saw that the river widened into a natural pool with deep water and a flat bank. There was a lane beyond the river and she realized it would take her back to *Osprey* or at least to the village, so she crossed to it on a small footbridge. She had almost reached *Osprey* when she saw a small figure walking back along the road towards her. It was Gracie. She was dressed in the same dark blue coat as before and was buffeted by the wind as she walked.

"Hello, Gracie."

"Who are you?"

"You remember me, don't you? On the boat. We had coffee."

"Oh, yes. I remember. The boat. I been at the boat but no one was there."

"I've been having a walk."

"I come to see you."

"Well, come aboard and we'll have another cup of coffee."

"I don't want no coffee."

"Come and sit down for a moment anyway."

She helped Gracie up the gangplank and got her seated in the wheelhouse.

"What did you want to see me about?"

"I didn't say nothing."

"Sorry?"

"I didn't say nothing to you about them." She pointed up to the house on the cliff edge. "Miss Ellen come to me and said what did I say? I told her I said nothing."

"About what, Gracie?"

"About anything. Especially about the body?"

"You mean the body of Tommy Lee?"

Gracie looked up at her darkly. "I ain't mentioning no name."

"All right, we won't mention any names, but if I said it was the body washed up here in 1961, is that what we're talking about?"

Gracie said nothing.

"Did you find it?"

"I ain't said nothing about finding it."

Alex could see that she was becoming upset. "All right. Look, I'm a doctor and I don't think you should be wandering about on an afternoon like this. Let me take you home and we can talk there."

"I mustn't talk. She said I mustn't. I'll lose the house."

"Come on, let me help you up. That's it. Now we'll get into my car and you tell me where you live."

She helped Gracie to the car and said, "Which way?"

"You just come from there," Gracie said. "You were on my road."

When Alex helped her from the car she realized that Gracie was weaker than she had thought. The house was cold and dark and she thought Gracie must have reached *Osprey* just about the time she had left for her walk and so had waited there for more than an hour.

She got Gracie into her chair and said, "Have you got a heater?"

"Just riddle the stove. It'll come up."

Alex had no idea what she meant until Gracie touched a handle on the stove with her toe. "Pull it and push it." Alex did so and soon the fuel begin to crackle.

"Room'll be warm in half an hour," Gracie said.

"When did you last eat something?" Alex said.

"Don't know."

Alex went to the cupboards. She held up a slice of veal and ham pie which had been cut into small pieces. "Is this all you've got?"

"Miss Ellen brought it but I don't like pie. Gives me heartburn."

"I'm going into the village to get something. Will you be all right?"

"I'll watch the fire."

Alex was back in twenty minutes with eggs, milk, butter, and bread and she had also stopped in at the chemist's and picked up some multivitamin tablets.

The stove was warm now and she made Gracie an omelette. The old woman ate it voraciously. When she finished she said, "I ain't had anything like that for years. I used to make omelettes; the Colonel loved a cheese omelette."

"So do I," Alex said.

Gracie seemed to expand and her voice was stronger. Alex took a chance and said, "Why does Mrs Blackhurst not want you to talk to me?"

"She thinks I talk nonsense. She thinks I got that disease that makes people forget things and talk nonsense."

"Alzheimer's? Is that what she says?"

"That's the word."

"Well, I don't think that at all."

"And you're a doctor?"

"Yes."

"Will you be my doctor?" It was said with a smile and Alex smiled in return. Gracie's relief was touching. "She said I would lose the house."

"It isn't yours, then?"

"It belongs to her."

"Who's her?"

"Miss Ellen. They bought it when the Colonel was alive so my father could live in it. It was a tied house, y'see."

"No, I'm sorry, Gracie, I don't see."

Gracie looked at her as though she was a dim child and said, "My father was ploughman for old farmer Hennesey. This was a farm cottage. So long as he worked for Mr Hennesey my father and me and my brother Harold could live here. But then my father got sick and couldn't work no more and he would have lost the cottage and where would he have gone? Harold and me, we would have bin all right, we was working; Harold on the boats and me up at the house. But Father couldn't work no more. So Miss Ellen says right, we'll buy the house and he can still live there."

"That was very good of her, wasn't it?"

"Now she talks of it all the time. Her house it is. And me to go to Bridmoor, she says."

"What's Bridmoor?"

"I don't like to talk about Bridmoor. It's for old people what can't think straight and — "

There was a rattle at the front door and it opened letting in a cold gust of wind. A man stood on the threshold. He was wearing an old tweed overcoat with frayed sleeves and below that was a pair of worn brown boots. His head was covered in a flat cap but there was something about the thin face that was familiar. Alex was almost sure she had seen him somewhere.

"I brought you this," he said to Gracie, holding out a small paper parcel. "Bit of cheese."

"What's wrong with it?" Gracie said suspiciously as she put it on the table beside her.

334

"That's a good bit of Cheddar. Nothing wrong with it at all."

Gracie turned to Alex, "Harold brings me food sometimes. But I can't eat it. Too hard." She tapped the cheese on the table. "Like this."

"I'll make you another omelette tomorrow," Alex said. "A cheese omelette. That'll soften it."

"You hear that, Harold?"

"I been praying you got enough to eat," Harold said. "And that the good Lord is looking after you."

"Harold talks to the Lord," Gracie said.

And then Alex knew where she had seen Harold. He was the evangelist who had insulted the Japanese tourists.

"Are you Gracie's brother?" she said.

"Of course he is," Gracie said. Then she said, "You ask Harold."

"What about?"

"About what you was asking me. You know something, don't you, Harold?"

"What about?" Harold said.

"About bodies what are washed ashore."

The old man's face contorted with apprehension and anger. "You're never to say nothing. You hear me? You'll go to Bridmoor if you're not careful!"

With that he turned and shuffled out of the room. Alex went towards him but he had already opened the front door and gone out into the night and when she turned back into the room Gracie had fallen asleep in her chair.

Alex turned on the lights and checked the fire in the stove. It seemed to be doing all right but she was no expert. She went to pull the curtains on the window next to Gracie's chair but there were none. The window was beginning to steam up. She stood uncertainly for a few moments not quite knowing what to do. Then she told herself that Gracie had got to a ripe age looking after herself and that there was nothing she could do for her at the moment. So she left.

The boat did not look inviting when she got back. It was pitching slightly at its moorings and the light in the wheelhouse was moving from side to side. She went aboard and put on other lights but even so it was cheerless and would remain so until the painting and refurbishing had been completed. She got into her car and went up to the pub to eat.

That was cheerless too. It was almost empty but for the group of Japanese tourists. She ordered a glass of wine and a sandwich. As she took them back to a table in the corner of one of the rooms she saw Frank Spender come through the street door.

He looked round the bar, nodded to her, and then went across to the Japanese and joined them. She heard him ordering champagne. Then Chris the fisherman came in. He was wearing jeans and a blue Guernsey and his hair, caught back in a ponytail, shone in the light of the bar. His cheeks were covered in light stubble and she thought how piratical he looked. He bought a pint and went to a chair and stared at her over the pot. She looked away and focused on the other group. Spender was asking what they would like to eat and then he went to the bar and placed the orders and she heard him say to the barman, "They're my guests."

"Right, sir."

The Japanese seemed to be enjoying themselves. There were two men and a woman and they were laughing a lot.

Alex became increasingly uneasy under the continuing gaze of Chris and decided she would be more comfortable in the boat after all. She finished her wine and abandoned her sandwich and left. She sensed, rather than saw, Chris leave his table and follow her. She thought briefly of spending the night at the Templar's Rest and then told herself not to be a fool and got into her car and drove back along the river, over the road bridge, and down to the hardstanding near the boat.

The distance from car to boat was less than fifty yards but it was very dark and she did not have a torch. There were odd flashes of moonlight but the clouds were passing quickly on the wind.

She walked along a stony path and then stopped. She had put most of the boat's lights on, especially those in the saloon. Now they were off. Or were they? The movement of the reeds and the movement of the boat made it difficult to see precisely what lights were on.

She heard a noise behind her. It was the scuffing of a shoe on the stony ground. She stopped, listened, but all she could hear was the wind.

She knew Chris had followed her out of the pub. She'd had to drive round by the road bridge. He could have walked over the small footbridge.

She was telling herself not to be afraid, not to panic and do something silly. For a moment she felt slightly stronger but then the memory of what had happened at the Meadowvale Estate flooded over her and she was more afraid than ever. She would have to go on or go back. If there was someone behind her she should go on. But what if the someone behind her came onto the boat?

She wanted to get back to her car but couldn't return the way she had come so she stepped off the path to work around another way and almost immediately sank into a foot of marshy water. She began to topple sideways.

Two things happened simultaneously: she grabbed a handful of rushes to stop herself falling and someone just to her right came bursting through the reeds and grabbed her.

She felt an arm go round her throat

and a hand grip her right arm and force it up her back.

"Help!" she yelled.

Then Mike's voice said, "Oh, Christ, it's you!"

* * *

"You frightened the life out of me," Alex said.

"Ditto and vice versa," Mike said.

They were in the boat and each held a strong whisky.

"I was sure you were Chris Cottis," she said. "I'd imagined he followed me from the pub. And I imagined that some of the lights had gone off in the boat. God, what one's imagination can do! But what I still can't understand is why I didn't see or hear your car."

"Because I left it up at the garage. It's got a slow puncture. I came over the footbridge and I saw yours and then I saw a shape in the reeds and of course I thought someone was either watching you in the boat or about to try and get aboard."

"Well, it was all pretty scary." She

340

drank from her glass and said, "Have you eaten?"

He shook his head. "I thought of having something in London. I was supposed to meet Rawlings in a pub in Chelsea but when he didn't show I thought I'd drive back before the traffic got bad."

"I'll get us something." Abruptly she put her arms around his neck and kissed him. "Oh God, am I glad to see you!"

"As I said before, ditto and vice versa." He kissed her back and held her tightly. "Now?" he said.

"Yes, now."

They went to the big bed and made energetic and cathartic love and the creaking of the springs was lost in the creaking of the boat's timbers as the wind picked up and the tide came in.

20

SHE watched Mike sop up the last of a cheese omelette with a piece of French bread. He put down his fork and said, "Why the hell can't I make omelettes?"

Alex smiled. "What you mean is if I can make them you think they must be easy enough for you to make."

"No, I don't."

"Well, that's what it sounded like, so I have to tell you that omelettes are not easy to make which is why I'm rather clever."

They were in the saloon in their dressing gowns, still relaxed and comfortable with each other after their sexual release.

She went on: "To tell you the truth omelettes are about pans and you've got a good pan so I make good omelettes. I made one for Gracie this afternoon in her pan and that wasn't as good as these but she liked it well enough."

"You mean the old woman who fell in the reeds . . .

" . . . and came aboard for coffee."

"Why were you making an omelette for her?"

"I've been doing rather a lot of things while you were in London. I've been talking to Bill Maitland and I've been to the local newspaper office and I've made an omelette for Gracie. I thought of not telling you because you'll accuse me of interfering and — "

"Interfering in what?"

"Well . . . in what you're doing, I suppose. To put it at its most basic you've made up a scenario and you're trying to bend the facts to fit it. It's like someone doing a jigsaw puzzle and using a pair of scissors to trim pieces that don't fit naturally."

She paused and he said, "Go on."

She was wary now but went on. "I just have a feeling that things are simpler than you think. I lived near here don't forget and Lexton isn't some drug entrepôt."

"Who said anything about drugs?"

"Well, musk, then. Same thing in the long run. What we're talking about is something that has a high value and for which, you say, people will kill."

343

"I say? You saw the body. You saw the wounds. You saw the musk. They're facts."

"Yes, individual facts, but don't you think you're linking them into something that might not be true? You've even got the Triads involved."

He shook his head in a kind of puzzled wonderment and said, "When you get a patient who's suffering from something you're not sure of — might be one thing or it might be something else — do you treat them for the most obvious?"

"If you mean the simplest, yes, because most illnesses are the common or garden ones and we'd look foolish if we didn't."

"Right, you tell me what the simple explanation is for what's happened here."

"Oh, God, Mike, I don't know. But what I do know is that real things have been going on here which people don't like to talk about and which might have something to do with what's happened. Years ago another body washed up just where the Chinese man's was."

She told him what she'd heard in the shop and how she had gone to Bill Maitland and what he had told her.

He said, "Two bodies being washed up in the same place doesn't mean a thing except that the tides are always the same around Lexton."

"I go back to Dommie. He's always been my most likely candidate. There's a violence in him that needs expression. I told you he had attacked some woman. The following day Mrs Blackhurst came to me to ask if there weren't any pills to check the sexual pressures in him."

"But what's that got to do — "

"Hang on. I haven't told you about the newspaper library."

He poured them each a glass of wine and cut into a piece of cheese. "You know what you're doing?" he said.

"What?"

"You're so worried I'm going to go into the musk-smuggling business that you're looking into everything so you can come up with a different hypothesis."

His voice was soft but he seemed to her to be relaxed and she said, "Look, Mike, you told me you weren't interested in going into the musk business. I believe you. Where is it, by the way?"

"Still wrapped in the flag."

"I don't think I've found out anything that would necessarily solve the mystery of the Chinese man and the musk, just things that I don't think people want us to know, which might or might not be significant."

"Places like Lexton are built on secrecy and closed mouths."

"Yes, but Dommie is part of the secrecy yet everybody knows about him and his predilections and who his father was but . . . hang on . . . let me finish about the newspaper. I came across references to the tragedy of Tommy Lee drowning but then I came across something else and that was the rape and suicide of a girl called Sylvie at the end of the war."

"You're not blaming that on Dommie, are you?"

"Very funny. Mike, how often haven't you said look for patterns in behaviour? Well, I've come across a pattern here in Lexton only I can't make the pieces fit. I mean, there's Gracie saying she would be sent to an old people's hostel if she told me a certain thing and her brother Harold threatening her with the same thing. Oh, yes, she's got a brother. I saw him Bible-thumping in the Square and being rude to Japanese tourists before I — "

"Rude to who?"

"Three Japanese tourists?"

"How do you know they were Japanese?"

"What do you mean?"

"How do you know they weren't Chinese? Can you tell the difference?"

"I knew they were Japanese because they were well dressed and carried lots of cameras and I saw them quite close up when they were with Frank Spender at the pub this evening and they were laughing a lot and you never seem to see Chinese people laughing. Not when they're with Westerners, anyway."

"With Spender?"

"Yes, and he was entertaining them. I heard him order the food and say they were his guests. He talks to the staff there as though he owns the place."

"He does."

"How do you know?"

"His name's on the licence above the front door. And he owns the garage. At least it's called Spender Motors."

"Good Lord, I've stopped there two

or three times and never noticed that."

"You'd make a great detective."

"At least I don't see Japanese tourists as Triads."

He looked irritated. "You accuse me of making up a story and trying to fit facts into it and now you're doing the same thing, except you haven't got any facts to fit. When I was in the Drug Squad I came across the Triads and I can tell you they make the American and the Russian mafias look like kindergarten kids. They've been going for hundreds of years and now they've spread as a criminal organization over half the bloody globe. They're into just about everything you can think of, but mostly heroin. They've got 'mule-lines' which are networks of carriers bringing the stuff from Hong Kong into places like Rotterdam, Marseilles, Hamburg, and London. Anybody can be a 'mule': airline cabin crews, Chinese seamen, and there are also professional couriers. So don't underestimate them or think they're just figments of an overheated imagination."

"And instead of heroin, musk?"

"At the price it's fetching, why not?"

She suddenly didn't want the evening to end in a row and said, "You're right. I'm just getting a little carried away. Tell me about your London trip. So Rawlings was a failure?"

He nodded. "I think he's so bloody scared of his wife that he stays locked in his flat with his Chinese girl. No, he wasn't any good, but Laddie Broakes came up with something interesting. He heard from the Dutch policeman I told you about, Van Hoogstraten. Apparently Dutch customs boarded the *Wilhelmina* where she was anchored near Rotterdam and they found that one of the holds had been partly blocked off by a false wall. Behind the wall were a dozen bunks and a chemical toilet. There was an air pipe from a deck vent and a few electric wires running to fans and lights. There were blankets lying about and the odd magazine on the floor. They were Chinese porn magazines published in Hong Kong."

"You mean the boat was bringing Triads over to Europe?"

"Not at all. Just the opposite, that the Triads are running an illegal immigrant scam. Anyway, that's my guess."

"Go on."

"Hong Kong is being given back to China by the British Government because the lease is running out. Hundreds of Hong Kong Chinese — maybe thousands — want to get the hell out with their money because no one knows what is going to happen. Canada is about the only country which has been taking a substantial number of Hong Kong people and they've mostly gone to Vancouver. But now it's cutting down on the numbers and making it difficult to get in."

"And you think . . . ?"

"I think that some illegals are trying to get into Holland. Don't forget it's got a big Asian and Chinese population from the days when it used to own half of South-east Asia. Hong Kong Chinese would have good contacts there."

"So give me the scenario."

"What happens is that the ship comes into the North Sea making for Holland with a dozen illegal immigrants. Something occurs on board and off the Suffolk coast one of the illegal passengers is stabbed — "

"Why?"

"Who knows? Maybe someone tried to steal the musk from him. There's a fight on deck and he goes over the side with the stuff. He either loops it round the buoy cable before he dies or it floats there by itself. And he comes on into the creek here and we find the musk. Simple?"

"Did you tell this to Laddie Broakes and get his opinion?"

"No, he was too excited about something else. Couldn't stop talking about it. He's leaving his job, leaving the security business altogether. Some big charity is setting up a police association and they've asked him to take over the crime section."

"What's a police association?"

"I don't think even he knows the details. But he says it'll be a body watching the police at work in terms of their interface — or some such word — with the public. I once knew a phrase for it in Latin though I can't remember it now. *Quis* . . . something or other . . . "

She nodded, "I knew it once too."

He said, "What it means is: 'Who will guard the guardians?' And in this case it's going to be Laddie Broakes."

★ ★ ★

"Your shake, Dommie," Ellen said. "That's it. Shake it well."

The dice rolled on the table top.

"Six," Dommie said.

"No, darling, it's a four. Move your counter four places."

"One, two, one, two, one, two."

"That's six. Go back two. Oh dear, you've got onto a snake. You go right down to the bottom of the board."

"I want to go up," Dommie said.

"When you get onto a ladder you can go up. Getting onto a snake means you go down."

"I want to go up," Dommie said.

"All right, darling, you go up on the snakes and down on the ladders."

"I want to go up on the ladders."

They played on. This always happened when they played snakes and ladders and she was used to it. His balding head was poised over the board and his cheeks were pink with concentration. She watched his powerful hands as they rolled the dice and moved the counter.

Would someone play snakes and ladders with him in an institution, she wondered? And was that where he was going to end up? He would if he went on tormenting women, no doubt about that. But what was she to do? Even if she decided to buy a woman for him every now and then who was there to buy? Betty Smith wouldn't cooperate any more, she was certain of that. In any case buying a woman for him wasn't something she felt able or willing to encourage. And of course she couldn't afford to even if she did.

She supposed she could ask Mike Harley for more money for his moorings. She might even allow boats to use her marsh. Turn it into something like the Norfolk Broads on a smaller scale. That meant she would look out of her windows over holidaymakers and pleasure craft and that wouldn't be nice; rather like having a caravan park on your doorstep. On the other hand it would mean she would have enough money to buy an old fisherman's cottage and move into the village with Dommie. But not even large amounts of money would answer the real question: what was going to happen to him once she was gone?

"I won, Grannie! I won!"

"You certainly did. What do you want to do now? Another game? Or are you going to bed?"

"Going out to clean my sticks."

"All right, darling, don't be too long, it's getting late."

She watched him go out to his 'castle' and switch on the lights. She'd give him half an hour then call him back. She turned on the television but could not concentrate. Was she doing right by Dommie? Could she be doing anything else? That woman doctor had said institutions were not so bad, but Dommie wasn't her grandson. She'd known her stuff about the pills, yet Ellen couldn't see herself feeding these to Dommie if there was a possibility of changing his character. She was full of doubts and worries and this new desire of his for women magnified them all.

She dozed.

Dommie cleaned one of his walking sticks then he picked it up and went out of his castle and down the road towards the marsh. The wind was blowing and the air was cold. He tested the stick by swinging it back and forth. It made a swishing noise. He came to the reeds and went off the roadway and onto smaller tracks which he knew well.

The boat was moving in the wind. There was the sound of water slapping on the steel hull. He went quietly to one of the portholes and pressed his face against it, but little curtains had been drawn and he could see nothing. He could hear voices though. He went along the creek bank to another porthole. Here the curtains had not been drawn quite so closely and there was a small gap. Again he pressed his face to the glass. This time he could see a woman's body, but not her head. She was wearing a dressing gown and where the folds had fallen away her legs, up to her thighs, were bare.

She was sitting at a table and Dommie wanted to get onto the boat and crawl under the table to be near her legs. But the gangplank was up on deck and there was no way onto the boat. He could feel his erection like one of his walking sticks. He opened his flies and, with his hot face against the porthole glass, comforted himself as best he could.

21

MIKE was still asleep when Alex woke and for a brief moment before she became fully conscious she thought he was Freddy. That brought her instantly into wakefulness. Then she saw his legs flex in that unmistakable way and she knew with relief that it was Mike. Sometimes she dreamed of Freddy and often the dreams were associated with guilt because it was she who had broken off the marriage. At other times she dreamed she was facing a choice between them. And there was frequently the dream about the cheque with her forged signature on it. In that dream the forger was someone she didn't know. In reality, of course, it had been Freddy.

That had been at the worst time of his gambling and she had threatened then that if he did it again she would pull her money out of the bank and open a deposit account somewhere else which he couldn't touch. He had and she did. And even after they had separated he used to come to her asking for loans.

They had met as medical students and then his gambling had seemed interesting and amusing. He'd taken her to the races several times and he'd also taken her to casinos in London and France. He was a brilliant card player and often won at blackjack and poker. But the more he won at cards the more he lost on the horses and at roulette.

It had taken five years of their married life for him to admit that he had an incurable disease and it was only when he realized it that she had been able to go with him to Gamblers Anonymous.

Sitting there in a crowded and smoky hall with Freddy standing on shaky legs saying, "My name is Freddy Elston and I'm a gambler," she had gone through deep feelings of guilt. Had she helped to make him what he was? Had she treated him without sufficient understanding and patience? And when the marriage finally ground to a halt she asked herself a hundred times: am I wholly to blame?

Was she now facing difficulties with

Mike? Was she trying to fit him into her pattern instead of fitting into his? What she desperately did not want to happen was that she should lose him.

These were some of the thoughts that had been going through her mind during a semi-wakeful night, but they all ended with one unavoidable fact: what she was doing excited her. She was entering a world that Mike had been trained to inhabit. It was his world, a closed world that held shadowy secrets. And the shadowy figure that she could half see in that world was always Dommie.

She put out a foot and pushed Mike's bottom. "Are you awake?"

"Mmmmm?"

"I'm going to make coffee. D'you want some?"

"Mmmmmm."

She got up and went to the galley. It was much colder now and she switched on a heater. She looked out and saw the reeds moving in the wind and a similar grey sky to the one of the day before. If anything the wind was stronger and the boat was creaking and groaning.

"What are you going to do today?" she

said, as they sat up in bed sipping the coffee. It was a careful, domestic question that she thought would not launch them into another argument.

"Go on with the painting. And you?"

"I'll give you a hand but first of all I must do some shopping."

People were wrapped up against the wind when she walked into Lexton. She did have shopping to do but that wasn't her first priority. She turned off the High Street and opened the door of the Lexton *Advertiser*. As she pressed the bell on the counter she felt the now familiar moment of excitement. She could hear the clang of wood on metal. After a few moments she rang again. The door opened and the editor put his head round it. This time his face had dark blotches on it and his hands were blackened to his wrists.

"Yes?"

"Archives, if I may."

"Cost you a pound."

"That's fine."

"Can't come at the moment."

"Would you trust me?"

He looked at her doubtfully then said, "I'm on the stone and it'll be an hour

360

before I'm finished. You've been before, you know where it is."

She went down into the same room and stood on one of the chairs. The collected editions started in one dark corner with the date 1928. She moved along the piles on the top shelf until she came to 1945. She began with January.

It took her more than two hours to flick through the pages of the fifty-two thin wartime editions for that year. There wasn't a headline about any rape. There were stories about US airbase workers helping with the local dance, helping with organizing and taking part in a cross-country run for charity, of marrying girls in Southwold and Orford, of doing many good and socially correct things, but not a word about rape.

Thinking she might have missed something she went back to January and started again. She had. But it wasn't a headline she'd missed, it was a whole page. She discovered the gap because she had read, just for interest, the main story on page one of the edition dated 12 May 1945. It was a deliriously happy local story about how Lexton had greeted the end of the war in Europe which had occurred three days before that. She read about the street parties and marches then turned the page to read on, but she couldn't find the continuation. She searched carefully. The front page story was supposed to continue on page three. But the page she was looking at was page five. There was no page three. She opened the paper as far as she could and looked carefully where it was held by the two long wooden strips. She could just make out a faint edge of yellowing paper where the page had been cut away.

She frowned. Then she opened the following week's edition. This time the front page was gone and she realized she had zipped through the papers so quickly the first time that she had even missed noticing that a page with the *Advertiser*'s banner was not there.

It did not take her long to go through the remaining editions checking for missing pages. She found that on each of the following five weeks the *Advertiser* had one page missing. Then, by the end of June, the papers seemed to be intact again.

She looked at her watch; it was nearly lunch time. The editor was in the editorial office. He had washed his hands and face.

Alex said, "Is there any other place with a collection of the *Advertiser* and the other local papers?"

"Why?"

He had a blunt inquisitiveness and she had anticipated the question. She had also decided not to get embroiled in the whole question of missing pages. "I'm doing some research on the area."

"What for?"

"I used to live in Southwold."

His manner changed. "Oh, you come from around here. That's different. Yes, go into Bury. There's a newspaper library there with all the little local papers including this one."

"Thank you," she said and made to leave.

"Archives are a pound," he said.

"I'm sorry," she said, and paid him.

All the way back to the boat she kept on asking herself two questions: Why were the pages missing? Who had taken them?

But when she put this to Mike he said, "Maybe the girl's family did? Who knows? It's all a long time ago." Then he said, "I phoned a contact of mine in the customs in Felixstowe. I'm going up to see him."

★ ★ ★

There was a banging on the front door and a voice called, "Ellen! It's me, Bill."

"I'm in the kitchen," she called back.

He came in on a buffeting wind. She sometimes forgot what a large man he was and he was looking bigger today with his heavy leather waistcoat and his knitted hat. He took it off as he entered the kitchen and his thick grey hair made him seem even taller.

"It's blowing up," he said. "Forecast's talking about something sizeable on the way."

"You haven't come all this way to tell me about the weather."

"No, no. What are you making?"

"A casserole for our supper."

"Looks good."

"Want some? There's going to be heaps."

"Thanks, but I've got a pie that needs to be eaten."

She saw him looking around, registering the cracks in the walls and the buckled floor.

"Ellen, I've come because I think I may have said things that weren't my business to say and I just wanted you to know what's what."

She was cutting up the beef into small cubes. "That sounds very mysterious."

"Harold Potter came to see me this morning."

"Harold? I haven't seen him for some time. Not to talk to, anyway. I pass him in the square sometimes. His congregations aren't getting any bigger."

"No. Poor old chap. I thought you'd better know that he thinks the people you've allowed to moor in the creek are starting to ask questions about Tommy Lee."

"How on earth would they be doing that?"

"That's what I've come to see you about. It's probably my fault. Alex — that's Dr

Kennedy — and Michael Harley and I have had a few meetings. He's interested in the Templars and the old town and wants to start what he calls diving safaris over — "

"Yes, I know all about that."

"I've had them to the cottage. In fact I find them pleasant enough. Dr Kennedy came to visit me yesterday and we chatted and . . . Ellen, she knew all about Betty Smith and when I asked her how, she said she'd heard it in the village."

"Well, you know how people talk."

"Yes, but she started talking about Dommie."

"What on earth for?"

"She's interested in him from a doctor's point of view. But I don't think she came to me maliciously."

"So you told her about him?"

"Well, I told her who his father and mother were, and that his father had drowned."

"Everybody knows that. There's no harm in her knowing."

"At least if she mentions it you'll know how she found out."

366

"Dear Bill. You do worry about me. Would you like some coffee?"

"If you're going to have a cup."

She got out mugs and a cafetière. He stood looking out of the windows towards the sea. A powerful wind was blowing and the shallow water had churned up the reddish sand so that the waves looked as though they were palely diffused with blood.

"You really should get out of this place, Ellen," he said as the kettle boiled.

"So people keep telling me."

"We could have — "

"No, we couldn't. If we'd got married I would have had to send Dommie to an institution. It wouldn't have been fair on you to bring him to the vicarage. Anyway, I don't think I was ever meant to be a vicar's wife."

"You'd have made a marvellous vicar's wife."

"Not after my affair with Frank Spender. Not nearly respectable enough."

"That's something I've never understood."

"I'm surprised at you. That's the sort of snobby thing John would have said."

"I don't mean it that way. I mean how

he could have let you go. I wouldn't."

She gave him the coffee and tapped his face with her hand. "That's a nice thing to say. The point about Frank was he likes young women and I was young then. He still likes them."

"I've seen them. Brainless plastic dolls from London."

"He's not after intellectual chats. But all this is beside the point. You said Harold Potter had come to see you."

"It follows on from my meeting with Alex . . . with Dr Kennedy. He says he went to Gracie's and Dr Kennedy was there and Gracie was saying she couldn't give her any information about the drowning, or anything else, otherwise she would end up in Bridmoor."

"Yes, I see."

"So apparently she told Harold that he should tell Dr Kennedy about Tommy Lee."

"And?"

"He says he didn't say a word. I'm not sure it would have made much difference since it's common knowledge. He seemed rather confused. And he was very upset. He was crying a little. Much more upset than I've ever seen him. I asked him if there was anything wrong but he shook my hand and left."

"I wonder what they really want."

"Want?"

"Why they're here."

"Couldn't they be here for precisely the reasons they say?"

"I don't know. I'm suspicious, that's all."

"Well, I don't think I am."

"You've always looked on the good side. It's being a priest, I suppose."

"Coming from you that's rich. What about the sacrifices you've made? That's what stopped you and me from getting married."

"What could I have done? I mean, the poor little boy."

"Nothing. You did the right thing. It's just that we might have done it together."

"There's no point in looking backwards like this, Bill. It wasn't on. And now I've got other things that worry me."

"Dommie?"

"Of course it's Dommie. And people who come here asking bloody questions."

After Bill had left Ellen put the casserole in the oven and went out and checked on Dommie. He was standing in front of his easel daubing yellow and green stripes onto a large sheet of white paper. She went back into the house and phoned Frank Spender but was told that he was away in London for a few days.

She felt unsettled and uneasy. She went into the drawing room and looked down on the marsh from the big windows. Below her she could see the boat. Two figures were standing on the deck. It was time they went, she thought.

22

ALEX left Lexton under racing black clouds and chose to go by the scenic route to Bury, taking a series of winding but beautiful country lanes instead of the dead straight Roman road. It was nearly an hour's run and when she was halfway there she became aware of the car behind her. It was a beaten-up grey Ford and she fully expected it to pass her when it got the chance. Instead, whenever she reached a straight without oncoming traffic, the Ford fell behind, sometimes so far behind that she lost sight of it. Then it would reappear. At first she thought nothing of it, then she began to react in a way she had never reacted before: she wondered if the driver was following her. She kept flicking her eyes to the rear-view mirror and back onto the road ahead. This is what happens when you play detective, she told herself; play becomes reality, at least in the mind.

She sought someone to blame for her nervousness and settled, without much conviction, on Mike. This morning he had got up early and driven away to Felixstowe to see this contact of his in the customs. It was then she had thought, to hell with it, if he is going to pursue his — what was the phrase the police used? . . . 'his own lines of investigation' — then she was going to pursue hers. What she wasn't going to do was spend a day of her holiday chipping away at rust.

And now she was being followed. Or she thought she was.

In Bury she parked on Angel Hill just off the square. She stood by the car for a few moments to see if she could spot the beaten-up Ford but couldn't. She found the tourist office and was directed to the East Suffolk Newspaper Library which was off the square on the east side of the ruins of the old monastery of St Edmundsbury.

In the library she half expected to be dealt with by someone like the editor of the Lexton *Advertiser*, who would say impatiently, "Archives, that's a pound."

Instead she got a young woman who was brisk and businesslike and who knew her stuff.

"None of the little country papers are on CD-ROM," she said, "but we've got a lot on microfilm and you can see them on one of the reading machines. They're all being used at the moment but I'll book you in next. In the meantime there's a good card-index system and a cross-reference system."

She took Alex into a large room with tables on which there were the reading machines. She showed her where *The Times* Index was kept and then the card indexes for the small country papers. There were half a dozen other people in the room using the reading machines so Alex got to work on the card index and made notes.

There were a large number of entries for the US airbase at Lister. They went from dances, to noise levels, to marriages, to bombings, to accidental deaths in crashes on take-off or landing, to the base after the war, to NATO exercises, and finally to its being released by the Ministry of Defence to the local council, who had turned it into a large housing estate.

Then she came to a heading that indicated a different picture. This said Criminal Proceedings and listed such crimes as Theft, Burglary, Motoring Offences, Assault, Fraud . . . and there it was: Rape. She looked up the index. There were more than a dozen rape and attempted rape cases, starting during the war but going on into the 1960s when the base, which had been taken over by the RAF after the war, came to the end of its life.

To look up all these would have taken her days but she had the missing page numbers of the Lexton *Advertiser* and so, when a reading machine became free, she got out the microfilm for the issues that had been mutilated.

The reading machine allowed her to bring up an edition swiftly, to isolate any page, and then to concentrate on any section of the page and read it through the magnifying screen.

And here, after her journey and the search of the day before, was what she was looking for. The headline jumped at her and she felt again a flow of adrenalin and a sharp stab of excitement.

LOCAL WOMAN ASSAULTED
THREE MEN HELD

A 21-year-old local woman returning from a party on Lexton beach to celebrate the end of the war in Europe is in hospital in Bury St Edmunds after being assaulted. Three men have been held for questioning in connection with the assault. The woman's name has not been released.

That was all there was and Alex looked at the story for another minute or two trying to read into it words that were not there: the word 'rape', for instance. Yet she knew that if it had been indexed under 'rape' she was looking at the right story.

She assumed that this was the only information released at the time or that the story had happened so close to edition time that this was all that could be squeezed in. She told herself that the war had just ended and that people were celebrating and that was the big story. Perhaps they simply did not want to read about something as unjoyful as a local rape.

She went to the next date on which there was a missing page in Lexton and hit paydirt.

RAPE CASE: WOMAN STILL IN BURY HOSPITAL
THREE YANKS HELD AT LISTER

LEXTON SHAKEN BY VIOLENT ACT — VICTORY CELEBRATIONS SPOILT, SAYS MAYOR

The young woman who was allegedly raped in Lexton after a beach party to celebrate the end of the war in Europe remains on the injured list at Bury St Edmunds hospital.

Three American servicemen who were helping police with their investigation have been returned to the Lister Airbase where they are being held in custody by the American authorities.

It is understood that if evidence is found to warrant charges being made against the men, whose names have not been released, they will stand trial at the base in a court martial.

The beach party near which the alleged incident took place was jointly organized by the local council and the Women's Voluntary Association and permission was given to increase rationing allowances so that there would be enough food to go round.

It is estimated that more than a hundred people attended the party. Mr. Harold Potter, 29, a local fisherman, said he had accompanied the woman to the party. They had spent three or four hours there.

Mr. Potter, who is a well-known churchgoer, said that at about nine o'clock in the evening three cars arrived bringing about a dozen American servicemen.

They were all wearing uniforms and they immediately joined in the party spirit. One of them had brought a piano accordion and began to play dance music.

As it grew dark, Mr. Potter said that fires were lit and people began to dance. He danced with his partner. All were enjoying themselves.

He said he had not been dancing long when one of the American servicemen wanted to dance with his partner.

Mr. Potter said, 'He told me it was an "excuse me" dance and that I must give up my partner. I was unwilling to do this but the man's friends said I had to do it. It was the custom.'

He said that three Americans danced with the woman in turn holding her very close. One of them tried to kiss her. They also danced very wildly, swinging her about, sometimes off the ground. Finally she managed to break away and returned to him.

The Americans tried to persuade her to dance again but Mr. Potter held on to her. She was crying.

'I asked if she would like to go home and she agreed.'

He said that they both lived in the village and the quickest way was to go along the little creek that flowed into the Lexton River and then across the footbridge.

While they were in the marsh, walking along the path from Lexton House to the town, they were attacked.

Mr. Potter did not see what happened for it was already dark. He remembers two or more men trying to pull the woman away from him. He says he fought them but was knocked down and became unconscious for a short while. When he came to neither the woman nor the men were there. He then went to the police.

The police found the unnamed woman on the edge of the creek. Her clothing had been torn away and she was partially naked. She was taken to the hospital at Bury St Edmunds.

Commenting on the rape, the Mayor of Lexton, Councillor George Smithers, said, 'This is a terrible tragedy not only for the woman in question but for the town. A dark cloud has been cast over what should have been a time of celebration and joy.'

The Revd. William Maitland, the local vicar, said, 'Everything was going well. We were expressing a deep sense of thankfulness that the war was over. And now this.'

There it all was and Alex could see it as plainly as a movie unfolding in front of her: the party, the fires on the beach, and the dancing that grew more and more boisterous until Sylvie — it had to be the woman called Sylvie by the newspaper columnist — until Sylvie had had been roughed up and started crying. Then she saw them go off the beach and onto the path by the creek and the men brutally assaulting Sylvie and Harold Potter. And she realized that Sylvie must have been raped close to where *Osprey* was moored.

She went on through the papers and found that the stories became repetitive which meant there were no new facts. There was one story saying that Sylvie had left the hospital, another that Harold Potter had visited Lister Airbase to give written testimony.

And then nothing. The *Advertiser* went on chronicling meetings of flower arrangers and competitions for vegetable growers, but there was nothing more on the Lexton rape.

Alex went back to the files. There was an index cross-reference to courts martial and she got that edition out. This was from the *Advertiser* for June 1946, more than a year after the alleged rape. The story read:

ALLEGED RAPISTS FREED IN AMERICA
NO EVIDENCE TO SUPPORT CHARGES, SAYS PENTAGON

Lexton was in deep shock this week as news came from America that the three men accused of raping a local woman on the night that Victory in Europe was being celebrated had been released by the USAAF.

A statement issued by the Pentagon said that there was insufficient evidence for the men to be charged and tried in a court martial. They were not permanent members of the air force but conscripts, so they had been released.

A spokesman at the Lister Airbase said the men had been taken back to America in March.

'In my opinion there was never going

to be a court martial,' he said. 'I was at the beach party and I remember seeing all the boys there until the time we left. If a woman was raped then it was not by any of our boys.'

Sgt. S. Freeman, of the East Suffolk Constabulary, stationed then in Lexton, and now retired, said, 'This is a big blow. Justice has not been done. We had evidence that three Yanks were seen leaving the beach party at the same time as Mr. Potter and the woman. How has that got lost?

'If you ask me the American authorities did not want anything to blight their reputation on that of all days.'

Underneath the story was the heading 'See Leading Article'. Alex moved on several pages and found it.

NO THANKS FOR THE MEMORY

Remember the song? Well, there are a lot of people in this town who will remember our glorious war allies the Americans but without any feeling of gratitude. Lexton is shocked and saddened by the cynical release of three men without trial for the attack on one of our women. No one's saying they did it, what we are saying and will go on saying, is that they at least had a case to answer.

So, no thanks, Yanks, for the memory. Not here. Not now.

And that was it, the last reference to the rape case in Lexton — or, Alex reminded herself, the 'alleged' rape case? Still, she had read the columnist who had described the rape victim — Sylvie — as having killed herself.

She went back to the index system and found a reference to Suicides. She spent the next hour looking up a series of inquests which described suicides at Lister. They were all of serving men either in the USAAF or later the RAF and they had killed themselves by hanging, car exhaust fumes, sleeping pills, and one had thrown himself out of the window of a hotel in Bury.

But there was no reference to a woman called Sylvie.

23

ELLEN watched Dommie get out his rod and said, "You're not going fishing, are you?"

"Going fishing."

"But, darling, the television said it was going to rain heavily and that there'd be high winds."

"Going fishing."

He put on his beanie and his coat and went into the larder for his water bottle.

"I wish you wouldn't." He didn't reply. "The tide's very high. Why don't you go out and do some painting. I'd love some pictures of cows."

"Going fishing." Dommie picked up his rod and went out through the ruined conservatory.

Ellen stood by the window and watched him. He stopped at the top of the path, turned, and she waved. She would normally have gone to the top herself but the day was unpleasant. She didn't think there would be any rod fishermen on the beach in the wind and if there weren't Dommie would come home. But you could never tell with fishermen, they were a hardy lot.

She went back through the house and looked down over the marsh. The boat was still there. Well, it was time. She went to the wall safe in her bedroom and took out a bundle of ten-pound notes. She stripped off several and put them in her pocket. She went down the hill. The wind was plucking at her and the air was filled with driving spray. When she got down into the reeds the wind made a hissing sound.

"Anyone there!" she called. "Mr Harley . . . ? Dr Kennedy . . . "

Osprey was rocking at her moorings but she looked deserted. Ellen went up the gangplank but the door into the wheelhouse was locked. She stood for a moment, undecided, then went back to the creek bank. Her fingers were fretting with the money. She didn't like giving him his money back, she would miss it, but there was no question now of him continuing to berth his boat in the creek;

not after what Bill Maitland had told her. Questions led either to answers or, failing that, to more questions. She didn't want either.

She walked back past the little stony beach where both bodies had washed up. She knew it was also where Sylvie had been found after she'd been raped, her clothes half torn away. It wasn't a place where she would have wanted to moor a boat; not with that history.

She went on up the path. The wind was higher now and she half expected to see Dommie but he hadn't returned.

When the wind blew like this Lexton House sounded like some great but deranged pipe organ. There were so many gaps under doors and windows that each produced a separate note. There were high notes where the gaps were tiny and low notes where the gaps were larger. She was used to a certain amount of noise but when the wind blew hard she liked to move into the middle of the house where the noise was less — and the middle of the house meant John's study.

She went in and closed the door and immediately the noise of the wind grew fainter. She didn't usually come into his room — that was how she still thought of it — except when the wind was high, and now she sat behind his desk, the desk where he had written his unpublished war memoirs. She could see them, two thick manuscripts done up in covers standing in his bookcase. No one had wanted to publish them. The war was over, the publishers had said. But that didn't seem to have applied to other ex-soldiers whose memoirs were published with enthusiasm.

She had always disliked this room. He used to call her in when he wanted 'to talk to her'. It was always when she had done something wrong, or something he considered to be wrong. There was the time when she had given Gilly some money to go off by herself soon after Tommy Lee had died. He'd been furious about that. When he asked her to come into the study it was like her headmistress back in her schooldays calling her in to chastise her. The room still made her feel nervous. The last time he had called her in had been the worst of all, given what had happened afterwards.

"Do you know what this is?" He was holding up a hypodermic syringe.

"Of course I know what it is."

"Do you know where I found it?"

She had felt her stomach clench because although she didn't know she guessed.

"I found it in Gillian's bathroom cupboard."

"Well, she may have had to use one. There may be some reason we don't know about and — "

"Don't talk rubbish! Anyway, she's admitted it. Told me it was nothing to do with me how she lived her life. My God, can you believe it?"

She had listened to him rant on and on. It became clear that his anger wasn't so much directed at Gilly for the damage she might be doing herself but at the reflection on himself as a father. At the time Ellen was so shocked that she had hardly taken in this aspect of his reaction. That had come later.

"What are we going to do?" she had asked because this was the question dominating her confused mind.

"Do? I'll tell you what we're going to

do, we're going to get her off the drugs. I've told her she's not leaving this house until I am absolutely certain that she's off them."

"Oh, John, that's not going to solve anything."

"It bloody well is! If she doesn't leave the house she can't get the drugs."

"How are you going to stop her?"

"I've locked her in her flat."

They had created a separate flat for Gilly after Dommie was born. Ellen walked out of John's study and went to her. The door was locked and there was no key.

"I'm keeping it." John had followed her. "No one's setting foot in there except me for at least a week."

"I'm her mother! I'm going in to see her even if I have to break a window!"

But it wasn't Ellen who broke the window. The glass had already been broken and Gilly and Dommie were gone. Ellen became frantic. She shouted at John; she told him she would never stay in the house with him again; that everything was finished between them.

She phoned the police in Ipswich and

Bury and Southwold and Orford and anywhere else she could think of and then she sat by the phone and waited. She could hear John in his study, hear the clink of bottle against glass. She waited all that day and all that night, and the following day the Bury police phoned and said they had found Gilly and Dommie and would she come and fetch them. John drove. He was grey faced from his drinking of the day before but she could smell fresh liquor on his breath.

The police were neither sympathetic nor unsympathetic, they were busy and matter-of-fact. A woman police officer took Ellen into the cells and said, "Your daughter was found begging in the square. She and the baby. We didn't want to prosecute her because of the baby."

Gilly was sitting on a bunk in the cell with Dommie on her lap. She did not greet her mother. Ellen put her arms round both of them. Gilly hardly reacted. She was dressed, as she had been the last time Ellen had seen her, in a long dress and a cardigan. Her feet were bare and dirty. In spite of the weather being warm, Dommie was dressed in a jumpsuit and a couple of blankets but looked cleaner than his mother.

"Come on, darling," Ellen said. "Let's go home."

Gilly said nothing and Ellen had the impression that had it not been for Dommie she would have refused.

Ellen took the baby and they left the police station. John was parked across the street and Ellen could see the flash of the hip flask as he put it away. He got out and said to Gilly, "You get in front with me where I can keep an eye on you." Ellen got into the back with Dommie in her arms. John drove out to the bypass and headed for Lexton. Nobody spoke for a while until they got onto the Lexton road, then John said, suddenly and savagely, "You think you can put something over on me! I'll bloody well show you what being confined to barracks means."

That was the last thing he ever said, for he had half turned to speak to Gilly, and had unconsciously turned the steering wheel slightly. It was just enough to take the car over the centre white line on the narrow road and the lorry coming towards them had no chance of avoiding them.

Ellen could not remember much about the smash. She sensed she had tried to hold on to Dommie, then there had been the terrible crashing noise and the rending of metal and she had woken up in hospital.

She herself had been only superficially injured but John was dead and so was Gilly. Dommie was alive, but only just. He had been flung forward from his grandmother's arms and his head had hit the door frame. He was in the children's intensive care unit and when she went in later to see him his head was almost the size of a football.

"Will he be all right?"

She had asked the question a dozen times of nurses and doctors until she had finally seen a consultant and he had said, "We'll have to wait. You can never tell with brain injuries."

They transferred Dommie to a children's specialist unit and it was nearly two months before Ellen could take him home. By that time Gilly and John were in the ground and some of her numbness was beginning to pass off. Having Dommie at home made the difference. He was something she could focus on, something she could love.

At the same time she knew that if it hadn't been for Bill Maitland things would have been infinitely more difficult. It was Bill who had come daily to the hospital, Bill who organized the funerals of her husband and daughter, Bill who officiated, Bill who finally brought her home. There was a kind of inevitability about their affair after that. It seemed just an extension of what had grown up between them and much of it on her side was gratitude. She knew this and knew equally well that gratitude was never going to be a base for a life together, not with the duties of a vicar's wife as well as Dommie to look after.

★ ★ ★

On Alex's way back from Bury, the rain which had been forecast began to come down. She didn't like driving in the rain, especially in an autumn dusk. She was irritated with herself for wasting time in Bury but she had spent so much of it in the library that it was mid-afternoon when she came out and she was famished. So she had had something to eat and then had looked at the shops and the afternoon had slipped away. Now she was in traffic — not heavy traffic by London standards, but heavy enough on a small country road in poor visibility. There seemed to be many lorries and she imagined that the drivers were pushing them hard to get home. All the way onto the bypass and then onto the narrow road to Lexton she kept looking into the rear mirror for the beaten-up grey Ford but it was nowhere to be seen and either it had been her imagination or the driver had found someone better to follow.

It was dark when she reached Lexton and she took the road along the river and stopped at Gracie's house. The light was on and she knocked.

"Who's there?" Gracie called.

"Dr Kennedy."

"What you want?"

"Can I come in?" She pushed the door and it opened. Gracie was sitting in her chair by the window. The stove was on and the room was warm. "I came to see how you are," Alex said.

"Ain't none of your business."

Alex smiled. The old fire and brimstone was back so Gracie was obviously feeling better.

"I brought you something from Bury."

"I don't want none of your food."

Alex opened a patisserie box and showed Gracie some chocolate éclairs and petits fours.

Gracie's expression changed.

"Please have one," Alex said.

"I'm not telling you nothing!" Gracie said, her eyes still on the contents of the box.

"I know that. Have one."

"You can't buy me, you know."

"I'm not trying to. I just thought you might like something."

"A taster," Gracie said. "I'll have a taster." She put her fingers into the box and withdrew a chocolate éclair. "I love these. I could make them once upon a time." She put one end into her mouth, bit, then sucked as the cream oozed out.

"Good?" Alex said.

Gracie ate a little more, then she said, "Good for a shop. Not as good as mine, though."

"Gracie, who was Sylvie?"

The end of the éclair went into Gracie's mouth. She chewed and closed her eyes.

"You're not asleep, I know that," Alex said. "You did that when your brother was here and I was fooled. You just pretend."

The eyes remained closed.

"I've been doing some reading in the newspaper library in Bury," Alex said. "I've been reading about what happened to Sylvie and about the three Americans and what happened to them and — "

"What you want?"

The eyes had snapped open now and Alex could see fear and anger mixed in them.

"I'm just interested, that's all."

"Who are you?"

"You know who I am. I come from this part of the coast. From Southwold."

This did not impress Gracie as it had the newspaper proprietor.

"They say your man is a copper," Gracie said.

"Who says?"

"I heard that."

"Well, he isn't. He was in the police but he isn't now."

"Once a copper, always a copper."

"Have another."

"No! I told you. You can't buy me. I ain't going to Bridmoor, you hear?"

"Of course you're not."

"You go now."

"Gracie, I want to ask you one more question."

But the old woman rose to her feet and began to bang her stick on the floor. Alex put the box of cakes on the kitchen table and left. She started her car and turned out of the small driveway in front of Gracie's cottage and her lights picked out a lorry parked in the trees by the river. It gave the impression of waiting for something and she realized that was precisely what it was doing when she read the sign on its side: *Purveyors of Meat, Poultry and Fish to the Catering Trade.*

The boats must be out, she thought, and it was waiting for their return.

The thought of the boats reminded

her that she was going to *Osprey* and Mike would probably not be back from Felixstowe. And she was right. The boat was in darkness. She went aboard and put on lights but the cabins felt damp and the rusty bulkheads absorbed the light and made it dim and dreary.

She made herself a cup of coffee and went into the saloon. There was a message on the answerphone. She pressed the replay button expecting to hear Mike's voice. But it wasn't his.

"Mike, this is Laddie Broakes," said a deep and hoarse voice. "It's fourteen hundred on Thursday. I've got something that might interest you. Give me a call. Message ends."

Alex wrote it down and left it on the saloon table. They were still at it, Mike and this Broakes man, still playing at being police detectives when they weren't. She had imagined her holiday here would involve lazy days on a comfortable boat, short drives to restaurants, a look at some of the churches, exploring the countryside and old towns like Bury — but doing all these things together and without pressure. Instead, Mike was trying to solve a case he had no business trying to solve, and hiding a valuable substance that wasn't his and was illegal anyway. And he was saying he wasn't going to try to sell it when she feared that was, in fact, what he was planning. The musk was 'found' treasure, wasn't it?

There was no place for her in this sort of life and yet she had made a place for herself. She was running about just like Mike and asking questions and finding out things — and the point was she didn't even know what she was finding out. She told herself that the whole thing was being done as self-protection, but it was more like self-indulgence and the sooner she stopped the better.

She would go and stay with Hannah for a few days and then fly off for a week somewhere — Morocco perhaps — and laze about and read novels and generally have a holiday kind of holiday before going back to prepare for the winter's 'flu epidemic. Mike might even decide to come with her but if he didn't she would go by herself.

She finished her coffee and was halfway to the galley to rinse the mug when there was a banging on the wheelhouse door. She paused, put the mug down softly, and went to the companionway. The banging came again. She turned the lights on up there and on the deck as well, then she went up.

There was a figure on the deck and when she got closer she could make out Harold Potter. She opened the wheelhouse door and he swung round to face her. His thin hair was plastered down by the rain and he was wearing shiny waterproofs.

"What do you want?" he shouted above the wind.

"What do *you* want, Mr Potter?"

"You bin asking questions. Checking up on things that ain't none of your business."

His face was streaming with water but in the deck lights she could see that it was red with emotion and that he was worked up into a froth of rage.

"Take it easy, Mr Potter, you could have a heart attack."

"You come here and you want to do us down."

"I don't want to do anyone down."

"You bin asking Gracie questions. You bin checking things."

"Yes, but only out of interest. I've been trying to find out who Sylvie was and no one should know better than you, Mr Potter."

He stepped back a pace and looked as though she had struck him.

"Can you tell me?"

"You . . . you can . . . you . . . " For a moment he was unable to get the words out. Then he said, "Thou shalt be smitten! Smitten to death!" Abruptly he spun round and made for the gangplank. She watched him go into the reeds and heard the noise of his car engine as it fired. Then a fishing boat came into the river from the sea with its lights blazing and in the glow she could see the car making for the road bridge. It looked like an old beaten-up grey Ford, like the one she thought had been following her into Bury. But at the distance and in the poor light, she couldn't be sure.

24

MIKE got back to the boat a little after eleven. Alex had been sitting in the saloon with all the lights on holding a book on her lap and trying to read. Every now and then a noise that didn't sound like the wind in the reeds or the slap of a wave on the steel hull caused her to imagine that there was someone else aboard. Twice she had gone round the boat checking that the portholes were closed and the curtains drawn over them and three times she had gone to the wheelhouse door and made sure it was double locked. None of these precautions gave her much confidence.

When Mike arrived she was both grateful for his presence and irritated with him for being late and allowing her to build up a load of apprehension. So her voice, when she mimicked the housewife's cliché, "Have a good day, dear?" was not exactly warm.

He picked it up instantly, "What the

hell's that supposed to mean?"

"It means exactly what it sounds like. You've been away all bloody day and I wanted to know if it had been good . . . worth it . . . a pleasure . . . "

"Well, if you want to know it's been a bloody awful day. You asked. I've told you."

He went into the galley and came back with a large neat Scotch.

Alex, having launched her offensive, wasn't about to be upstaged and said, "What happened? Wasn't your little friend nice to you?"

"Have you been saving this up?"

"Only over the last four hours or so. You said you'd be back about seven."

"OK. Things went wrong. I wasn't back at seven. Some days are like this. You win some, you lose some. It's what it's all about."

"Oh, God, it's not what this is all about! This is a holiday for two people who want to be together. That's what this is all about."

"You finished?" It was said quietly and she knew she was getting near the danger area.

"Yes, I'm finished." It was on the tip of her tongue to talk about flying off to Morocco either with him or by herself but she held onto it. "I'm sorry. Why don't you get me a drink too and tell me about it."

He came back with a glass of wine for her and said, "I got there just after lunch. He was giving evidence in court. I waited. I went to the pub and had a sandwich. Went back to court. He was still there. Went back to the pub, had another sandwich. Went back to the court. Waited and waited and waited. He came out at four. Said he had to see his chief about something. I went to his office and waited. That's all I did all bloody day. When he came out he said he could give me fifteen minutes because he had to pick up his kid. So I said, 'All right, come and have a drink.' But he didn't have time. So in the car park I started asking him questions about migrants and smuggling and he said there was a hell of a lot to talk about and why didn't I book into the hotel and stay over and he'd see me the next day. What about lunch and then we could have a good old talk? So I said, 'Well, thanks a million but I've got to get back and I'll be in touch . . . '"

"Oh dear."

"See? That's the sort of day I've had. Now it's my turn. Have a good day, dear?"

She laughed and felt the tension snap. He took her face in his hands and kissed her on the lips and said, "I've been wanting to do that all day. When I was having my second sandwich I thought, what the hell am I doing here? I want to be with Alexandra and I want to be kissing her and putting my hand — "

"Oh, that sort of day. Well, I wouldn't have been here."

She told him about Bury and what she had found in the papers. She could see she was losing his attention so she switched to the car she thought had been following her and then what had happened on the deck earlier that evening.

He was instantly alert. "Smitten? He said, 'Thou shalt be smitten'? 'Smitten to death'?"

"That's how he talks. You've never

heard him in the town square as I have."

"It may be biblical as hell but the way he said it, it's also a criminal threat."

She stretched and shrugged and said, "I shouldn't have taken it so seriously. He's just a poor old man with a religious complex."

"But why would he threaten you?"

"Ah, you finally got there."

"What d'you mean?"

"I mean you're interested. Suddenly interested and only because someone has threatened me. When I said I thought there were secrets here, you weren't interested."

"I don't like people threatening you. That's one thing. And I want to know why he's threatening you. That's another. You say he said you'd been asking questions and checking — "

"And he said, 'come to do us down'."

"So there are others."

"Others what?"

"Involved."

"Involved in what?"

"In whatever it is."

"There you go again," she said.

"You've taken another step. I've been sitting here thinking and thinking and saying to myself exactly what you've been saying. With what I found in Bury and also at the newspaper library here I think what we are on the edge of is a cover-up. It's like a carpet under which something has been swept and I've picked up a corner and I'm looking underneath and the only problem is I don't know what it is I'm looking at — or for. But he doesn't know that, he thinks I know exactly what I'm looking for and will recognize it when I find it."

"And what are you looking for?"

"The answer to a conundrum I haven't even thought of yet."

"Well, I know what I'm looking for. The car. We'll go together to Potter's place and you can tell me if it was the one that was following you into Bury."

In the morning, Mike looked up Potter's address in the local telephone directory and then got directions to his street. The day was wet and windy, the rain slamming down in squalls as it had all night.

The house was on the edge of the little

town, a bungalow built in the 1950s and standing by itself on a corner behind tall and unkempt cypress hedges. They stood at the gate and glanced in. The garden was neat, mainly given over to vegetables.

"He's a late sleeper," Mike said.

"How do you know?"

"Curtains are still drawn."

A little rutted drive ran round behind the house and Alex said, "The garage must be at the back."

"Bugger."

"What are we going to do? We can't just go up to the front door and say, 'Have you been following me?'"

"You told me you'd said if he wasn't careful he might have a heart attack. You could just be checking up to see if he's all right. I'll see if there's a back gate, there usually is. While you're talking to him I'll nip in and look at the garage."

"I don't think so."

"Why the hell not?"

"Mike, this isn't really my kind of thing. Anyway, I don't want to talk to him."

"Listen, it's all basically because of

you, so let's get it over, I'm getting soaked."

He went around the corner and she went unwillingly down the path to the front door and rang the bell. The curtains in the windows on either side of the little porch were closed. She rang again but no one came. She knocked on the door. Still no one. She walked round to the back door and knocked on that. Nothing. The garage was nearby. One of its doors had come unfastened and was banging in the wind. The place was eerie and lonely and she wanted to leave.

"Mike!" she called, but her voice was whipped away on the wind. She waited for a few moments and then realized that the hedge at the back had no break in it, so there was no back gate. She turned to retrace her steps and meet him at the front gate when she remembered why they were there. It would only take a moment to glance into the garage. It was unlikely there was anything there, for Mr Potter was clearly out and probably in his car. But she might as well check.

The garage faced side on to her. She went round to the door that was banging and pulled it open against the wind.

That's when he grabbed her. He must have been standing just inside the door and his arms went round her head. She wrenched backwards, screaming. The arms lost their grip. She turned and fell backwards into the garden. Mike was coming down the track.

"He's in there!" she shouted. "He grabbed me!"

There was an old spade on the ground and Mike snatched it up. The garage door had slammed shut again in the wind and he raised the spade as he went to it.

"Mr Potter!" he shouted. "Don't try anything!"

He got no reply.

"Come outside!"

He raised the spade.

Alex said, "Mike, be careful!"

Mike caught hold of the door and pulled against the wind. It opened partially. Arms came at him. So did legs. A whole body. It swung and turned and the wind pulled it backwards and forwards on the rope that was strung round its neck. Harold Potter was hanging from a beam just inside the door.

"Oh my God," Alex said.

Mike dropped the spade, went forward and touched the twisted face. "I'm pretty sure he's dead," he said. "It's cold as ice. Should you try?"

"I must."

They cut the old man down. He was not very high. He had only had a wooden box to step off, the rope had stretched and his feet were almost touching the ground.

They got him onto the concrete floor just ahead of the bumper of an old beaten-up grey Ford and Alex examined him.

"He's strangled himself," she said. "Been dead for hours."

"I'll call that police sergeant. What's his name?"

"Somers."

"Right, I'll go inside if the back door's open and phone from there."

"But what'll we say? I mean why are we here?"

"We're here because you were worried about him last night. He came round to

411

see you in the rain because he wanted to . . . "

"Wanted to what?"

"No, forget that. You told me you saw him at his sister's, didn't you?"

"He brought a piece of cheese for her."

"Right. You're worried about her not getting enough to eat and you just wanted to ask him about it. Good Samaritan stuff. Good medical practice."

"My God, the things I've been doing would get me struck off!"

The back door was unlocked and Mike went into the house to make the call. She didn't fancy being outside with what was left of Harold Potter so she fastened the garage door and followed Mike into the kitchen.

"Phone's in the passage," he said.

She heard him dial. The kitchen was sparsely furnished and looked as if it too came out of the 1950s or before. There was a sink with a wooden draining board, an old electric stove which stood on metal legs, a brown painted food larder, and, in one corner, a mangle. She had never seen one except in movies of the period.

"He's coming," Mike said as he entered the room. "Says we must stay, which of course is procedure." He paused and said, "I wonder why?"

She didn't have to ask what he was wondering about. "He seemed almost unhinged when he came to the boat. I think I was more frightened for him than for myself. But I didn't think it was going to end this way."

Mike had brushed against the kitchen door as he came in from the passage and now it slowly closed revealing a mirror on the wall behind it. A piece of paper had been stuck to it and in bold lettering were the words, *To who it concerns. I do this with my own hand.* Then below that was written, *Forgive me Sylvie. Forgive me Lord.*

25

"**G**OD, I hated that!" Alex said as she and Mike walked back to the boat through the village. The rain was coming down in buckets but she was hardly aware of it.

"Somers has been waiting for that chance ever since I was rude to him about mooring where we are."

"You know, Mike, I think you may have picked the wrong village for diving safaris."

"I'm beginning to wonder."

Somers had kept them at Potter's house for nearly two hours as he laboriously wrote out their statements, got them to spell their names, made them give him their London address, and then made them wait for a police doctor to arrive and certify Harold Potter dead. It was only when the ambulance had come and taken the body off to the mortuary where the post-mortem would take place that he allowed them to go.

"He wanted to show us who was who," Mike said. "Don't forget Inspector Brady humiliated him in front of us and that had to be paid for."

"Do you think he believed all that about Gracie and food?"

"Why not? It makes perfect sense. Anyway, it's true, because you have taken Gracie food which means you were worried about her. So forget Somers and his bloody village mentality."

They crossed the square and went on down towards the river. All the fishing boats were at their moorings. In the rain the picturesqueness had vanished and the area looked derelict.

Osprey felt damp and cold when they got aboard and Mike said, "I'll phone Laddie Broakes now, see what he wants."

Alex made the bed and began clearing up. Her mood, brought on by the suicide of Harold Potter and the change in the North Sea weather, was not that of someone on holiday and she remembered when she was at school in Southwold how often the days had been like this. The Suffolk coast was known for wind and fog and cold. When it was nice, it was very, very nice — as it had been when she had first joined Mike on the boat — but when it wasn't, it was bloody.

Mike came into the cabin and said, "He's out."

Alex plumped up the pillows and pulled the duvets straight. "Mike, I want to say something."

"That sounds ominous."

"No, it isn't. Listen, this is supposed to be a holiday and it isn't at the moment. I'm sick to death of all the unpleasant things that have been happening since we found that bloody musk. I've got some holiday money tucked away and . . ." She saw his expression change. "Oh, Lord, I knew you were going to be like this. But I don't care. All I'm saying is, let's go away for a week to somewhere sunny and nice and it'll be my treat."

He turned away from her. She went on, more forcefully, "For God's sake, why not? You're not being fair. Being here with you is your treat. It's your boat, you're paying for the food and drink. Why can't I do the same?"

"Lots of reasons, but the main one

is the fact that there's got to be an inquest on the Chinese man. We'll have to attend."

"I don't know as much about the legal system as you do but from personal experience I've known inquests to be delayed for a year or more from the finding of a murder victim. You're not telling me we have to stay in one place all that time."

"No, of course not."

"Then what about Morocco or the Seychelles? Mauritius, maybe? Hand the musk over to customs and let's get out of here — just for a week."

A voice called, "Hello! Anyone there? Mr Harley!"

He looked out of the porthole. "It's Mrs Blackhurst." Alex followed him on deck.

Ellen said, "Mr Harley, I want to see you."

"Come aboard."

Alex said, "Come and have some coffee."

"No, thanks."

Mike went down the gangplank and Alex leaned over the rail.

Ellen's face was wet with rain and she was wearing a yellow fisherman's sou'wester.

"I hope there's nothing wrong," Mike said.

"I'm afraid there is. I'm going to have to ask you to vacate the mooring."

"What?"

"I'm sorry, but I've changed my mind." She dug an envelope from her pocket and held it out to him. "I'm returning your money."

Mike put his hands behind his back. "We had an agreement. You allowed me to moor here for an agreed sum of money."

"There was nothing in writing."

"Doesn't have to be."

"Mr Harley, don't you understand? I don't want you here any longer."

"Oh, I understand what you're saying, but I don't understand why. I mean, we haven't done anything wrong and — "

"I suppose you think what you did to Harold Potter wasn't wrong! My God, I've known that nice old man for more than thirty years and a short time after you get here you go out to his house and pester him and he makes an end of himself."

"Now wait a moment . . . "

"No, I'm not going to wait. You get your boat out of this creek. Here . . . here's your money."

"I'm not taking it! I'm not going to let you order me about like some bloody peasant." Her head jerked back as though she had been slapped. He went on, "And we didn't do a damn thing to Harold Potter. All we did was try to find out if his sister was getting enough food."

"And leave Gracie alone!" Ellen pointed up at Alex. "You've been asking her questions and prying and that's what you did to Harold. I want you out of here or I'll go to the police!"

Mike said, "And if you do I'll go to them about Dommie."

"What about Dommie?"

"He's been aboard this boat and burglarized the interior. He also hit me with his stick. And he's a peeper. He comes here and looks through the portholes."

"Rubbish! You've no proof of this at all."

"What d'you think the social services will say if I tell them not only that but about the attempted rape the other night?"

She stared at him for a long moment and said, "You bloody sod!" Then she turned away and walked back up the road to her house.

Mike came up the gangplank. His face was drawn but that was the only reaction Alex could see. She knew that if she had had to face the same barrage she would have been shaking, but Mike's hands were steady as rocks.

They went down into the saloon. "Is that right about the agreement?" Alex said.

"Not being in writing? I think so. There is such a thing as a verbal contract and I paid her the money, and you know that — so I've got a witness."

"I always thought she was a rather nice woman."

"Something's happened," Mike said. "I don't know what, but something."

"Of course something's happened. Harold Potter has killed himself and we're held to blame."

"You realize she already knew that he'd killed himself."

"That's the thing about villages, especially on this coast. Word gets round fast."

"She practically accused us of going over to his house and supervising his suicide."

Alex said, "I thought that too at first but it's really the questions and the prying that she's blaming us for."

"Prying? All you did was ask a few questions about the far past and he puts a rope around his neck and jumps! People don't do that sort of thing unless . . . "

"Unless?"

"Unless they have something to hide."

She patted his hand. "Welcome. You've arrived."

"All right, you can say I told you so."

"Well, I did tell you. The only trouble is we still don't know what we're looking for."

He was sitting in one of the swivel chairs and began to turn it from side to side until he put unexpected strain on his left knee and winced. "Listen," he said, and she could see his trained mind begin to tick over. "We come to this village which isn't really a village but the bit left over after most of a town has gone under the waves. That's enough to give most places a distinct feeling of insecurity. But English villages have a kind of secrecy paranoia, at least the ones I've been into. Half the time they won't tell you what the weather's going to be like tomorrow. So into this village floats a dead Chinese man with knife wounds in his chest. A little later a valuable and illegal Eastern substance is found near where the body floated. Am I right so far?"

"Exactly right."

"Soon after that our boat is attacked, not once but twice — I'm counting the loosening of the mooring ropes as one because I'm damn sure I tied them well enough — and in the second I get hit on the head."

"I heard what you said to Mrs Blackhurst. Suddenly it isn't the Triads who hit you, but Dommie."

"I had to say something to her, didn't I? It might have been Dommie. It might have been the Triads."

"It also might have been Chris Cottis."

"I told you the boats were out."

"Yes, but there's a place the fishermen can get ashore without anyone knowing. I saw it the other day when I was on a walk. I'll show it to you. It means you can't write him off."

"All right, but for the moment let's say it was Dommie. His grandmother probably believes that and I don't see how she can get us to go if she thinks there may be some truth in it. Can I go on?"

"Of course."

"So, soon after this you start finding out odd things about Lexton from the local newspapers and also what you hear in shops and what Bill Maitland tells you. Now my question is, do these things have anything to do with a Chinese gent and musk?"

"Well, it depends. You've left something out."

"What's that?"

"Another body, the one that Gracie says she found."

"And you've left something out too

— the Japanese group at the hotel. If they *were* Japanese."

"I'm sure I'm leaving out lots of things. All I'm really saying is that from the beginning you made up your mind that this was big time crime: smuggled migrants, Triads, illegal musk."

"And you've been saying it's just a little village problem. Well, I don't buy that."

"You said you didn't count Chris Cottis either. Now I've told you there's a place — "

He looked suddenly impatient and said, "All right, all right, show me."

They put on their wet-weather gear and Alex led the way through the reeds and along the dykes. The wind was thrashing the water in the polder-like marshes into foamy yellow waves and the reeds were bending at severe angles.

They walked for about fifteen minutes and then Alex cut along a dyke towards the river. They were now well beyond the village and ahead of them all was flat and reedy and wet.

"Look," she said. "See how the river comes up and broadens out? Well, I saw

424

a boat almost stop here the other day." She pointed to a flat bank with deep water at its edge. "Any fisherman could jump ashore if he wanted to."

They looked out over the choppy water of the river. On the far side of it Alex could see Gracie's house.

Mike said, "This is a turning basin. I've seen them in Lincolnshire. When I first came I wondered about the river. It's very narrow. And Bill told us how much broader it was in the old days. What this means is that the boats can come up here and turn without worrying about manoeuvring in the narrows by the village."

There was a footbridge up past the basin and they crossed. The grass was flattened on the bank and the water was deep.

"I see what you meant," he said. "You could easily bring a fishing boat up here."

"So you see, Chris could have left his boat here and walked down to *Osprey* and no one would have been any the wiser. My only problem is I don't see why he should be so violent."

Mike said, "He warned me, not once but twice. These guys are very anti-strangers. Fishermen always are. They don't want competition. We've heard it from Bill. Remember he told us about the man who wanted to dive on the Old Town. He couldn't get a mooring either and had to berth his boat up the coast at Hallows. And because he had to travel the extra distance he was drowned in a storm."

She had been looking past him while he was talking. "Mike, there's no smoke coming out of Gracie's house."

"So?"

"She has the stove lit all the time, I had to light it myself when it went out. Do you think I should go in and check?"

"No, it's nothing to do with us."

She knew he was thinking about Gracie's brother and the police. But that was precisely what she wanted to check.

"I'm going up, Mike."

They went through the reeds and up the path to Gracie's front door. Alex knocked.

There was no answer. Mike went to

426

the living room window and put his hands on either side of his head to cut the reflection. "No one there," he said.

"Try the door."

He turned the handle and it opened. "You want to go in? It's not allowed, you know."

"Stop being a policeman. She may be ill."

But Gracie wasn't in the house. In the little bedroom upstairs a few old suitcases were piled on the stripped bed. One had clothes in it but the others were empty.

Mike said, "She's packed up and gone."

"Where would someone like Gracie go?"

"Maybe to her brother's house."

"I doubt it."

"And I think we should go too before someone comes along."

They went out into the rainy wind and started down the road to *Osprey*.

"I don't like it," Alex said. "You don't pack a bag to go to a house where someone has just committed suicide."

"Who knows what people do in a place like Lexton."

427

"She might have collapsed and been taken to hospital. She wasn't eating properly. And, anyway, think of the shock when she heard about her brother. I think I'll ask Bill Maitland."

His cottage was on the way back to the boat and looked dwarfed by the great Church of the Meres that stood blackly against the grey windy sky.

He seemed less than his usual welcoming and friendly self. He took them into his untidy sitting room but kept standing. Alex told him what they had found. His big face fell into a frown and he looked at his watch.

"I was just going to her to see that she was all right."

"You've heard about her brother?"

He nodded. "Yes. What a tragic thing. You found him, I understand."

"The word gets round," Mike said.

"I was his priest for many years. It's only natural I was told."

"We wondered if she might have gone up to her brother's house," Alex said. "There were signs that she'd packed some clothing."

"She wasn't there when I went round.

428

But I wasn't there for long. I just went in case there was anything I could do."

"Is there anywhere else she could go?"

"Not that I know of, but I'll ask. A suitcase? That's rather odd. I was going to take her some fried fish and chips. She likes that."

"Will you let me know if she's all right?" Alex said.

"Yes, if you want me to."

They left and went on down to the boat.

"He's changed," she said. "He's lost the warmth he had."

"Someone's got to him."

"About what?"

"About us."

"What have we done?"

"We've been asking questions."

"And not getting any answers."

The memory of Gracie's empty house and the cold stove and the suitcases on the stripped bed remained with her all day.

26

THE notice said BRIDMOOR HOUSE. The lettering was white on a black board attached to a post inside big iron gates. A drive curved away between tangled rhododendron bushes. Once there had been a lawn but now it looked more like a cut field. Two tall cypress trees added to the gloom. Alex opened the gates, drove through, closed them, and went up the drive. The nursing home was much as she had expected because she had been to others near London which looked similar. Like so many of the big houses once built for wealthy families this had now been put to other uses. It was Victorian Gothic, red brick, turrets and black-tiled sloping roofs. It looked much as it might have done soon after it had been built except for one difference, the bars on the windows.

Alex parked the car at the side of the house and sat for a moment before getting out. She was feeling nervous and anxious in about equal proportions and the questions in her head were the ones that Mike had asked her several times before she left the boat.

"Why are you going?" he had said. "What business is it of yours?"

And she had blurted out, "Injustice is everybody's business."

"That sounds a bit pompous," he had said.

She winced now as she thought of that because it had been pompous and she had instantly regretted saying it.

She had still been holding the note they had found stuffed under the wheelhouse door when they came back from a late lunch at the pub. All it had said was, *I understand Gracie has been placed in Bridmoor. Yrs. Bill Maitland.*

"She's not your patient," Mike had continued. "She's nothing to do with you."

And then Alex had said what had been in her mind since she had read the note. "She's in there because of me. If I hadn't started asking stupid questions she'd still be at home and for that matter Harold

Potter would probably still be alive."

"You can't possibly make assumptions like that."

"Oh, yes, I can. Look, I've clearly been heaving at some rock that's been in place for years and there's something nasty underneath it which no one wants out in the daylight — and I'm not even sure I want it out."

"All you did was ask a few questions."

"And I wouldn't have done that if it hadn't been for you."

"Me?" The tone was outraged. "How the hell do you account for it being my fault?"

"If you hadn't gone off like some hyperactive boy detective I wouldn't have dug through the old newspapers and I wouldn't have asked Gracie and her brother questions."

She stopped then, and said, "I'm sorry. That was awful. And I don't mean it. It's just me trying to shove the blame and guilt on the nearest body. No, it might have started off because of what you were doing, I mean in self-defence, but then it got going under its own steam and I was asking questions because I got a charge.

Now one person's dead and another has been carted off to a home for mentally ill geriatrics — and I'm going to get her out. It's the least I can do."

But now, sitting in the car park at Bridmoor House, she wasn't so sure of herself.

She went to the big oak front door and rang the bell. It was opened instantly by a stocky woman with short grey hair and a square face. "Yes?"

"I'm Dr Kennedy," Alex said. "I've come to see Gracie Potter."

"Who?"

"She was brought in today."

"Oh, Dr Morris's patient."

"I don't know who Dr Morris is but — "

A uniformed woman came into the hall behind the square-jawed woman and said, "Mrs Ramsay, there's no milk left."

"Damn. I told someone to order extra."

"Well, it never came. And supper's in half an hour."

"They'll just have to do without, then."

Alex looked at her watch, the time was

now a little after four o'clock. Old people in places like this ate early.

Mrs Ramsay turned back to her and said, "Sorry . . . what was it you were saying?"

"I was saying I wanted to see Miss Potter. I know that her GP has died and she asked me to look after her." The words Gracie had used, "Will you be my doctor?," were said, Alex knew, probably in playfulness, but they had been said and that was what counted.

Mrs Ramsay ran her fingers through her hair. "I don't understand that. Dr Morris signed the papers."

"I don't understand it either. Now may I see her, please."

When Alex assumed her present tone it was as though some chilly voice from the General Medical Council was speaking.

"God, if only someone would tell me what's going on," Mrs Ramsay said. "I've only been here a month and I'm supposed to know everything! Come with me, please."

She led Alex to a room on the first floor and opened a door without knocking. "Here you are, Gracie," she said. "Your doctor wants to see you." Then she said to Alex, "I'll leave you with her but they have their supper in a little while."

Gracie was sitting upright on a narrow iron bed with her back to them. There were two other women in the room, which was very cold. There was a large patch of damp on one wall and the place smelt of mould. One old woman was asleep in an armchair. The other was standing by the window. She was small and birdlike with bright robin's eyes. As Mrs Ramsay left she came over to Alex and touched her face. "Hello, beauty," she said. "Are you my thingy? My . . . girl? Is that the name of the thingy? Are you?"

"No, I'm not your daughter," Alex said. "Does she come to see you?"

The little birdlike woman picked up Alex's hand and kissed it. "Jam tart," she said.

Alex managed to free herself and went round to the other side of the bed. "Hello, Gracie."

The old face was closed like a door is closed, shutting out the light. She stared past Alex and did not move.

"I've come to help you, Gracie. I'm your doctor, don't forget."

"Wax polish," said the little woman.

Gracie's eyes flickered and Alex realized she had heard what she had said and had taken it in.

"I want to get you out of here. This isn't a place for you."

The eyelids flickered again, more rapidly.

"Waltzing thingy," said the little woman and gave a little skip.

Alex tried to ignore her. "Gracie, I'm very sorry about your brother and I'm very sorry that this has happened to you. But I don't want you to worry or think about it. I want to find out why you were sent here and why Dr Morris signed the papers and what — "

The woman in the chair snored heavily.

Suddenly Gracie spoke. "Phil Somers brought him." The woman in the chair snored again. Gracie went on, "'You're very tired,' he says, 'and I'm going to send you to a place that will look after you.'"

The birdlike woman gave a little curtsey

and held on to Alex's hand. "Are you my thingy?"

"No, I'm not your daughter," Alex said. "Look, Gracie, we can't talk in here. Shall we go for a little walk?"

They went out into the corridor. The smell of human waste and old cooking was very strong in these airless passageways. "Let's go this way." Alex led Gracie off to her right. "But be careful." There were several buckets catching drips from the ceiling and some of the water had come onto the floor. It was a long dim passage but there were windows at the far end and Alex made for them.

"Tell me exactly what happened," she said.

"He come to me . . . "

"Who?"

"Phil Somers. He come to me and said, 'Gracie, Harold's dead by his own hand.' Then he said they'd taken the body to the place in Bury where there's going to be an inquiry. So I said, 'Harold's killed himself?' 'Yes,' says Phil. 'With a rope.'"

They had reached the end of the passage and Alex saw a conservatory down a flight of stairs.

"Let's go down there," she said. "Perhaps there are chairs."

Once the conservatory had been a beautiful place. Now its woodwork was rotting and the glass, some of which was broken, was stained by green lichen. There were still a few potted palm trees, which must have been there for years, Alex thought; probably put in by the previous owners. There was a pile of plastic garden chairs in one corner and she brought out two and sat Gracie down opposite her.

"Go on, Gracie. What happened then?"

"Phil said a doctor was coming. I should have known then. I should have been suspicious but I was thinking about Harold."

"Suspicious of what, Gracie?"

"They wants me out of the way."

The little old face was puckered with anger and unease.

"They?"

Gracie ignored her. "Put away so I can't speak. I thought you would have known that, you been asking and asking and I been telling you I can't say nothing."

"Hang on, Gracie, are you saying that 'they' have had you put in here because 'they' were afraid you might tell me things?"

"Why'd you think they brought that Dr Morris? I never seen no Dr Morris. My doctor was old Dr Willis before he died. And Phil Somers says, 'This is your new doctor and he's come to see if you're all right after the shock.'"

"That's the shock of Harold's death?"

"Harold and me was never close. His head was always in the scriptures and there were things I could tell you about Harold. Well, I mean — "

In the distance there was the sound of a dinner gong. Gracie looked over Alex's shoulder as though someone was coming into the conservatory to take her by force and said, "I don't want none of their food."

"You must eat something."

"None of their slop."

"All right, I'll get you something else. It's early yet. But you were telling me about Dr Morris. Can you remember exactly what he did?"

"He had a machine and he put that cloth round my arm and he pumped."

"Blood pressure. Anything else?"

"He looked in my eyes with a light and he says to me how am I feeling and I says I'm feeling very well. And he says can I tell him my name and when I was born and things like that and as I'm telling him an ambulance arrives and he says he just wants me to go for a little ride to a hospital where I can rest for a few days after the shock, and they pack a suitcase and take me."

Alex was confused but decided that for the moment she'd just go along with what Gracie was telling her.

"Are you saying that it was the police sergeant who organized Dr Morris?"

"Well, I didn't."

"Isn't that a bit unusual?"

"It's more than unusual, it's a downright liberty. I don't want to be here. This is where they said they'd put me and I don't want it!"

"Who said?"

"Miss Ellen said."

"I thought she was your friend."

"Friend? I was her skivvy. I cleaned up after her and her husband and Gilly and Dommie. For years and years. Then she give me the house after my father died and now she's saying it's not my house but hers and if I don't be good then it's Bridmoor. And here I am!"

The last sentence was uttered in a voice full of anguish and fear and it touched Alex deeply. She leaned forward and took one of Gracie's hands and said, "Don't worry, Gracie, I'm going to have you out of here. But you've got to tell me a bit more so I'll know how to go about it. What was it they were so worried you would say?"

Tears began to form in Gracie's eyes and then spilled over the lower lids and ran down her cheeks. "Are you my doctor?" she said.

"You asked me once in your house if I'd be and if you still want me then I am."

"I dunno why they was worried," Gracie said. "If it's the other death then it's what the village knows about."

"Which death is that, Gracie?"

"The first one."

"The body in the sea?"

"Long before that. I saw Sylvie's body."

"She was the girl said to be raped by the Americans, wasn't she? You saw her when?"

"After they cut her down. That's why Harold done it that way."

"Hanged himself?"

"Used a rope. Because she done it that way."

"You mean he's been in love with her all these years and — "

Gracie gave a slight snort and said, "If Harold was in love then he had a fine way of showin' it."

"What do you mean, Gracie?"

"I mean she killed herself because of what he done or I should say of what he never done."

"I thought she killed herself because of what happened to her that night."

"That's true enough. But Harold might have changed that. I mean if he had loved her he would have tried to help her. I know 'cause I was at home lookin' after our dad when Harold come running in white faced and frightened. He says he's

442

been fighting some Americans who took Sylvie off him. But there was no blood or bruises and you can't tell me that three men would have had much trouble with Harold."

"So you're saying he didn't try to help Sylvie?"

"That's what I am saying. But afterwards he told the police and the newspapers what a fight he had."

"All right, so he was lying. Or perhaps just exaggerating. But would she kill herself for that? I mean, it could happen to many couples. He might have gone off for help."

"Harold never even tried. I know that because he changed his story three times. First he knocked down one of them buggers and then gets knocked down himself. Then he didn't knock him down but kicks him in the privates. Then he never did neither but hits him with a branch he picks up off the ground. But I was going with the police sergeant in them days and he told me as far as he can see none of them was even scratched."

"That was before the American air force people came for them?"

Gracie nodded. "I never said nothing about it. My dad was sick and Harold being my brother. Couldn't, could I?"

"Was Sylvie badly affected?"

"She was a poor weepy thing and she never got over it. If Harold had stayed with her, been with her, it would have made the difference. But what's she got at the end of it? Been raped by three men and the man she loves and is going to marry runs off into the reeds and leaves her to her fate. That's a funny way of showin' love."

A voice behind them said, "I'm sorry, we don't have visitors here."

Alex turned and saw Mrs Ramsay.

"Oh, it's you, Dr Kennedy. Supper's been on for ten minutes."

"Yes, I'm sorry, the time got away from us. I'll bring her in now."

Mrs Ramsay turned and left the conservatory, her square-jawed face looking irritable.

Gracie had risen to her feet. "I ain't going in."

"Come on, Gracie. You mustn't starve yourself."

"I don't want to be here!"

"I know you don't and I'm — "

"You're my doctor. You said I ain't got that disease!"

"I know I did, and you haven't."

Gracie went down onto the floor and gripped Alex round the legs. "Please . . ." she cried. "Please . . ."

"Gracie, I promise."

"Come along now! None of that!" Mrs Ramsay was back. She stooped and pulled Gracie to her feet. "Supper time!"

"Just a moment," Alex said. "I said I'd go out and get something for her. She has a dietary problem."

"Dr Kennedy, this is an establishment that has to keep to a timetable. I simply can't have — "

Alex said coldly, "Mrs Ramsay, I've seen enough so far in this place to make a report to the Suffolk Health Authority that will have the inspectors here in a matter of hours. If you force me to, I will. In the meantime let me say this: Miss Potter enjoys cheese omelettes. Please have one made for her. I shall be back to see her in the morning. Have I made myself clear?"

The anger in Mrs Ramsay's eyes had given way to anxiety, and now she said in a voice hollow with obsequiousness, "Yes, Doctor."

Alex left the still weeping Gracie and went out to her car. She felt jangled and unhappy and filled with her own anger. She knew she had to get Gracie out and she knew that meant more questions. But the excitement of discovery had vanished. Too much had happened. Now there was only a feeling of unease.

27

ALEX drove back to the boat past Gracie's house. She had an idea that she would try to find a way of locking the front door to make it safe for the night but when she stopped there she found the door already locked. Had Mike locked it when they had checked the house earlier?

Fog was rolling in over the marshes and soon the house would be engulfed. It looked cold and dark and she got back into the car feeling even more wretched at the thought of Gracie in Bridmoor. At least here, even if it was bleak, she had her own things and a hot stove and it was home.

She drove slowly down the lane by the river. The fog was patchy, one moment she was clear, the next she couldn't see a thing, and it reminded her of when *Osprey* had nearly been run down by the other boat when Mike was diving. God, how she wished they had never gone out there in the first place, never found the musk, never become embroiled in the contemporary violence surrounding the dead Chinese and the past violence surrounding the village itself.

On that foggy lane in early evening she came to a decision: she was absolutely and definitely not going to remain in Lexton for the rest of her holiday. If Mike wouldn't come away with her, Hannah might. But that was only after she had secured Gracie's release from Bridmoor. How she was going to do that she wasn't sure but there had to be a way. If Gracie stuck to her desire to have Alex as her doctor then that was a possibility. Especially now that she had Mrs Ramsay under threat.

The figure was abruptly right there in front of her, huge and threatening in the fog. She braked hard as the man turned sharply away. Then she saw it was Bill Maitland. She stopped and brought the window down. He was standing on the side of the road looking at the car but she had the impression that he was hardly seeing it. His face was deathly white.

"Are you all right?" she said.

He didn't seem to hear her and she repeated the question. "All right?" he said. "Yes, yes, I'm all right."

"You don't look it. Get in, I'll run you back to the cottage."

"What?" He spoke, she thought, as though he was only half hearing what she was saying or only half listening. But she wanted to talk to him and she was not going to let the opportunity slip.

"Get in." She opened the passenger door. He came in and fog came in with him.

She drove slowly down the lane unable now to see more than five or ten yards.

"I went to Gracie's house," he said.

"So did I."

"I went to make sure it was all right."

"I thought the door was unlocked before."

"She kept a key under a flowerpot. We all knew where it was."

"So it was you who locked it." She stopped at the cottage gate. "I'll come in for a minute, if you don't mind. I want to talk to you about Gracie."

"I've been wondering when you'd come."

The fog was so thick now that from the car she could hardly see the cottage at all.

He stood in his living room as though it were her house and he was waiting for her to invite him to sit down.

"I've been to see Gracie," she said. "She's very unhappy."

"Poor Gracie." He went to the window and stared out at the fog. Then he said, "Alzheimer's is a terrible thing."

"Yes, it is, but she isn't suffering from it."

He turned to her frowning. "But I thought . . . I mean that's what was said."

"By whom?"

"Well, Ellen's said so a couple of times. I spoke to her earlier. She said a doctor had been to see Gracie and was sending her to Bridmoor. She said that Harold's suicide had affected her."

"I don't think there's anything the matter with Gracie except the slight confusion of old age. Her short-term memory seems good enough. And talking about doctors, she asked me a few days ago if I would be her doctor since hers had died."

"That's true. Old Doc Willis died some months ago."

"Well, it isn't possible for me to take her on since I have a London practice but there is nothing to stop me looking after her while I'm here. Or I hope there isn't because I'm damned if I'm going to let her stay there."

"What can you do?"

"I don't know. Stir things up. That's why she's there, I think, because I stirred things up, so if I stir them up again it may work the other way."

"You have stirred things up, you know. You've stirred up old bones that were buried long ago."

"I realize that. It's something I wasn't planning on. It just happened."

"You came and talked to me and I told you things and . . . I think I upset some people."

"People in this place get upset pretty easily."

He began to walk slowly up and down his room avoiding the piles of books on the floor without even looking at them. She watched him rub his hand over his mouth and then both hands together and she wondered if this was the way he behaved when he had to give a sermon.

"Lexton's always been a secret place," he said at last. "Right from the time those first Templars arrived in their cob from France. They were fugitives and wanted no one to investigate them; today we'd say they didn't want any publicity. So everything was cloaked in secrecy. And I suppose that's what the place has been like ever since. The tragedy of the erosion hasn't helped. It's been a closed town. A place you don't pass on the way to anywhere. It's the end of a road."

He went on pacing and she began to think that he had almost forgotten she was there. His eyes seemed to burn in the dead white face and he said harshly, "Even I don't know all the secrets. I know some, but I'm like a cuckolded spouse, the last to know others. Some people come to me in *extremis* because they think I represent God, but that's about all."

"And do you represent God?"

"In the way that Anglican priests do, I suppose." Suddenly he shook his head violently. "No, no, that won't do!"

His hand went up to his mouth again and he wiped it across his lips. Then he said, "This is why you've come, isn't it?"

"Why?"

"So that you can say I've left God's shadow. Well, I know that. I knew that a long time ago."

He began to pace up and down more rapidly now, his big frame casting huge shadows on the cottage walls.

"The real point . . . the absolute point . . . is that I bowed to the secrecy. No, not only bowed, but wanted it because I knew that whatever it might be, whatever I might discover, would change my life . . . No! That's not true! Yes, it is, but only up to a point. I suppose you do things for selfish reasons and my reasons were selfish. I wanted privacy. I was in love with someone and I wanted to marry her. That was what I wanted." He turned and made the same gesture with his hand. "There's a point where you can know too much. People don't like that . . . And one's ministry depends on being liked . . . Otherwise it means empty churches and empty hearts . . . "

He seemed to run out of words and Alex, embarrassed at his obvious unhappiness, said, "I've just come from Gracie. She wasn't in any state of shock about her brother's death. She wasn't even very fond of him."

"Oh? She never told me that."

"Gracie has been keeping her silence too. It's part of the secrecy you talk about, isn't it?"

"I suppose so. It depends what she was keeping silent about."

"Her brother. Or that may only be part of it. Now that she's in Bridmoor I think she feels she no longer has to keep quiet because she's ended up where she expected to end up only if she was guilty of talking."

"Poor Gracie," he said again. "She wasn't one of mine. I suppose she thought that one in the family was enough."

"Harold?"

"He was a very earnest Christian even as a boy."

"I heard him in the square. But Gracie

told me that to an extent he lived a lie his whole adult life. She says that when Sylvie was raped he cut and ran. She was at home when he arrived. She says he was untouched though he claimed to have fought on Sylvie's behalf. Then he let the police and the newspapers believe that too."

Maitland nodded slowly. "I didn't know that but it makes sense. That's what I mean about secrecy and about me only knowing some of the secrets. He came to me yesterday and he was *in extremis*. I've never seen him so overwrought."

"That's probably after he followed me to Bury. He must have seen me go into the newspaper library and guessed I was looking up what had happened all those years ago."

"He started talking about the old days. About Sylvie and himself. And then he began to cry and asked me if I would hear his confession and I said no I didn't hear confessions but if he wanted to tell me something and it would help him then he was to go ahead."

Maitland paused then and held up his

hand as though to stop her questioning him and said, "I'm only telling you this because he's dead now and it can't hurt him but it may help both of us to understand him. You see, when Sylvie killed herself we all thought it was because of the attack on her, but it wasn't. The real reason was because Harold wouldn't have her. That's what did it. She told him a couple of months later that she was pregnant by one of the men and he broke the engagement. No one knew that, of course, because she killed herself the following morning. But that's what he's been living with and that's what he was afraid you were looking for. His guilt was very deep and conflicted every day with his Christian beliefs. You just can't be a servant of God, a lay preacher, a devoted Christian — and have a past like that which you're keeping to yourself."

"But he'd lived with it for years."

"Only because no one knew. And when he told me, when he 'confessed' to me, he already knew what he was going to do. He must have had the rope ready and he must have had it all planned out."

"But didn't Sylvie's family know?"

"She didn't have a family, only a brother, and he was away at sea."

★ ★ ★

It was dusk when Alex got back to the boat. She had stayed with Bill Maitland for another hour. There had been moments when she thought he was going to break down completely and she had comforted him as best she could. All the time she watched him and saw his burning eyes and white face she knew that underneath that first layer of information about Harold Potter and his rejection of Sylvie were other layers, and other secrets, which he was not going to share with her. She realized this when she saw how close to the edge he had reached.

By the time she left him she was still feeling bruised from her meeting with Gracie but added to that was the energy she had spent on him. So as she crossed the road bridge and saw the boat and thought of Mike, her spirits rose. She realized that *Osprey* was much higher in the water than when she had left. Then she saw that the creek itself was almost to the top of its banks and remembered that the forecast had been for very high tides.

The rain was still coming down in sheets and she ran to the boat and climbed aboard. She was nearly thrown off the gangplank for *Osprey* was jerking at the moorings like an animal.

"My God," she said as she came into the saloon. "There's a real storm blowing up."

Mike was sitting in one of he swivel chairs at the chart table and said, "I've doubled the mooring ropes. We'll be all right here."

She took her wet coat off and put it away and as she did so she noticed that on the table, half hidden by his shoulders, were the packets of musk. Next to them was a pad with columns of figures on it. She frowned. She didn't like what she was seeing.

She dropped into one of the other chairs and said innocently, "What are you up to?"

"Just doing my sums. I'm working out what happens if we can't stay here. I'll have to have another try at getting a mooring in the river."

"It's only Chris Cottis stopping you, isn't it? I mean, surely it's a public waterway?"

"I don't know. But what I have found out is that the whole fishing industry here is owned by Spender. He might have riparian rights on the river frontage just as Mrs Blackhurst owns the creek. So I'll ask him. The thing is I'm not going up the coast to Hallows or anywhere else. I don't want to be sailing twelve miles through stormy seas like that man Howarth was doing when he was drowned."

She had never heard Mike talk like this. There was the faintest edge of defeat in his tone.

"What's brought this on?" she said.

"Remember what we said when we came back from Potter's house? That Lexton mightn't be the place for me? Well, it might just be true."

This is what she had subconsciously been hoping for, she realized, an end to Mike's absurd adventure. Yet now that she heard him hint at it, other thoughts rushed in: if he wasn't going to carry out his plans, what was he going to do? The memory of him day after day in her flat during the bad times came back to her.

"So what are you thinking of?" she said.

He flicked the pad. "Just working out what I might get for the boat if I sold it."

She opened her mouth to speak then let the breath escape silently. She had realized why the musk was there: he was putting that into the equation too. The boat plus the musk.

Quickly she said, "It's the weather and poor old Harold Potter that's made you feel like this. When the sun shines again we'll both feel better and we'll find a way."

"Sure."

It was said without passion, simply a flat reactive answer. He threw down his pen and said, "What about Gracie?"

She told him about the damp, foul-smelling home into which Gracie had been unwillingly placed.

"And you think you can get her out?"

"I don't know, but I'm going to have a damn good try. I've dealt with cases of Alzheimer's and I'm pretty certain she isn't one. The only thing that bothers me is that her secrets, if you can call them secrets, don't seem important enough to send someone to what is really a kind of imprisonment. All she told me was that her brother had lied about his involvement — or his non-involvement — in the attack on Sylvie. To quote your good self, who really cares after all these years?"

He put down his pen. "I remember something that Laddie Broakes once said to me. He said, 'Just remember we're putting together jigsaw puzzles but we don't know what the pieces look like till we find them.' And he said the people with bits of information often didn't even know they had them. So what I'm saying is that this bit that Gracie has about her brother just might be important if we can link it with another piece."

She heard the word 'we' for the first time and smiled cynically to herself. It was far too late for that. There was no 'we'. There was no anything. She was going to get Gracie out and that was that. Then she was going on holiday somewhere nice and if Mike decided to stay on here and found a mooring, well, that would be a set of circumstances she would face in the months to come. It was the immediate future that was engaging her. And the immediate future was Gracie.

"What are you going to do about Gracie?" he said. "Kidnap her?"

"I'll go and see Mrs Blackhurst tomorrow. Gracie says it was her doing. There's the whole business of this Dr Morris. He's not Gracie's doctor, or at least she says he isn't. And he was taken to her by the local policeman."

"Somers?"

"That's what she says. Can that be right? I've never heard of it."

"Not unless there's a court order. No copper is going to take a doctor round to someone like that. He'd be suspended instantly."

"Well, she says that's how it happened and until someone tells me something different I believe her."

"OK, fine. There's another thing. While you were away I was thinking about something you showed me. You know, that basin where the boats turn.

Well, I began to wonder — if someone like Chris could get ashore there then why not — "

The phone rang. Mike listened for a moment and then said, "Hello, guv'nor, how are you?" He put his hand over the mouthpiece and whispered, "Laddie Broakes," then turned back to the phone. "Yes, I got your message and I phoned but you weren't in."

Alex went into the bedroom. The talk of Gracie had made her uneasy. What if the old dear *was* mentally ill? She went over their conversation in her mind and could find nothing that pointed too solidly to that. And as she went over it she again got a picture of Gracie going down on her knees and grasping her round the legs, pleading to be taken away. It was pitiful. Well . . . she'd have her out tomorrow, or at least she'd try. She'd go and see Mrs Blackhurst and . . . but why leave it until tomorrow? Why not go now? Then she could get things moving and get Gracie out and she'd be free to fly away to wherever she wanted.

She went back to the saloon. Mike was

sitting back in the swivel chair with a faint frown on his face as he listened to the rumbling of the voice from the other end. She put on her coat and waved at him. He hardly seemed to see her, then as she was turning away he raised his hand and waved goodbye.

It was dark now and the rain was still coming down. She decided not to walk up to the house but got into the car instead. She turned and drove up the hill. All she could see of the house was a massive black shape.

28

ON Alex's trip to America with Freddy they had gone, between race meetings, poker sessions, and crap shooting, to Hearst's Castle at San Simeon. It had been on a wild and stormy day and she was reminded of it now as she drove up to Lexton House. The Californian road had been steep and windswept but at least it had not been muddy. This one was, and as the drive wheels slipped and the car lurched she became ever more regretful of coming at all. What was she going to say? How was she going to interfere with the arrangements of someone like Ellen Blackhurst who had lived here most of her life and who knew the right people? And yet she had to interfere because her mind kept going back to Gracie in the same room as the birdlike woman and she knew she couldn't leave her there.

The house was mostly in darkness though she could see several lighted windows. There was also an outbuilding near the cliff edge which was lit. The car heaved over large undulations in the driveway and in the headlights she saw that the ground had been twisted as though by an earthquake.

She got out of the car and was nearly blown off her feet. The wind up on the cliff top was powerful and she could hear the roar of the surf below as it thundered into the base of the cliffs, and taste the salt in the air. She bent her head and made for the front door of the house and almost immediately her right foot went down into a fissure in the ground and she toppled forward onto her hands and knees.

"Oh, damn!" she said out loud.

The fall changed her attitude. She was feeling sore and damp and emotionally drained and abruptly she was filled with a compensating anger. Any feeling of apprehension or anxiety was swept away.

Hands gripped her. "I can help," a voice said. The hands were under her arms and pulling her upright. She tried to fight them off, but they were strong. She twisted her head and looked up into

Dommie's rain-streaked face.

"I'm all right," she said.

"I can help," he repeated. "I help Grannie."

"That's good," she said, and withdrew her foot from the fissure.

He held her arm with his left hand and offered his right in greeting. "Dommie," he said.

"Hello, Dommie."

He kept his grip on her hand and arm and began pulling her towards the outbuilding. "Putting pictures in my books," he said.

She pulled against him. "Dommie, I'm going to see your grannie."

"See my books."

She tried to prise his fingers from her arm but they were too powerful. "Not now, Dommie. I'd love to see them later when I've talked to your grannie."

"Want to show books."

The door was to their right. The place was brightly lit. It might be better than arguing with him out here, she thought.

"All right, I'll come and look at your picture books, then I'll go and see your grannie."

They went into the outbuilding. It was sparsely furnished with a table and chairs and an easel on which there was a blackboard. There was a range of walking sticks hanging on special hooks on the old walls. Dommie was dressed, in spite of the weather, in a short-sleeved shirt which was now wet from the rain and seemingly moulded onto his powerful torso.

"Grannie's in Grandfather's room."

"Oh?" Alex ran her hands through her hair, taking out some of the rainwater. "What's Grandfather's room?"

"Dunno."

She wondered how long to stay and thought a few more minutes might do it. She looked at the blackboard and saw squiggly lines of yellow and blue chalk and said, "What are you drawing, Dommie?"

"Fish."

"That's what I thought. It's very beautiful." Then she saw at the top of the board in white capital letters the words OMMIE'S CASTLE.

"Is this your castle?" she said.

"My castle," Dommie said.

He was standing very close to her and his strange slightly slanted eyes were half closed against the bright light. He was looking at her breasts.

She closed her coat. "Did you write it?" she said, and moved slightly towards the door.

"Grannie."

"Oh, your grannie wrote it."

She took another step.

"Wouldn't your grannie have written it D-ommie? That's O-mmie."

She saw that if she got to the blackboard she would be more than halfway to the door. The anger she had felt a few minutes ago began to be replaced by an empty feeling of apprehension. She picked a piece of white chalk from the table and went to the blackboard. The door wasn't far now.

"Look, I'll add the D," she said, and wrote it to match the other printing.

"No!" Dommie wrenched the chalk from her. He scored it over the D, then rubbed out the mess. "Dommie," he said.

He had somehow got between her and

the door and she tried to move round him. He moved too.

"I think it's time I went to see your grannie." Her feet grated on the flagstoned floor as she moved towards the door. "Won't you draw something for me?" she said. "What do you draw, Dommie?"

"Cows." He tapped the blackboard squiggles. "Cows."

"Oh, yes, I see, cows."

His face had changed from the simple face of a young man to a face she had not seen before. It seemed twisted like the ground outside.

"Fish," he said.

"That's right. Cows and fish. I see them. They're very beautiful."

He moved quickly and took a silver-headed cane from the walls. She thought, "Oh God, he's going to hit me," and stumbled backwards, holding up her arms.

But he simply held out the stick to her. She couldn't grasp what was happening for a moment and then she said, "For me?"

"Stick," he said.

470

He pushed it at her. He was holding it horizontally and she felt it against her breasts.

"It's a lovely stick, Dommie, but I — "

"Stick," he said pushing it at her again.

Abruptly she thought of the woman who had had a fish pushed down her throat by Dommie and she knew what he wanted. The stick was payment in advance.

"I'm going to see your grannie now," she said. "And when I come out I'll take your stick."

"No," Dommie said.

"You'll see. I won't be long. I'll just talk to her for a moment and then I'll come back and" — he was still pushing her backwards — "and we'll play some games, just the two of us."

He was scowling at her, his face very close. Abruptly his expression changed into a smile. "Games? Play games?"

"Oh, yes, Dommie. Lovely games."

"Promise?"

"Yes, I promise and — "

"Dommie!" A voice came from the doorway. "Stop that now!"

Dommie was still pinning her with the

stick. She looked over his shoulder and saw Frank Spender in the doorway.

"That's enough, Dommie! Grannie wants you."

"Games," Dommie said.

"Not now," Spender said.

Dommie turned back to Alex. "You promised."

"That's right, Dommie. I promised. And we will."

Dommie relaxed the stick.

"Go to Grannie!" Spender's words were cold and hard.

Dommie shook hands with Alex and then with Spender and went out into the gale.

"Are you all right?" Spender said.

"I'm fine, but glad to see you. I'm a little nervous with Dommie."

He came slowly into the room. She remembered him the last time she had seen him, which was in the pub. There he had been the same person she had originally met when the Chinese man had been found and he had arrived in his big motor cruiser. Now he seemed different. His face was set, his eyes were cold and his iron-grey hair was held down by a tweed cap. Some of the good looks seemed to have vanished and he looked older.

Alex said, "I came to see Mrs Blackhurst, and Dommie wanted to show me his picture books."

"What did you want to see Mrs Blackhurst about?"

She was caught off guard by the question. "Oh, just . . . " then she collected herself. "I'm afraid that's private."

"If it's about the use of her mooring, she's already told you she wants you to leave."

There was no hint now of his earlier friendliness and Alex felt her anger begin to return. She was about to tell him it was no business of his until she remembered that Mike was going to ask him about a mooring in the river.

"Mr Spender, we have to moor somewhere."

"Not here. You were told." There was an echo there of Chris Cottis's voice talking to Mike.

"Well, where do people moor when they come here?"

"They don't."

"What about the river? I know Mike was going to come to see you about that."

"Why me?"

"Because your fishing company owns the rights."

He paused then said, "How did you find that out?"

"I asked."

"You've been asking a great many questions."

"And getting very few answers."

"Why should you get any answers at all? This isn't your territory."

The phrase was sophisticated yet the voice that said it was full of the drawn-out vowels of the Suffolk coast.

He went on, "Anyway, there's no room in the river for more boats."

She decided to be less aggressive. "Look, Mr Spender, we didn't come here to try to muscle in on the fishing or take anything away from anyone. What Mike Harley is trying to do is start a new business, diving on Old Lexton. Nothing to do with fishing. And if the fishing's so bad at least you'd have his boat on the river and it would mean rental for moorings."

He gave a dry laugh. "A few measly quid!"

"But better than no measly quid."

"Are you being funny?"

"Not at all, I'm just — Oh my God . . . !"

He had come closer as she spoke and now he was standing next to the blackboard and her eyes had flicked across to it and a thought had come so powerfully that she felt her breath go.

"Yes?" he said.

She shook her head, trying to unlock her mouth and throat.

"Go on."

She whispered to herself rather than to him, "It's Gracie!"

"What about Gracie?"

"She knows something and she's been put away."

"There's nothing Gracie knows about moorings."

She hardly heard him. "But she doesn't even know what it is she knows or why she's been put away."

"I told you, Gracie's got damn all to do — "

"But I think I know what it is! And it's got nothing to do with her brother or the rape or the body she says she found."

"I don't know what the hell you're talking about."

"I'm talking about what Gracie has seen out of her window. I'm talking about 'little people' and 'eat'."

"You're mad!"

"Not at all. Because I've seen what Gracie saw. Not all of it but I've seen the lorry." She was talking rapidly almost feverishly. She hardly registered that Spender was in the room, he was just a figure to concentrate on and communicate to. Dommie would have done just as well. "Listen . . . you know how it is when someone draws the silhouette of a face in a few disconnected lines? You, the viewer, connect them and complete the drawing in your head."

"It's time you went."

"Look at the blackboard. That's what I should have noticed right away. What do the words on the top say?"

"For Christ's sake, you — "

476

"No, read them to me."

"They say DOMMIE'S CASTLE, of course."

"No they don't. They say OMMIE'S CASTLE. You've put in the D in your head. And that's what I did. I saw the lorry in the reeds near Gracie's house. It had a notice on the side. I can't remember it completely but it said it was selling meat, fish, and poultry to the catering trade. Except it didn't say 'meat', it said 'eat'. The letter M had fallen off. I just corrected it in my mind. But Gracie didn't."

"Go on." Now there was a different tone in his voice but Alex didn't hear it. She was so febrile and her own train of thought was racing at such speed that she might have been explaining it to Mike.

"All right, so what did Gracie see? Gracie saw 'little people'. Why not Hong Kong Chinese? They're small. And she saw them in the early morning getting into the lorry that had come to pick them up."

He nodded slowly. "Yes, I can see how you could think that. But you'd be wrong. Chinese don't just appear in the

North Sea to be picked up by fishing boats."

"Not by fishing boats, by one boat. Chris Cottis's boat. And the Chinese come in ships with special holds built to accommodate them. At night one of the fishing boats meets the ship and takes off the Chinese. Then they're landed upstream of the village where there's a turning basin, and a lorry takes them south and they disappear into London's Chinatown. But the other night something went wrong. One of the Chinese was stabbed and ended up down there in the creek."

"Well, well. You really have been busy. I thought your boyfriend wasn't in the police any longer."

"He's not. He's interested, that's all."

"Fine. Good. So he's not going to be a problem."

"Problem? Why should you — Oh God, wait a minute . . . " It was only then that she realized what she had been saying and to whom. "It's not Chris Cottis, is it? He's not the head man." A few moments earlier all the facts that had been just under the surface of her mind had come bursting out like oil from a gusher. Now she caught herself and said softly, "What does that mean, that Mike's not going to be a problem?"

Spender said, "Well, he doesn't know, does he? It's obvious you've only just put things together."

"I can't answer for what Mike knows or doesn't know."

"Bullshit. If he knew he'd have discussed it with you."

She was suddenly afraid. "Look, Mr Spender, I didn't come here to talk to you about this. I came to see Mrs Blackhurst and tell her I couldn't allow her to put Gracie into Bridmoor."

"What are you really saying?"

"I'm saying that Gracie is not mentally ill."

"But she's seen illegal immigrants being landed. You also said that, didn't you?"

"Yes, I did."

"And now what're you saying?"

"That it isn't my business what she sees. It's not what I came for. It has nothing to do with either Mike or myself." She cringed internally as she heard herself saying this.

"Let me tell you something." Spender's voice was harsh and full of anger. "I came from nothing. Just a common fisherman. Now, as you say, I practically own this place and I've got other assets in London and the Far East. I'm no longer a common fisherman like Chris or the others. Lucky, that's what they say about me. But it isn't luck. It's hard work and it's taking care of things when they go wrong. And you think I'd take a chance on some nosy couple who come up here and start asking questions? Don't make me bloody laugh!"

"Look, Mr Spender — "

"Keep your mouth shut. I'm tired of listening to you."

He had been talking so fast she had not realized he had closed the gap between them and now he grabbed her.

"You stupid fucking bitch, you think you can come here and ruin me. Jesus!"

He had pushed her back against the wall. She clawed at him but he was stringy and powerful and his arms were longer than hers.

"You came here to the house . . . " he said. "You parked your car . . . you

480

weren't sure which way to go to the front door . . . you came too near the cliff edge . . . and the wind was blowing a gale . . . That's what they'll say . . . "

"Mike's on his way! He'll be here in a few moments!"

"It only takes a few moments to go over the edge — and with that sea running . . . !"

She felt one of Dommie's sticks hanging on the wall behind her and scrabbled for it. He saw her. He wrenched it from her hands and broke it across his knee. "You must think I'm bloody stupid," he said. This time he caught her right arm and twisted it behind her back. She yelled out in pain.

"Games?" Dommie was in the doorway. "Games now?"

"Fuck off!" Spender shouted. "Go on! Get out!"

"Games," Dommie said again and came towards them.

"Dommie, help me!" Alex shouted. "Dommie, he's going to kill me!"

Dommie was laughing. He stood in front of them, not allowing Spender to pass.

"Get out of the way, you dim-witted bastard!"

But Dommie danced about in front of them, preventing them from leaving the building.

"Go and get Grannie!" Alex shouted.

But Dommie didn't seem to comprehend. "Playing games," he said.

"Get out of the bloody way," Spender shouted, and threw the pieces of the stick at him.

For a second Alex thought Dommie might react to the stick but it was as though he had not registered it. Instead he went on dancing in front of them and once more shouted, "Playing games!"

And that was the last thing he ever said for as he spoke there was a deep rumbling as though a volcano or earthquake had suddenly come to Suffolk. The rumbling grew louder and Alex looked at the doorway through which Dommie had just come and it seemed to melt away against the dark night. Spender dropped her arm and began to run towards the huge hole in the wall where the door had been. Dommie, laughing and dancing, held him back as though in a waltz.

The hole was growing larger and larger until most of the wall had gone and then the building seemed to rock and shake and there was a roar as bricks and flints came down in a great avalanche.

Everything moved sideways. Alex fell. As she did so the stone-flagged floor moved sideways too. Part of it split and she fell through a shallow opening and lay amidst dust and old human bones and acrid smells. And then the roof came down on top of her.

★ ★ ★

Mike Harley put down the phone. He had been talking to Laddie Broakes for half an hour and what he had heard had caused a large upheaval in his thought processes.

"Alex," he called. She did not reply. He went into the cabin and only then dimly remembered her waving to him and saying she was going up to the Blackhursts' house. He couldn't remember why, even if he had known, but surmised that it had something to do with Gracie, since Alex seemed obsessed about her. He went out on deck, still churning with an unfamiliar excitement, and looked up at the dark outline of Lexton House. It sat on its cliff, a black mass against the cloudy moon. In the gale that was blowing it was easy to imagine it as a Templar castle, a small Krak perhaps, out of place and out of time.

He was irritated that Alex wasn't in *Osprey*, for what he had to tell her would change everything. He stood on deck for a few moments longer. The rain had stopped but the wind still howled and the clouds were racing past. At that moment they opened, showing a full moon, and at that moment too the house on the cliff changed shape. It was as though he was looking at the dark silhouette of a huge sandcastle which was suddenly partially eaten away by waves on the beach. It took him some seconds to realize what it was he had seen, for the reality was so unfamiliar and so shocking that he couldn't take it in. But he knew at the end of those few seconds that the shape of the house had altered because part of it had collapsed. As the truth sunk in he began to run. He ran with one knee stiff giving him a kind of sailor's roll. He ran to the car and drove fiercely up the slippery road and when he got to the top he witnessed the enormity of what had happened.

Of the house itself only half remained. In the moonlight he could see that the end closest to the cliff edge had collapsed and part had dropped away into the churning sea below. What was left reminded him of newsreels and pictures he had seen of London's bomb damage in World War II. Rooms had simply been split. Wallpaper strips blew in the wind. Carpets hung like dark waterfalls still held to floorboards at one end of a room but not at the other, for those floorboards had vanished. Dust rose from the inside of the wrecked rooms only to be blown away the moment it came above the broken walls. A heavy Aga cooker lay on its side with oil running from a broken pipe. A fridge had burst open and food lay in the mud. There was a smell of central-heating oil in the air.

"Alex!" Mike yelled. "Alex!"

He ran into the part of the house that survived. Doors had been wrenched off their hinges, floors were canted, walls

485

leaned inwards. He knew he might only have minutes before the remainder of the house either collapsed where it was or more of the cliff was gnawed away by the sea and it went down into the waves.

"Alex!"

The wind was gale force and his shout was whipped away. He thought he heard a voice. He went deeper into the morass of fallen pictures and bricks and cupboards and papers and ornaments and chairs and tables.

"Alex!"

He heard it again. A faint cry.

"I'm coming! I'm coming!"

He clambered over a settee that had ended against a doorway and entered a room where books were spread on the floor in jumbled piles and bookcases lay upended. He saw someone.

"I'm here," he said. "I'm here."

Ellen Blackhurst said, "My leg's crushed. I can't move."

"I'll help you."

Part of a wall had come down on her. Mike clawed at the bricks and woodwork but there was no way he could move enough. Ellen was whimpering in pain. He could see dark stains on her face and realized it must be blood.

"I'll phone for help," he said. "Where's Alex?"

The voice was weak. "I think . . . she's outside . . . in Dommie's room . . . "

"Right. I'll be back."

He ran to the outbuilding. "Alex!" he shouted again.

Most of it had collapsed but the rear end, furthest from the cliff, still stood. He saw a coat he recognized.

"Alex!"

He found her. She was lying in a hollow. Her face was resting next to another face, that one a skull. Her teeth were almost touching its teeth. A heavy wooden beam had come down and was pinning her to the collection of bones. And then he made out the most bizarre thing of all. In the hollow was a pair of old and perished tennis shoes. She was covered in dust and mud and, he realized, the same dark stains that covered Ellen Blackhurst. He felt for a pulse and found it.

"It's all right, my darling," he said to

her unconscious body. "I'll look after you."

He ran to the car and phoned emergency services and then went back to the ruins to hold her hand.

29

"GOOD morning, Dr Kennedy, all ready to go?"

The nurse came into Alex's room and closed the door. She was, Alex thought, a few years younger than herself, yet her whole demeanour seemed to suggest she was older and wiser.

"All set," Alex said.

The nurse was small and short and had a northern accent and might have sounded just a shade too fierce except for the fact that she had a round face and wore a constant smile. She checked the strapping on Alex's chest and then the bandage on her foot.

"Have they given you a crutch?" she said. "Oh, yes, there it is. You probably won't need it after a few days." She talked all the while she was examining Alex and then said, "You'll do for someone a house fell on. Are you being picked up?"

"Mr Harley's coming. He should be here any minute. Have you heard from

Mrs Blackhurst's doctor? I really would like to see her before I leave."

"Oh, yes, sorry, I forgot. He says she's strong enough now. But she'll make the decision."

"And has she?"

"I'll go and ask her."

Alex settled herself back in the chair. She was dressed, her bag was packed, all she had to do now was wait. But waiting had become a problem for her. She did not like being alone, just as she had not liked it after her parents had been killed. Hannah had known that and had spent much of the first few months in the same room. Now she wanted Mike.

She had wanted him with her from the moment she had regained consciousness in the ambulance — and he'd been there, holding her hand. In fact he had not even released it when they got to Bury General Hospital, and when she was wheeled into casualty he had walked beside the stretcher, still holding it. They had almost had to prise his fingers from her. She had floated in and out of consciousness then, but each time she came to he was beside her.

At first when the cliff had eroded and pulled down Dommie's castle she had thought it was a dream. Then for a brief moment she had known it was reality: that the skeleton she was lying on was composed of real human bones; that the bodies of Dommie and Spender which she could see in front of her were real bodies, and that both were crushed beyond saving. She remembered Mike fighting to get the beam off her and his knee giving way and not being able to manage it and then the fire brigade arriving with cutting tools and slicing the beam up and pulling away the masonry. And one of them had said, "She was only saved because she fell into a grave." And then she remembered the paramedics in the ambulance and Mike hanging on to her hand.

She had no idea what had happened to Ellen Blackhurst, indeed she had not thought of her until she had been lying in her hospital room. It was then Mike told her that she had been badly crushed and was in the same hospital having a leg amputated.

That had been three days before, and

491

now Alex was up and moving and Mrs Blackhurst had lost a leg and two people were dead.

There was a knock on the door and Mike put his head round. "Hi. How're the ribs?"

"They're much better."

He kissed her on the lips. "You're looking better."

"I'm feeling better."

The nurse was back. "Mrs Blackhurst's OK at the moment. She says she wants to see you."

They went along the corridor, Alex hobbling on one leg. Her right foot was swollen to such an extent that with the bandages it looked like a football.

Ellen Blackhurst looked very small in the large bed. There was a bed cradle where part of her right leg had been. Her hair was almost white against the pillow. She said, "I wanted to see you to say how sorry I am that you were hurt."

"I'm very lucky only to have a few cracked ribs and some bruises," Alex said. "You're the one who's suffered. You and Dommie. How are you feeling today?"

"Oh, I'm fine for a one-legged septuagenarian."

Her voice was stronger than Alex had anticipated and she said, "Do you feel able to talk for a little while? There are some things I'd like to get straight, and this is possibly the last chance I'll have for some time."

"That's what I'm going to have now, lots of time. The police have already been in, and they'll be occupying a great deal of it to start with. But I'm going to have a lot of time. I'll have to learn to walk again, of course."

"That takes time," Mike said.

"I won't have Dommie now. He took up a lot of time. I mind and yet I'm glad. I mind for selfish reasons but the stronger emotion is thankfulness. It happened quickly, didn't it? I mean for him?"

"Oh, yes. In an instant." Alex was lying, she didn't know, but she said it anyway.

"I couldn't have asked for anything better. One minute alive . . . "

"And dancing. He was dancing then."

" . . . alive and dancing. The next

gone. And now he's safe."

There was a knock at the door and Bill Maitland came in. "I can come back later," he said. He was dressed in a jacket and tie, which made him look strange, Alex thought.

"Don't be silly, Bill, take the other chair." She turned to Mike and Alex. "He was with me just before they operated and still there when I came round. Isn't he a dear man?" She turned back to Maitland. "Dr Kennedy was just telling me how Dommie went. It was all over in a moment. Isn't that wonderful?"

Maitland had been looking unhappy since he had come into the room and now said, "Yes, Ellen. Marvellous."

"Bill's going to help me walk again. And he's found me a cottage on the river. So I'm going to be all right provided the police don't want their pound of flesh. A man called Brady came to see me. I can't say I liked him much."

"He's been to see me too," Alex said. "I'll come to the point. Did you know Frank Spender was smuggling illegal immigrants into the country?"

"I knew he was smuggling something.

494

You don't get as rich as Frank in the fishing business, not these days. I thought it might be wines and spirits from France. That was always the cargo in the old days, wasn't it?"

Mike said, "It's drugs and people now."

"Well, at least it wasn't drugs," Ellen said. "I wouldn't have stood for that, not after . . . well, not after what happened here . . . " She didn't mention Gilly's name but the three of them knew what she meant. "Who was he bringing in? Pakistanis and Indians?"

"Hong Kong Chinese."

"Isn't it strange — the French Templars were smuggled in. And after them some of the Huguenots came through Lexton. And many of the French aristocrats who were running away from the Revolution. Now it's the Hong Kong people . . . "

"That was a Templar sarcophagus that saved me, wasn't it?" Alex said. Maitland nodded. "But they weren't Templars' bones."

Ellen turned slightly in pain and then said, "No, they were the bones of poor Tommy Lee, Dommie's father."

495

"How did they get into the sarcophagus?" Alex said.

Maitland half rose and said, "I don't think Mrs Blackhurst needs to answer any more questions."

But she held up a hand and said, "Why not? I've told the police. You see, I didn't know myself until after John was killed. Then, when I was going through his papers, I found one of those *To whom it may concern* letters tucked away in his desk. He liked to have things written down. His army training, I suppose."

"Ellen, this isn't the time for — " Maitland said.

"Hang on, Bill, these people have suffered too. And so has Gracie, for that matter." She looked at Alex. "I must tell you I didn't know Frank was going to have her sent to Bridmoor. As far as I was concerned that was always just a threat to get her to keep her mouth shut. You see, if something had happened to me, if I'd been arrested by the police, who would have looked after Dommie?"

"I'm going to get her out today," Alex said.

496

"Poor Gracie. She was involved right from the very beginning, you know."

"Because she was Harold's sister?" Alex said.

"You know about the rape?"

"Yes, I've been reading about it."

"Frank said he was sure you'd found out. Harold went to him, you know, before he killed himself. He told him you were investigating the old business."

"He came to me too," Bill said. "He was in the most dreadful state."

"Well, it all goes back to that time," Ellen said. "If you've read up about the rape I won't repeat the details, but nothing you could have read will tell you how Lexton felt. The people here felt badly cheated that no one was ever going to face charges. I mean those men were just let go. The worst affected, of course, were Harold and Frank."

"You mean Frank Spender?"

"Sylvie was his sister. He was very bitter."

"I'd never been able to discover who she was. Neither Gracie nor Harold would talk about her."

"Bill's told me about Harold's last visit

to him. It's not surprising he wouldn't talk to you. And Gracie wouldn't because I'd told her not to." She paused then said, "Now you must jump more than fifteen years to a time when Tommy Lee came to Lexton. Bill tells me he's told you about Tommy and you've probably read up on him too. But what you don't know is that my husband John saw him raping our daughter Gilly. That's what it says in his *To whom* letter. I don't believe it. I believe he spied on them and saw them making love down on the beach. Gilly had reached a point where she wouldn't have cared what he saw. She was on drugs by then. You knew that?"

"No, I didn't," Alex said.

"Well, she was. So was Tommy, I think. Anyway, I took her to London in an effort to get her away from Tommy and while we were gone John got Harold and Frank to help him 'try' Tommy."

"Try him? How do you mean?"

"Court-martial him. For rape. John promised Frank and Harold the chance to get some justice — his word — for what had happened to Sylvie. They brought

Tommy up to the house and 'tried' him for rape, and found him guilty of course, and then John flogged him. He writes in the letter that he used a knotted rope. But he went too far. He killed him. He said in the letter he believed Tommy died of a heart attack. But even if he did it occurred during or after the flogging. There's not much point in even wondering about that now. The real point is he died. Then the three of them got into Harold's boat and took Tommy out to sea and threw him overboard and made it look as though he'd had a fishing accident. For that John gave Harold and Frank five thousand pounds each — Harold bought his own little house with the money and Frank got started in business. But that wasn't the end of it."

Alex said, "Tommy Lee's body floated back."

"Yes, he came back. Whatever they'd tied on to him wasn't good enough, and he was brought in by the current they call the Herringstream. That's the one that brought the Chinese man in. So John and the others put him in that old sarcophagus in what became Dommie's castle. John had always known it was there under the flagstones. There was never anything in it, though there may have been long ago."

Mike said, "And that's when Gracie saw him, when he floated into the creek."

"She saw the marks of the flogging on his back and John said he had been fishing and must have fallen overboard and that they were made by rocks. But then he said how would Gracie like to have a house of her own — her father was ill in those days — so we bought a cottage and let her live there rent free. She knew there was something strange, of course, but John said Gilly would be upset enough to kill herself if she knew Tommy was drowned, so they were going to bury him elsewhere and Gracie must keep her mouth shut. Well, she knew that Gilly had overdosed once before after a love affair had gone wrong, so she did keep her mouth shut. She went on working for us for years and we looked after her and then when she retired she still had her house."

"But she became a bit confused, didn't she?" Alex said.

"A bit. And she began talking about the old times. Not that there was much she could say. I mean, she had seen a body washed ashore in the Sixties. Who would believe her now?"

Alex said, "Except now another body was washed ashore and we arrived and began asking questions and looking up old newspaper stories. And then we met Gracie who did know something. She knew about the illegal immigrants being smuggled in — but didn't know she knew."

"You'll have to explain that," Ellen said, and Alex did. Then she went on, "And I got so foolishly excited when I realized this that I told the one person I shouldn't have told."

"Frank?"

She told them what had happened. Their faces became grimmer. "It's ironic but the fact that the building collapsed probably saved my life."

She waited for Ellen to comment and finally she did. "A long time ago I loved Frank as much as I could love anyone. Oh, Bill knows this only too well. And I've loved him over all these years even though there hasn't been anything between us for a long time. So I hear what you're saying and part of me believes it, for Frank was a very hard man, but part of me still says . . . " She turned again in pain and said, "I think that's enough for now."

But Alex hadn't finished and said, "He implied that the man Howarth — "

Maitland said, "I think that's all. Mrs Blackhurst is exhausted and she's in pain." He got up and stood in front of Alex, blotting out, with his big body, the woman in the bed.

★ ★ ★

As they were driving back to the coast Alex said, "If Bill Maitland hadn't come we could have stayed a bit longer."

"Maybe it's better we didn't. She's pretty weak."

"Not too weak to side with Spender. My God, when you think about it! Do you believe her about what was in that letter of her husband's?"

"Sure. It was one way of guaranteeing Spender and Harold Potter wouldn't talk because they were as guilty as he was. It's called conspiracy."

"Well, she wouldn't either. She covered things up!"

"Why not? Tommy Lee was dead. So were her husband and daughter. All she had was Dommie. And what would have happened to him if she'd gone to prison for — oh, I don't know — but something like perverting the course of justice? He'd have had to go into an institution."

They drove on for a while and then she said, "Mrs Blackhurst doesn't believe me about Spender, you know."

"I think she does. I saw her face. She probably just wasn't letting on to us. Don't forget she said she'd been in love with him. Probably had an affair."

"Even so . . . "

He put out his hand and covered hers. "Don't forget, he's the one who's dead."

"I know. But, oh God, it was close."

"Are you going to do anything about it?"

"I've told Brady everything I know. He was a bit better this time, probably because you weren't with me."

503

"What's he going to do about Chris? The trouble is we've no proof that he was bringing in the illegal immigrants."

"I told Brady what we thought and he said he was going to look into it."

"Did you tell him about the attack on the boat?"

"Which one?"

"Not the first. If that wasn't Dommie then it was my fault. I might not have tied her up as well as I thought. No, the second. When I was hit. I'm pretty sure that was Chris. Look, this is my scenario: Chris Cottis brings those Chinese off the *Wilhelmina* on Spender's orders. Clearly he's been working for him. One of them has the musk. It's what's going to support him financially. But it looks to everyone else like drugs. So someone goes for him, another Chinese, trying to steal the stuff. The first one goes overboard with the musk but he's already been stabbed. He comes to the buoys over Old Lexton. It's foggy. He wraps the packages round the buoy cable and hangs on himself. Then he dies. His body floats out to sea on the tides and is then picked up by this current they talk about and

504

brought into the creek. But Chris has seen the stabbing and he's also seen what he thinks are drugs. He goes to look for them. Sees *Osprey* out there, almost runs us down, thinks we've found the drugs and comes to look for them. I turn up — and bang! I get it on the head. How does that sound?"

"Perfectly plausible."

"So did you tell Brady about the burglary?"

"No. Because I would have had to talk about your other theory. The Triads."

He looked slightly shamefaced. "You know those Japanese people you saw with Spender? Well, they weren't Japanese and they weren't Triads, they were Taiwanese."

"Spender told me he had business interests in the Far East, so that fits. Go left here."

Bridmoor came up within half a mile and Mike opened the gates and drove up to the nursing home.

"They said she'd be ready when we came," Alex said.

They had said more than that. When Alex had phoned from the hospital she had used her General Medical Council voice and the superintendent of Bridmoor had been unctuously cooperative. "Oh, Dr Kennedy, we've given her her own room. And don't worry, she'll be ready."

When Alex had mentioned this to Mike he had said, "It's no wonder she was glad to get rid of Gracie. Don't forget her boss is dead and she must be wondering who is going to pay her salary. She'd probably give you them all if you asked for them."

Gracie was sitting in the foyer with her suitcase beside her. Alex hobbled to fetch her and Mike took the suitcase.

"You'll be home in a few minutes," Alex said.

Gracie was hurrying to the car and gave not the slightest indication of hearing. She opened the door and got into the back. Alex hobbled up and said, "Mike's bought you food and lit the stove so the house'll be warm."

She might have been talking to a wall for all the notice Gracie took. She went on talking until they reached Gracie's house. The old woman did not speak once.

"Here you are, Gracie. Home."

Mike took the suitcase and he and Alex went with her to the front door.

"Put it down there." Gracie spoke for the first time, pointing to a place in her sitting room.

"Is there anything I can get you?" Alex said. "An omelette?"

But Gracie was standing with one hand on the front door knob.

Alex said, "Gracie, I'm sorry about what happened but it wasn't our fault. You were put into Bridmoor by Frank Spender."

Then she said, "I'm not one of them people. Never was. Never will be." And she closed the door with a bang.

Alex smiled and said to Mike, "Well, at least Gracie's fine."

They reached *Osprey* and Mike said, "I got some champagne to welcome you back but I'm not sure how you're feeling."

"I'm feeling great and champagne would be great."

They went down to the saloon with a bottle and a couple of glasses. There was a message on the answerphone.

A rich voice said, "Mike, this is Laddie Broakes. Have you made up your mind yet? End of message."

"About what?" Alex said.

"I wanted you back here and in your right mind before we talked about this. He's offered me a job on this new police association. Wants me to work with him. I'd just put down the phone and gone out on deck when I saw the house begin to collapse. Honest to God, I forgot about the whole thing until yesterday."

"And?"

"Well, it'd mean giving up this whole plan."

"And coming back to London?"

He nodded. "He says the office will be in Euston."

"That's only ten minutes from the flat."

"I know."

"Mike, I don't want to influence you. You must make up your own mind. But I think you know what I'd like best."

"I've been thinking about it off and on since yesterday. I think I know what I want too, and Lexton doesn't really figure. Not after what's happened."

She felt drained and excited at the same time. "You could always moor the boat at Southwold and we could use it at weekends."

"Maybe. We can see about that."

"Mike, can I ask you one thing? What are you going to do about the musk?"

"It's gone. I put it back in its cardboard boxes and handed it into the customs. Said I'd found it washed ashore. Let them make what they can out of it. I bet they think it's drugs just like we did to start with."

She felt a surge of pleasure.

He poured her another glass and touched her cheek with his fingers. "My God, it's good to have you back."

"If you're thinking what I'm thinking then let me tell you we can go and try. Love will always find a way round bad feet and cracked ribs."

At that moment there was a grating noise on the boat's hull.

They looked at each other in sudden apprehension. "Oh, Christ!" Mike said. He got to his feet and went up the companionway. Alex followed more slowly. The grating noise came again.

They peered over the side into water that was now discoloured by all the rain and high tides. There was something that looked like a body scraping along the hull.

It turned slightly and moved . . . stopped and moved again. Then they saw it wasn't a body but the waterlogged trunk of a small tree. It floated just under the surface of the water to the little beach where first Tommy Lee and then the Chinese man had ended up.

"That does it," Mike said. "Let's get the hell out of here and go somewhere warm and sunny — and where no one's heard of the sea."

THE END

Books by Alan Scholefield
Published by The House of Ulverscroft:

BURN OUT
DON'T BE A NICE GIRL
WILD DOG RUNNING
BURIED TREASURE
NIGHT MOVES

TO FIGHT THE WILD
Rod Ansell and Rachel Percy

Lost in uncharted Australian bush, Rod Ansell survived by hunting and trapping wild animals, improvising shelter and using all the bushman's skills he knew.

COROMANDEL
Pat Barr

India in the 1830s is a hot, uncomfortable place, where the East India Company still rules. Amelia and her new husband find themselves caught up in the animosities which seethe between the old order and the new.

THE SMALL PARTY
Lillian Beckwith

A frightening journey to safety begins for Ruth and her small party as their island is caught up in the dangers of armed insurrection.

THE WILDERNESS WALK
Sheila Bishop

Stifling unpleasant memories of a misbegotten romance in Cleave with Lord Francis Aubrey, Lavinia goes on holiday there with her sister. The two women are thrust into a romantic intrigue involving none other than Lord Francis.

THE RELUCTANT GUEST
Rosalind Brett

Ann Calvert went to spend a month on a South African farm with Theo Borland and his sister. They both proved to be different from her first idea of them, and there was Storr Peterson — the most disturbing man she had ever met.

ONE ENCHANTED SUMMER
Anne Tedlock Brooks

A tale of mystery and romance and a girl who found both during one enchanted summer.

CLOUD OVER MALVERTON
Nancy Buckingham

Dulcie soon realises that something is seriously wrong at Malverton, and when violence strikes she is horrified to find herself under suspicion of murder.

AFTER THOUGHTS
Max Bygraves

The Cockney entertainer tells stories of his East End childhood, of his RAF days, and his post-war showbusiness successes and friendships with fellow comedians.

MOONLIGHT
AND MARCH ROSES
D. Y. Cameron

Lynn's search to trace a missing girl takes her to Spain, where she meets Clive Hendon. While untangling the situation, she untangles her emotions and decides on her own future.

NURSE ALICE IN LOVE
Theresa Charles

Accepting the post of nurse to little Fernie Sherrod, Alice Everton could not guess at the romance, suspense and danger which lay ahead at the Sherrod's isolated estate.

POIROT INVESTIGATES
Agatha Christie

Two things bind these eleven stories together — the brilliance and uncanny skill of the diminutive Belgian detective, and the stupidity of his Watson-like partner, Captain Hastings.

LET LOOSE THE TIGERS
Josephine Cox

Queenie promised to find the long-lost son of the frail, elderly murderess, Hannah Jason. But her enquiries threatened to unlock the cage where crucial secrets had long been held captive.

THE TWILIGHT MAN
Frank Gruber

Jim Rand lives alone in the California desert awaiting death. Into his hermit existence comes a teenage girl who blows both his past and his brief future wide open.

DOG IN THE DARK
Gerald Hammond

Jim Cunningham breeds and trains gun dogs, and his antagonism towards the devotees of show spaniels earns him many enemies. So when one of them is found murdered, the police are on his doorstep within hours.

THE RED KNIGHT
Geoffrey Moxon

When he finds himself a pawn on the chessboard of international espionage with his family in constant danger, Guy Trent becomes embroiled in moves and countermoves which may mean life or death for Western scientists.

TIGER TIGER
Frank Ryan

A young man involved in drugs is found murdered. This is the first event which will draw Detective Inspector Sandy Woodings into a whirlpool of murder and deceit.

CAROLINE MINUSCULE
Andrew Taylor

Caroline Minuscule, a medieval script, is the first clue to the whereabouts of a cache of diamonds. The search becomes a deadly kind of fairy story in which several murders have an other-worldly quality.

LONG CHAIN OF DEATH
Sarah Wolf

During the Second World War four American teenagers from the same town join the Army together. Forty-two years later, the son of one of the soldiers realises that someone is systematically wiping out the families of the four men.